REE REYES BOOK THREE

HEXOMANCY

MICHAEL R. UNDERWOOD

PRAISE FOR MICHAEL R. UNDERWOOD

"If *Buffy* hooked up with *Doctor Who* while on board the Serenity, this book would be their lovechild. In other words, *Geekomancy* is full of epic win."

> – Marie Lu, author of the Legend trilogy, on *Geekomancy*

"Michael R. Underwood just keeps getting better and better. We need more urban fantasy like this."

> – Seanan McGuire, New York Times bestselling author of *Discount Armageddon*, on *Celebromancy*

"This is truly a unique spin on the typical Urban Fantasy story and one of the most genuinely fun stories I have read in a long time."

> – KristenD, Bitten by Books, on *Attack the Geek*

"Come for the geeky world and fun storyline, stay for the fabulous characters, relationships, and action. I thoroughly enjoyed the whole series; I simply loved *Hexomancy*. I commend it for your reading pleasure. Seriously, pre-order today."

> – Joe's Geek Fest, on *Hexomancy*

"Heroes, villains, and a world like no other."

> – Joe's Geek Fest on *Shield & Crocus*

" . . .a bright and exciting space opera in the cosmic comic book style of Marvel's *Guardians of the Galaxy*. In a galaxy that has been dominated by the mollusk-like Vsenk for a thousand years, three treasure hunters stumble across an artifact that will shake the foundations of an entire empire . . .Underwood's prose is brisk and funny without ever sacrificing his skilled sf world building. Highly recommended for fans of action-packed space opera and anyone else looking for a fun and fast-paced read.

– Booklist (Starred Review), on Annihilation Aria

"In this entertaining space opera from Underwood (the Genrenauts series), a married couple—one an affable archaeologist from Earth who was accidentally transported across the universe with no way home, the other a warrior woman from a devastated alien culture who utilizes songs to enhance her combat skills—becomes embroiled in a mess of galactic proportions after they "liberate" a dangerous artifact from a long-lost temple . . .This is a rollicking good time."

– Publisher's Weekly, on Annihilation Aria

"*Annihilation Aria* is the found family space opera you've been waiting for."

– Adam Rakunas, author of Philip K. Dick Award-finalist Windswept

"*The Younger Gods* is a solid urban fantasy with an interesting premise and characters you can't help but get invested in."

– Bibliotropic

"This is fun . . .Readers will be looking forward to Leah and company's next trip to a story world."

– Library Journal, on *Genrenauts: The Shootout Solution*

"This is one of those high concepts so irresistible, you can't believe no one has come up with it before. This first installment is a rollicking exploration of western tropes, with hints of a larger conspiracy afoot. Underwood has plans for a lot more of these, and I can't wait to read them."

– Joel Cunningham, Barnes & Noble Sci-Fi & Fantasy Blog, on *Genrenauts: The Shootout Solution*

"A Tardis of a novella, *The Shootout Solution* is packed full of ideas . . . The possibilities are endless . . . Tor.com continues to blaze a bookish trail in terms of both originality and diversity. More like this, please."

– Geek Syndicate, on *Genrenauts: The Shootout Solution*

"*The Shootout Solution* is Genre blending fun."

– Fangirl Nation

"A clever, exciting, and seriously fun twist on portal fantasy that sends a geeky stand-up comedian into the Wild West. Sign me up to be a Genrenaut, too!"

– Delilah S. Dawson, NYT-bestselling author of *Star Wars: Phasma*

"I have this sinking feeling that the Genrenauts series, with its raucous meta-commentary upon the stories of pop culture, is going to say important things that I might not be clever enough to catch the first time around because I'm too busy enjoying the books."

– Howard Tayler, Hugo Award Winner and creator of *Schlock Mercenary*

2ⁿᵈ edition
Copyright © 2015, 2022 by Michael R. Underwood
All rights reserved, including the right to reproduce this book or portions thereof in any form whatsoever.
For rights inquiries, contact info@morhaimliterary.com
ISBN: 9780998060682 (Paperback)
          9780998060699 (ebook)

Cover by Deranged Doctor Design (derangeddoctordesign.com)
Also available in audiobook

First edition by Simon & Schuster Pocket Star Books September 2015
1st edition ISBN 9781476757810

MORE BY MICHAEL R. UNDERWOOD

The Ree Reyes Geeky Urban Fantasy Series
Geekomancy
Celebromancy
Attack the Geek
Hexomancy

Genrenauts
#0 -The Data Disruption
#1 -The Shootout Solution
#2 - The Absconded Ambassador
#3 -The Cupid Reconciliation
#4 - The Substitute Sleuth
#5&6 - The Failed Fellowship
#7 - The Wasteland War

The Space Operas
Annihilation Aria

Other Books
Shield and Crocus

The Younger Gods

Born to the Blade
(with Malka Older, Cassandra Khaw, and Marie Brennan)

To Meg, my dearest heart

CHAPTER ONE

Cause I'm Leaving, On a Steam Cruise

SUMMER

The clock ticked toward 9 PM entirely too quickly as Ree hustled to finish her closing tasks at Zombie Café. She appreciated Charlie giving her the shift, but it was hard to concentrate on overnight baking to-do lists and inventory when she was due in court in an hour. Especially when *court* meant "facing a homicidal Hexomancer bent on murdering your erstwhile mentor and anyone who tries to stop her."

Fortunately, Ree's friend Priya was on hand to help keep her grounded. Ree's worrying mind could focus on talking with Priya, while her productive mind could work down the checklist the way she'd done five hundred times before.

Ree Reyes (Strength 10, Dexterity 14, Stamina 13, Will 18, IQ 16, Charisma 15—Geek 7 / Barista 3 / Screenwriter 3 / Gamer Girl 2 / Geekomancer 2) rolled out a length of plastic wrap over the d6 cupcakes, draped one side over her forearm, pulled the wrap taut, then pulled the other side up, cutting off a perfect square. She tucked the plastic wrap around the sides, careful not to smoosh the icing. It was a delicate art, and one she was glad to have not forgotten. She hadn't needed to do any baking at Grognard's, but it'd take longer than eight months for her to lose her edge.

Zombie Café hadn't changed much in Ree's absence over the last year. The twenty-by-twenty front room had well-worn tables and seats. Murals and paintings of rocket ships, superheroes, and dragons filled one wall, bookshelves and gaming merch lined the other, and between them, a cash-wrap overstuffed with collectible cards and pastries.

And while Ree worked, Priya talked. Priya Tharakan (Strength 8, Dexterity 13, Stamina 12, Will 15, IQ 17, Charisma 15—Geek 3 / Professional 3 / Seamstress 4 / Steampunk 4 / Goth 2) was in "casual mode," an earth-toned scarf over a black top and slacks, her duster draped over the one table with chairs not already stacked up for closing time.

"The best thing was the music. Half of the bands were pretty much Mumford with Gears On, but whatever you call them, they were excellent," Priya said, recounting her time as an invited costuming guest on a Steampunk cruise. "This one band had ten members, including sitar, djembe, and banjo, and they actually had backstory to explain the fusion aspects—they were supposed to be the crew of an airship that traveled the world escorting dirigible freighters."

"That sounds pretty awesome. Did you grab their album?" Ree asked, dumping out the decaf coffee.

Priya pulled a CD case out of her purse and held it aloft like a prize. "Ta da!"

"Sweet. Can I borrow?"

Priya held the CD out toward Ree, a twinkle in her eye. "Keep it. I figured you'd want a copy, so I got two."

Ree took the case with excited reverence. "Best friend is best." The last month had been rough on the finances, hence her needing to take shifts at Zombie Café.

"So you're headed off to the catering job after this?" Priya asked.

"Yeah. The company has been losing customers, so I really need to take this one, or the boss is likely to write me off."

"What kind of events do you cater for?" Priya asked.

"Mostly private parties. Tonight is a soiree some muckety-muck lawyer is throwing for her friends and clients," Ree lied.

Every time Ree had to make shit up to cover for her magical life, it was like walking over burning embers. She'd learned to mute the pain, but it never quite went away. Other than her magic-world associates and her dad, only Anya knew about the magical world. The other two Rhyming Ladies had been kept in the dark to try to minimize risk. The result was . . . messy. Especially with Priya dating Drake Winters, one of Ree's constant companions in All Things Weird.

"What kind of food did they serve on the cruise?" Ree asked, turning the conversation back around, both so she didn't have to extend the lie, and because she was genuinely interested. It'd been harder to keep up with the Ladies with her whacky Urban Fantasy life, and Priya had put off an evening of engineering to come hang out, so she should get as much out of the short evening as she could.

Ree crossed a few more tasks off in as Flash-like a fashion as possible while keeping her end of the conversation going, converting nervousness over the coming trial into speedy efficiency. It was better than the alternative, which was to stop long enough to consider the long list of a million and one things that could go wrong at the trial.

After all, it wasn't often that a member of Pearson's magical community was tried by her peers in a massive underground cavern decked out like a mash-up of the Goblin Market and the Origins Game Fair. And that was precisely where Ree was headed, as soon as she got the café in ship shape and the clock struck 9.

The cashwrap clock read 8:47.

One thing at a time. Cupcakes first, doom later, Ree thought.

Life since Lucretia d'Fete had ruined Grognard's Grog

and Games with a cascade of Hexomantic curses and several waves of monsters had been, in a word, *fucked*. Grognard didn't have the money to pay her for more than about five hours a week, which she spent throwing out trash, making capital repairs, and mourning the tens of thousands of dollars of geeky merchandise that the events of that sucktastic Saturday night had destroyed, throwing an adamantium crowbar in the wheel spokes of her already shaky life.

Priya pulled her back to reality, gushing about the cruise. "And they've already asked me back to be a guest on the spring voyage, which is awesome. Being a guest pays a cool grand up front, plus room and board, and the chance to sell my merch and services. Two of these a year and I might be able to hire an assistant for the grunt work! And then I could make enough to finally pay off the Student Loan Fairy."

Ree stopped counting down the drawer, scribbled a note to keep her place, and looked up. "That's fantastic, Pri. And if you need a charming merch-booth lackey, remember that I happen to love cruises." Ree punctuated the line with the biggest, most obvious wink she could.

"Yeah, but if you came with me, I'd come around my merch booth to find you playing *Pathfinder* with all of my customers," Priya said, referring to the one time (one!) that Ree had run merch for Priya at a totally dead one-day Steampunk con in Pearson.

"Hey, that was one time," Ree protested. "And that older lady bought a corset."

"Which was my only sale that day."

"Yeah, but even the hat and fascinator folks were having a crap day. There was nothing to be done with that festival."

"As evidenced by the fact that the con was a one-and-done." Priya packed up her bag.

"Okay, I should probably let you finish up, yeah?"

"Yeah, I'll need to book it to make the job in time. Thanks for coming by, and remember what I said about the cruise. I could use a vacation."

Ree scurried out from the cashwrap to give Priya a hug, and then locked the door behind her friend after she left.

Okay, what's left to do? she asked herself, scanning the room.

Eastwood had asked Ree to make it to market by 9:30, which wasn't going to happen. She was shooting for 10, and cutting corners wasn't going to help. Julio Reyes didn't raise a sucker, and walking into the Midnight Market to square off against Lucretia at the trial was going to take every single bit of Ree's Geek-fu, and she wasn't about to walk in unarmed.

Ree booked it across the U-District, weaving among college students on the early stops of their weekend pub crawls on a sweltering summer night. Someone had scooped up a big bowl of Midwestern summer soup weather and dumped it on Pearson in a flagrant violation of the Pacific Northwest Climate Accord that kept her beloved city free of the kind of miserable humidity she'd learned to despise as a kid.

Adrenaline hurled her up the five floors toward the Shithole, her and Sandra's apartment. These days, the Shithole was much closer to earning its usually inaccurate name, thanks to Ree and Sandra's life erupting into matching fail-nados within a week of each other. Sandra's admin job at the dentist had gone poof when the practice got tanked by a malpractice suit, sending Ree's roommate back to the job market.

But there was no time to clean now (had there ever been?), so Ree dashed into the bedroom, thankful that Sandra seemed to be out once again. It'd been hard enough to keep her best friend and roommate in the dark over the last year, especially with Anya already knowing about magic and everything, and Priya dating Drake.

The having-a-crush-on-her-friend's-boyfriend thing didn't help either, but time was making that piece of angst slightly easier to digest.

Slightly.

Ree had laid out her arsenal on her bed before leaving for work, prepping ahead of time for a quick-change armoring session. Her old boss Bryan had agreed to let her pick up some shifts, as long as she didn't bring her magical business to Zombie Café. And that included the gear.

Clothes came first. She switched out her black-on-black work garb, stained many times over by frosting, coffee grounds, and steamed milk, and replaced them with her last remaining Urban Fantasy Adventure outfit—black jeans (with only a few tears and holes), black undershirt, the quilted armor of convention shirts Bryan had given her last Halloween, and the magically-always-fitting-and-self-repairing buff jacket Drake Winters had given her on permanent loan. She tied her shoulder-length black hair up and back, pinning it with a Wonder Woman barrette.

She cleaned the shift's accumulation of crud off her old glasses, catching a quick glimpse in the mirror of how tired she looked. Puerto Rican heritage saved her from taking on the mime-esque chalky paleness that white folks got when they were wrung out, which she was sure she'd have if she'd taken more after her mom's Irish coloration.

And now the weapons.

Her Force FX lightsaber went from her purse (what Bryan didn't know couldn't hurt him) into the outside right pocket of the jacket, along with her *Deep Space Nine* phaser. She grabbed a rubber-banded stack of cards, flipped through the top to triple-check her selections, and then stuffed the sideboard into her left pocket. Along with those, she pocketed the last handful of health and stamina potions from her copy of *Descent*, a handful of dice (for ritual miscellany), and an external battery for her phone.

Such were the tools of a Geekomancer. Ree sometimes marveled that it'd only been eight months since she discovered that she had the power to use her love of pop culture to do physics-defying magic, but if ever she needed those skills, tonight was the night. In her hands, the lightsaber and phaser were as real as they were to Luke Skywalker or Benjamin Sisko, brought to life by the collective nostalgia of fans worldwide.

The sideboard of collectible cards gave her access to one-shot effects—one card, one spell. And the phone was her own personal Power Ring, loaded with video playlists organized to grant specific powers. A quick rewatch of the opening to *The Matrix* could bestow limited Wire-fu, and smiling along with *Spider-Man* as he webbed his way across the city could make her a Friendly Neighborhood Spider-Gal—for a time.

And now it was 9:21. Ree double-checked everything and turned around in place to make really, *really* sure she wasn't forgetting a tool or weapon. She retrieved a slice of Turbo's pie from the fridge to nom along the way, one final power-up for the night's misadventures.

✕⊗✕

The doorman at the Midnight Market got obscure on her, which was cute. She didn't have time for crap, especially considering how many gnomes were still wandering Pearson's sewers. They'd been stirred up last month and hadn't settled down.

"What's the first appearance of Karnak?"

Since she'd used a copy of *Fantastic Four* #45 just last month during Lucretia's attack, she rattled off the reference as easily as her phone number.

Three bolts and locks slid open, and Ree entered the Midnight Market, leaving behind the smell of sewage that had gotten entirely too familiar to her this last year.

She nodded to the bald doorman and strode down the hall, which was suspiciously low lit. Was this their version of flying the flag at half-mast? Three of the people who had left Grognard's that night never made it home: Tomas, Alexi, and Siobhan.

The Midnight Market filled the room, more stalls and booths this month than she'd seen in months. Were they all here for the trial? Ree'd never been to a Pearson Underground trial, though Eastwood and Grognard had gone over the details with her what seemed like a hundred times.

Kiosks, booths, and wandering traders spanned twelve rows deep, hand-painted signs erected at the open walkways between booths. Ree passed comics-backlist sellers, action figure gurus, 3D printers, miniatures sellers, and costumers.

Farther down the lane was her traditional neck of the woods, where Grognard's cart would be parked at the corner of Geneva and Talsorian. The cart had been lost in one of Ree's all-too-frequent adventures in the sewer, but the space was still occupied by the man himself. Grognard was dressed in his Saturday best, a stain-free shirt with a leather jacket.

Grognard aka "Just Grognard" (Strength 15, Dexterity 10, Stamina 15, Will 18, IQ 15, Charisma 10—Geek 7 / Collector 4 / Geekomancer 3 / Brewmaster 5) was a living statue of a man, built thick with muscle, head shaved clean. His beard was immaculately kept, and for the first time at market, he was packing. It was a halberd rather than a gun, but considering Grognard topped 6'2" and two hundred fifty pounds, he usually didn't need anything in the weapons department to feel safe.

Beside him, shifting his weight side to side like a pendulum of nerves, was Eastwood. The former Console Cowboy (Strength 11, Dexterity 14, Stamina 14, Will 18, IQ 18, Charisma 7—Geek 8, Astral Cowboy 4 / Geekomancer 5 / Thunderbolt 2) stood just a few inches taller than Ree, with a well-worn trench coat (yes, even in summer) over a blazer and slacks. Ree'd never seen Eastwood in slacks. He still wore his weapons belt slung low like the Cowboy he had been and remained.

Eastwood had been on edge since that night at Grognard's, but tonight, he was more put together than she'd ever seen him. His beard was freshly trimmed, his hair shampooed and combed. He looked, frankly, like he was going to court.

But he was still off—pale, slightly red around the eyes.

Ree gave the chin nod of companionable silence as she walked up, joining the two men. They returned the nod, and Grognard pulled out a flask from his jacket and held it out to welcome her.

"Care for a sip?"

Ree looked at the flask. "And this is?"

"Critical Hit ale. Figure we can use every bit of help possible."

"You okay?" Ree asked Eastwood.

Eastwood snorted back snot by way of answer. "No. I caught the frakking flu. I might as well be a snot elemental." He pulled a handkerchief from his blazer and blew. And kept blowing.

Ree grimaced and took a sip from the flask. She felt the tingling of magic, felt the universe slide into the booth next to her and offer a tipsy high five, saying, *You got this! Woo!*

Whatever was coming, she felt just a tad more prepared. "Everything set?" she asked.

"As set as it can be," Grognard said. "Drake's not here, and neither is Wickham. But Talon, Chandra, Shade, and Uncle Joe are; that's more than enough testimony to back our story. Plus," he said, reaching into his jacket again, "we have this."

The brewmaster pulled out Lucretia d'Fete's handwritten note that basically admitted her guilt. In a U.S. court, this would be an open-and-shut case. But this was the Underground, and she hadn't seen thousands of hours of *Law & Order: Pearson* to give her the confidence of familiarity. She imagined Eastwood and Grognard as cop and lawyer for *L&O: Pearson* and chuckled.

"What's that for?" Eastwood asked.

"Just imagining something weirder than our life. Perspective is handy," she said.

Eastwood sneezed, dramatically undercutting his badass demeanor. "Don't go daydreaming too much, kid. Eyes on the prize."

Ree held the flask out toward Eastwood. "You need some of this? Maybe Crit your way out of that flu."

"I get the vaccines, I take my old-man vitamins, and still, this frelling thing." Congested, Eastwood's gruff voice sounded dangerously close to that of a Muppet.

Ree felt the hairs on the back of her neck go up, Spider-sense-style, and she turned to see Lady Lucretia d'Fete walking down the aisle. Lucretia (Strength 9, Dexterity 13, Stamina 11, Will 17, IQ 15, Charisma 14—Strega 9 / Hexomancer 3 / Seamstress 3) held her head high, her makeup perfect, black hair styled in a complicated updo maintained by a half-dozen spikes and needles.

She was followed by Sven Carlssen, her frequent sellsword bodyguard. Sven was loaded down like a warrior in an Obsidian RPG—a half-dozen weapons visible over his coat: bow, crossbow, sword, daggers, another sword, and a fuck-off-size Bat'leth on his back.

If it were anyone else, Ree would snicker at the preposterousness of wearing that many weapons all at once. But she'd crossed blades with Carlssen. If he was wearing all of those weapons, she was betting that he was in a position to use them.

Lucretia walked past the corner of Talsorian and Geneva, head held high, actively refusing to meet Ree's or her companions' eyes.

A smart woman would let it sit there, would allow Lucretia to pass without incident.

Ree felt like being ridiculous. "You ready to take a fall, Lucy? NordicTrack here isn't going to save you from the long arm of geek law."

A hand gripped her arm, squeezing ever so slightly too tight. It was Grognard. She restrained a snarl and watched Lucretia miss half a step, the comment slipping past the woman's cool demeanor like a dagger under the folds of plate.

That won't be the only sting tonight—you can bet your ass, sister, Ree thought, tossing her angry thoughts at the Strega.

"Harassing her isn't going to help our case," Grognard said.

"Yeah, but we were all thinking that, right?" Ree looked to her boss and her former mentor. Both shrugged, grinning.

"That's what I thought."

And so they went to court.

CHAPTER TWO

Time to Face the Chiptune Music

Most months, the Midnight Market hosted a grand auction, where members of the Pearson Underground put up items of magical significance for sale. Bids came in the form of barter, and the process could get as nasty as the hotel queue for San Diego Comic-Con.

But tonight, with the trial supplanting the auction, the crowd was as big as ever. Bigger. Pearson had lost three of its own last month, and while people in the Underground seldom all saw eye to eye, they looked out for one another. Lucretia hadn't done a great job of making friends along the way, even outside Grognard's crew.

The steel-eyed and silver-haired Auctioneer stood atop the podium, still wielding her gavel like a badge of office. She'd preside over the trial, since she was as close as Pearson got to an impartial observer.

Eastwood took the lead, with Ree second and Grognard pulling up the rear. They strode down the aisle, making their way to the front table opposite Lucretia.

Ree still wasn't sure why they couldn't have just bound Lucretia into fixing all the damage from Grognard's and been done with it, but every community had their own method of self-policing.

She just hoped that it would actually work. Lucretia wasn't the sort to go into a situation without at least a few trump cards up her crinoline sleeves.

The three took their places at the table, and after a minute of audience rumbling, the Auctioneer raised a single gloved hand and the crowd went silent.

That was power. Ree'd never spoken to the woman outside the context of an auction. *I should change that.* It never hurt to have friends in high places. Too late for the trial, though.

The Auctioneer's voice filled the cavernous room, seeming to come from all sides. It was either magic or a well-hidden PA system.

"Welcome, everyone. We are called here today to resolve the matter of serious charges leveled against one of our own."

The auctioneer looked at Lucretia. "Lucretia d'Fete, you stand accused of indirectly causing the deaths of three members of our community: Tomas, Alexi, and Siobhan. You also stand accused of direct assault on Eastwood, Grognard, Ree, and Drake Winters, as well as damages totaling fifty thousand dollars to Grognard's Grog and Games. How do you plead?"

Lucretia waited a moment, as if savoring the silent anticipation. "My actions were right and just. If Tomas, Alexi, and Siobhan were arrogant enough to get in the way of the justice I am to mete out for Eastwood's crimes, then that is regrettable, but I deny culpability. Those and any other actions were taken in pursuit of my mandate as a Strega, and are above reproach."

"You are not above reproach, Lucretia. It is right here, waiting for you." The Auctioneer spread her arms, indicating the crowd. "I will now hear testimony from the accusers."

Grognard stood, leaving his halberd on the table, point directed at Lucretia. He took center stage below the platform, looking at the crowd.

Filling his lungs, Grognard began. "Last month, on the second Saturday, I had eighteen patrons in my store, most participating in a *Vampire: the Eternal Struggle* tournament. Some of you were there with me. Ree Reyes, Eastwood, Drake Winters, Uncle Joe, Chandra, Shade." As Grognard listed off the names, Ree watched the heads nodding in the crowd. Even Uncle Joe had cleaned up for the trial, though his version of cleaning up appeared to be putting a cabbie's hat over his comb-over and wearing a new T-shirt.

"Around nine PM, the lights went out. The breaker sparked when I tried the fuse box, and the office door was locked and warded, surpassing my own wards."

Grognard walked to the right, approaching the crowd. "I closed down shop, and most of the patrons left, in groups and on their own. Minutes later, they returned with gnomes hot on their heels. We provided refuge, and for the next several hours, fought off wave after wave of monsters trying to break down my doors and kill everyone inside. Ree, Eastwood, Drake Winters, Chandra, Uncle Joe, and even Abigail Wickham joined the defense, in a display of heroism and teamwork that reminded me why I founded Grognard's Grog and Games: to bring people together to relax and celebrate our shared interests."

Ree'd heard Grognard talk a lot on that Saturday, but not this much. This was rehearsed. How many times had he practiced this speech? A hundred? Her boss was many things, but a public speaker was not one of them. Especially outside of his bar. *Keep going, boss.*

"Later in the evening, something caused my merchandise to come to life and attack everyone in the bar. Miniatures, board games, weapons, and more. Nearly my entire stock put to the task of trying to kill me. Thanks to the ingenuity of Drake Winters, we were able to break the animation curse, but not before we were forced to destroy hundreds of pieces of merchandise to protect ourselves.

"I assumed it was the same thing that caused the monsters to come knocking, and I was right." Grognard walked back and stood in front of Lucretia. "During a lull in the fighting, this flew under the front door." Grognard held the note aloft for all to see. He stepped back and handed it to the Auctioneer, who read the note aloud.

"The note reads:

Dear Anthony,

By now you will have had the fortune of enjoying the first phases of my vengeance for your despicable affront and robbery last fall. As revenge is a dish best served cold, I decided to inflict my fury on all those who would associate with you, including the nursemaid Grognard, with his childish clubhouse; your erstwhile upstart apprentice; and, well, whoever else happens to be around.

I thought it might be appropriate to turn your little ritual tools against you. Perhaps robbed of your crutches, we will see what you're truly made of.

I look forward to gazing down on your bloodied broken corpse and reclaiming that which was stolen from me. And then I will leave you out in the street as a message to all in Pearson that to cross Lucretia d'Fete is to invite death and ruin.

With coldest regard,

Lady Lucretia d'Fete"

A couple of gasps and a few boos leaped up from the audience. *That's what I like to hear. This should be an open-and-shut case, so why is Lucretia wearing that I-know-something-you-don't-know smirk?*

The Auctioneer set down the paper and nodded to Grognard.

"When we finally cleaned out the rest of the monsters, Eastwood and I, then Ree and Drake, pursued Lucretia, leaving the others to hold down the fort. Around the corner from my store, we were transported into Spirit, into some kind of labyrinth, again via Lucretia's magic. We pursued her through the maze, facing several more life-threatening creatures and situations, and finally captured Lucretia and her accomplice, Abigail Wickham. Wickham confessed, and Lucretia admitted that the entire evening's destruction had been her doing, all because Eastwood stole back the Claddagh ring he had rightfully won in the Midnight Market last October."

"Lies!" Lucretia said, bolting to her feet. "Eastwood's death was foretold! The river of fate must be corrected. It is my sacred duty. This entire trial is a sham." Lucretia turned to the assembled audience. "I have been a part of this community for more than a decade. I have been protecting you all, keeping the eddies of fate from carrying this city and its people off course. And now Eastwood stands before us, when his own crimes against the city have been unpunished. He contributed to the suicide of four youths, ready to offer them up to the Thrice-Retconned Duke of Pwn! But where is his trial?"

And there it was. She'd been planning to flip this on Eastwood the whole time. Had she wanted to get captured? If she wanted him tried, she could have just made the accusation and skipped the whole *Jumanji* act. But this way she got to have her chaos and eat it too.

Eastwood stood. *Great, this is definitely not spinning out of control.* "I'm not on trial, here, Lucretia. And this river of fate is just a bunch of *go-se* you dreamed up to justify your revenge!"

"*Silence,*" the Auctioneer said, gavel striking the table and echoing throughout the chamber like a thunderclap.

Eastwood sat, but Lucretia remained, her arms crossed, defiant. *Woman knows how to stick to a story, I'll give her that.*

"You will be seated, both of you, and allow Grognard to finish his testimony." Lucretia had a short stare-down with the Auctioneer, then sat.

"Please continue," the Auctioneer said.

Grognard took a breath and talked past Lucretia to the crowd. "Lucretia submitted to a giese to not attack me or any of the others, and that she would report to the Midnight Market for her trial. She has held to those terms, and now here we are. Three people dead, my shop in ruins, and a self-confessed killer in your midst."

"Thank you," Grognard said, and then sat.

The Auctioneer left time for people to whisper and harumph and boo and hiss. Ree wanted to be a part of the latter but managed to restrain herself this time.

See, Dad? I do have self-restraint!

"Lucretia, you may now give your testimony."

With a smile, Lucretia answered, "No testimony is needed. I request trial by combat."

The crowd erupted into another round of chatter and jeering.

Eastwood snarled, then coughed, reaching for his handkerchief again. As the primary accuser, he'd be the one matched up against Lucretia. And given the fact that he was currently chilling in Sicktown, odds were not looking good, even with his probably superior fighting skills. Her hexes could make his weapons malfunction or turn him into a flopping slapstick farce. The only way she'd found to beat Hexomancers was to throw so much at them that they couldn't Hex fast enough to stop you.

The Auctioneer slammed the gavel again, this time without the crack of thunder. "Silence. We respect the right to trial by combat, though typically, that right is requested before testimony begins."

Lucretia's grin ticked one size bigger. "Grognard had been preparing that little speech for so long, I didn't want to deny him the chance to tell his little tale. But Eastwood is my accuser, so I will face him in combat to prove my innocence and worth to this community. And to bring him to justice for his crimes."

"Not so fast, sister," Ree said, standing this time. "Eastwood's in no condition, so you get to fight me."

"No," Eastwood said. "I can handle her." Eastwood stood, then wavered and slumped back to the table, undercutting his point just a little.

Ree caught her former mentor and set him back in his chair. "Sure thing, boss. That sounds like a great idea." Ree reached into her jacket and produced her lightsaber. "So, we just do this right here and now?"

"I wish," Grognard said.

Lucretia's smile was approaching Cheshire dimensions.

The Auctioneer's booming voice called out, "Trial by combat. As the challenger, Lucretia, you have the right to choose the weapons."

"I thought Duello went the other way," Ree said.

"We don't use the Code Duello," Grognard answered.

Lucretia turned so she could face the crowd and Ree at once. "Since Ree was such a fan of our last jaunt to Spirit, I choose a game of *Incarnate*. Best of five falls."

"No shit, *Incarnate*? I didn't take you for a FPSer," Ree said. *Incarnate* had taken the video game world by storm just a month ago. It pitted rival sorcerers against one another on massive battlefields, with NPC foot soldiers and archers on each side. But the casters were the real challenge, with each player customizing their set of spells and foci.

The primary resource in the game was mana. Each spell cost temporary mana, which was paid into a larger Incarnation pool. The mana pool regenerated constantly, but slowly, requiring players to be tactical with their spell casting, choosing between keeping magic on hand for emergencies and casting more to get a temporary advantage and/or to fill the Incarnation pool.

When a player's Incarnation pool was filled, they could unleash their Incarnate spell, which summoned a magical construct capable of laying waste to entire brigades by itself. Ree'd heard the game had originally been conceived as an SF mecha combat setup, but moved to fantasy to set itself apart from *Halo* and the like. Since her cash flow made a dripping faucet look like a raging river, she'd played only the *Incarnate* beta, and only that one weekend.

"Where are the rigs?" Ree asked. There were no computers on hand to complete the fantasy redux of *The Wizard* that she suddenly found herself in and was not-so-secretly excited by.

"Oh, my dear. I've gotten you confused again, it seems. We won't be playing on computers. We'll be doing the fighting ourselves . . . in Spirit."

Lucretia sleight-of-handed out two marbled orbs, each the size of a baseball. Ree's was blue, Lucretia's red.

Not interested in taking anything handed to her by Lucretia, Ree turned to Grognard. "So we're doing this *Tron*-style?"

The brewmaster nodded. His voice was thick with annoyance. "It is her right as the accused to set the challenge in Spirit. The precedent goes back to the days when Shade was the young gun in town, throwing down with Street Samurai in the early days of the Wild Wild Web."

Eastwood forced his way through a coughing fit and grabbed Ree by a lapel, pulling her close. "How much do you know about this game?"

"I played a couple days of the beta."

Eastwood's eyes went wide, then he collapsed forward into another coughing fit.

"This won't be like noodling away at a controller on your couch," Grognard said. "When you play in Spirit, you feel the pain, the wind on your face, the shock in your legs when you land. It might as well be real."

Eastwood sucked in air to delay a coughing fit, then continued.

"The pocket dimension is a simulation, so dying there won't kill you. The Auctioneer will make sure of that. She'll be watching very closely. But you better fucking believe that Lucretia will find some way to cheat. You have to beat her, and you have to do it clean, otherwise the ruling won't stick."

More coughing. Ree grabbed Eastwood's hand, trying to hold him still. A few moments later, he recovered, still flushed.

"Lucretia's going to go long-distance, I can just about guarantee. The way you move, you'll want to close, use utility spells that will let you keep your troops alive and close the distance." He pulled a piece of grease-spotted thermal paper from his coat and started scribbling notes.

"Here're your options for spell selection. Your troops will respawn on a timer."

Eastwood tried to keep going, but the Auctioneer coughed audibly. Ree took her seat.

"Kick her ass, okay?" Eastwood added. "Let's be done with this bullshit."

Ree squeezed Eastwood's hand once more, then stepped toward Lucretia, seated a few paces away. "I catch you cheating, and I'll pull your organs out through your nose and parade you around as a crinoline mummy. You get me?"

"Armor yourself with all of the smugness you can muster, child. The game doesn't care about how angry you are. Besides, you're the hotshot Geekomancer—this should be easy for you, yes?" Lucretia held out the blue orb.

Ree grabbed the orb, then passed it between her hands, feeling its heft. "I've been around this scene long enough to know that you'd never pick a battleground you didn't know by heart, Lucretia. But I've spent more time behind an FPS HUD than some pro gamers," she said, stretching the truth like taffy. "Let's do this."

A few folks stepped out of the crowd and pulled the tables away, leaving two chairs facing the crowd. Shade, recovered from the injuries he sustained during Lucretia's attack, worked a control pad, and above, a massive projection screen descended on the far wall, behind the Auctioneer.

"Why don't we use this to watch movies all the fucking time?" Ree asked.

Grognard chuckled. "The bulbs to work these cost about

a thousand dollars apiece in alchemical components, and last two hours."

"Only two grand? I'd kick in," Ree said, all bluster. She took her seat, Lucretia beside her. If it weren't for the mounting pressure, the fear of unfamiliarity, and the dead certainty that Lucretia was about to cheat worse than a hungover frat boy in Chem 101 with answers printed on the inside of his vitamin water label, she'd be excited. She'd dreamed of going inside a video game ever since her dad had shown her *Tron* as a kid.

The Auctioneer stepped in front of them, holding a yellow globe of her own, half again as big as the other two. "Red player, are you ready?"

"Ready," Lucretia said.

"Blue player, are you ready?"

"Ready," Ree lied.

The Auctioneer raised her arms. "Prepare for Incarnation."

The orb in her hand grew hot, and she felt crushed inward and expanded outward at the same time.

"Game on!" she shouted as her world went blue.

CHAPTER THREE

Would You Like to Play a Game?

Blue-black faded to sapphire, then faded again into a volcanic landscape. They were on the crags of Valos, the battlefield where the ragtag Cohort makes their final stand against the Starii Federation in the game's campaign mode.

Ree looked down to see herself in the badass robes of a high-level Cohort mage, leather and silks wrapped together in an outfit that managed to be powerful without being featureless. Too often the outfits for female avatars in games came in two flavors: 1) three-quarters-naked sex kitten, or 2) matronly robes. This one actually split the difference in a way that she could get excited about. In her right hand she had her twisted ash staff, and her left hand glowed with faint blue light.

As she stood still, a menu popped up, dominating her vision. She had three choices of Incarnation spells, the massive Spirit constructs that gave the game its name: Stalwart (the tank), Guardian (the all-arounder), and Doombringer (the artillery).

Remembering Eastwood's advice, she took the middle path, choosing the Guardian.

Next was the spell list. All characters got a levitation spell for free, plus four spell slots.

She chose Shield, Haste, Fireballs, and Mana Sink. Defense, a buff, damage, and a counterspell.

Those selections done, the menu disappeared, showing her the world again. When the displays popped back up again, they were as a heads-up display at the edges of her vision: Mini-map, spell list, mana pools, and health bar.

A squadron of foot soldiers charged past her on the left, and to her right a trio of Treefolk shook the ground as they marched.

The Auctioneer appeared in the sky, half-transparent and three times larger than the sky-dominating moon.

"Prepare for Incarnation!" her voice boomed like thunder, then she disappeared, and the chaos took off.

With NPCs, there were a hundred entities per side. The game had elements of a MOBA, since in some modes, you could quite happily rack up the score by mowing down enemy minions without ever crossing the opposing casters or Incarnates. But this was Deathmatch, so everyone else was just an obstacle. Only caster kills would count. Get Lucretia three times before the Strega got her. The whole thing would take maybe twenty minutes. A really, really intense twenty minutes with life-long implications. No pressure.

"You better run, Lucretia," Ree said as she set off, boots crunching the loose volcanic rock. She oriented herself toward the red dot that indicated Lucretia's position. *Thank you, mini-map gods*, she thought.

The field sloped up toward a crevasse.

She had two options:

1) *Bear right and head down through the inside of this volcano, dodging lava flows but with cover from archer fire from above.*

2) *Take the long way around to the left and get the higher ground so she could rain death down on Lucretia and her troops, but take archer fire along the way.*

She decided on the second choice as she fell in with a squad of fast-moving skirmishers. Their leader raised his sword to salute her, a feature she hadn't remembered from the beta.

"Friendly caster with us! Deliver her to the enemy, blades!" the woman's voice called.

Ree smiled, excitement finally bubbling over, worry temporarily forgotten.

"Forward!" she shouted, pointing toward Lucretia's dot with her staff. The group charged ahead, moving even faster.

As they rounded the hill, exposed as they headed to high ground, a wave of arrows arced up toward them. Ree thrust her staff forward, casting her Shield spell. Blue mana coursed through the staff, flowing out to create a dome over the skirmishers. The arrows snapped and shattered on the shield, raining detritus down on all sides.

"Go!" she yelled, dropping the shield. That had tapped a chunk of her mana, down payment on the Incarnation spell.

The field beyond was spotted with skirmishes—cavalry and pikemen, archers and infantry. The units were small, ten to fifteen each, but they added up to a messy melee right quick.

Lucretia was still a ways off, standing on a ledge above a lava flow, red contrails of magic swirling around her like a music visualizer.

A squadron of heavy infantry stepped into their path, two-handed weapons ready. Her skirmishers wouldn't last long against the armored opponents. It was her turn again.

"Step aside!" she said and took her staff in both hands like a lance. She tapped out her barely-recovered mana pool to toss a trio of fireballs. A couple of the soldiers dove out of the way, but the blasts caught the rest of the squad, setting them alight.

In the game, they'd just burn up and drop to the floor. Here, she could smell burned flesh and slagged steel. And hear their screams.

"Fucking hell," Ree said, terrified of what she'd done even as she knew that the soldiers were nothing more than magical constructs. She'd been killing digital mens for decades, but never had it felt quite so real as now.

Focus, kid, she heard in Eastwood's voice, her mind internalizing his advice. Her skirmishers dove on the remaining heavy infantry and put them out in moments.

They regrouped and pushed on. "We need to get to that caster. Cut me a path!" she said.

Lightning split the air, and when the flash receded, Lucretia's Incarnate form loomed over the field, thirty feet tall, glowing red. It looked like a cross between Lucretia and a Fade spirit out of *Dragon Age*. Lucretia had chosen the artillery-esque Doombringer, surprising absolutely no one.

The Incarnate reached forward, and a red vortex formed, charging with the sound of a thousand stones grinding against a thousand mills.

That's my cue to take cover, Ree admitted, jumping behind a rough outcropping of volcanic rock. According to video game logic, the cover should protect her, even if a real explosion would still envelop the area. To be safe, she cast her Shield spell again as the blast hit.

Her mana pool gave out as the blast faded. She was two-thirds of the way to her Incarnate spell, and she'd been casting almost all-out. Lucretia must have used an artifact to charge her spell this fast. Or she'd cheated. Same difference. The likelihood that the Auctioneer was going to step in, even if Lucretia cheated, was about zero.

Reassuringly, this wasn't too different from being a late twenty-something with two jobs and a life trying to play an FPS with teenagers who basically lived on the multiplayer queues. She just assumed everyone knew more and had more stick time, and she made do.

Ree peeked out from the rock formation to see Lucretia Sauron-ing her way through Ree's army, knocking cavalry and Treefolk aside like they were LEGOs.

She called up her Mana Sink spell, designed to damage Incarnates, and saw that her pool was still empty. She needed to rack up some minion kills to speed her mana recharge, or find another way to take on Lucretia.

Neither option seemed terribly viable with her Doombringer dominating the field. Ree snuck around through cover, hoping that Lucretia was focused enough on rampaging that she wouldn't notice one little sorceress wandering around.

A searing bolt vaporizing a pillar in front of Ree told her that those hopes were entirely, head-deskingly unrealistic. She broke into a sprint, slaloming her way between rocks, trying to make it harder for Lucretia to aim her blasts. The detonation of a fire burst seared her left side before Ree could dive between the seams in one of the mini-volcanoes.

Falling down toward the lava, Ree activated a levitation spell (which was blessedly free, mana-wise, unless you wanted to ramp up the speed), which let her drop back onto the ledge. The heat was nearly overwhelming, but Ree forced herself to remember that it was all special effects. Spectral effects, maybe, but still not really real.

But real or not, it wouldn't take long for Lucretia's Incarnate to close the distance and fire down at Ree, fish-in-a-very-hot-barrel-style. *Keep moving. That armor's around here somewhere, right?* Ree pulled up the details from the last time she and Charlie had talked about the game during a Zombie Café shift a couple weeks back.

Ree searched the volcano cavern, looking for the golden chest that would contain the level's best artifact, a suit of lava armor able to turn aside both fire damage and the attacks of an Incarnate.

"But it only shows up after a hundred minion deaths, so you can't just go sprinting for the loot," Charlie had said. The memory shook loose as she jumped over a chasm, bubbling lava just feet from her boots.

With Lucretia's rampage, it might not take long for the kill counter to grow that high. The sound of charging magic echoed down the cavern, and Ree looked up to see the chasm filling with fire. Ree raised her staff for another Shield spell.

The protective dome turned aside Lucretia's magic.

For a second.

The spell's upkeep zeroed out Ree's mana pool, and then fizzled with the pathetic sound of spent carbonation.

She felt a moment of intense heat, and then nothing.

The world reset after a flash of white.

First point went to Lucretia.

1–0.

Ree respawned at another part of the battlefield, away from her original muster point. She stood on the bloodied field, beside a freshly-spawned group of cavalry.

"Friendly caster!" their leader said, acknowledging her as the skirmishers had done before.

Ree made for the head of the column. "We have an enemy Incarnate, which means we need to fight smart!" Her Incarnation pool was two-thirds full, close enough to shape how she could play this life.

Ree paid into the pool again with Haste spells, increasing the cavalry's speed even more. Then she levitated her way up to a horse, riding behind one of the cavalrywomen.

"Up and to the right—we're going to come at her from behind and above, charge down that hill!" Cavalry had limited usefulness on this level, since the ground was so uneven. But there were a couple of pathways where they could build up to charging speed, and that hill was one of them.

Ree looked at her mini-map and saw two other squads on that path, along with an enemy unit. In the distance, Lucretia and her armies dominated the center of the battleground.

The cavalry charged their way through the narrow path, each step carrying them farther and faster than it should, thanks to her buff. Her mana pool refilled, slowly.

She needed to rack up some kills if she was going to keep up these buffs.

Around the corner was a unit of pikemen.

"Fucking great," Ree said. Pikemen were the rock to the cavalry's scissors in the balancing act of the game.

Again, it'd be up to Ree to lead. She had the chance to strike first, since the pikemen needed to be dug in to properly break the cavalry's charge.

Ree tapped out her mana pool for another burst of fireballs, crisping nearly half the pikemen and clearing the way for her unit. Their numbers reduced and the remaining ones flailing around in DoT-land, the cavalry broke the pikemen with only a few casualties.

Beyond, they met up with a trio of Treefolk, freshly respawned. The Treefolk gave a *Harrooo!* in greeting and fell into step. Ree cast Haste again, bringing the molasses-slow elementals up to human infantry speed.

With two strong units now at her back, Ree forged ahead, making her way to the center of the field. Her Incarnate spell was almost ready.

Payback time, Ree thought, urging the cavalry forward.

Ree charged down the hill with her troops, Treefolk forming a wedge at the front, which her cavalry split around to strike at the corners. Her cavalry trampled over a unit of skirmishers, and was plowing their way through heavy infantry when Lucretia turned her attention to this side of the battle. She dissolved the ground beneath the cavalry. Horses and riders alike fell, breaking legs and shattering spears. Ree jumped off her horse, landing softly thanks to her Levitation spell.

Next, Lucretia turned to the Treefolk. Ree activated her Mana Sink spell, which shot out with a *twhorp* sound. The Mana Sink took a motorcycle-size chunk out of the Incarnate, and all of a sudden, the Treefolk were forgotten, the Strega turning her attention directly to Ree.

Ree slid to the side, using another rock outcropping for cover as Lucretia retaliated. Ree pumped some mana into her Levitation spell to get limited flight, taking to the sky and firing the Mana Sink again. Lucretia tried to slide her Incarnate out of the way, but the Artillery form was the slowest.

The burst of counter-magic took another chunk out of the Incarnate, and Ree plunged back down to the battlefield. Ree fired one more Mana Sink, but this time Lucretia didn't move, pressed from the other side by a team of Elephant riders, a rare unit span.

At last, some luck on my side.

The ground rushed up at her, as Ree dropped down on Lucretia's Incarnate. She kicked on her Levitation spell to avoid going splat, and landed on the back of the Incarnate. Lucretia's magical form clawed at its back, trying to tear Ree off its vulnerable neck.

"Take this!" Ree shouted, charging up a final Mana Sink spell, and unloading it into the back of the Incarnate's head. The spirit exploded, sending Ree flying back and up onto the ledge.

She'd taken a beating, but beaten wasn't dead. Ree pulled herself up with her staff and saw that Lucretia was gone.

1—1.

"Form up!" Ree shouted to her forces, which were making short work of the opposing units, no longer bolstered by the Incarnate.

The Mana Sink spells hadn't filled her Incarnate pool at all, since it was magic used to cancel magic, so she waited for her pool to refill and then applied buffs to the Elephant riders.

The sky went redder than normal as the big volcano nearby erupted. Soot grew thicker in the air, and bursts of lava started raining from the sky.

"Cool!" Ree said, dodging the burning hail. The battlefield hadn't done *this* in the beta.

Out of the volcano, riding a flow of lava, came Lucretia, already in her Incarnate again.

"How the hell?" Ree said as the crimson-and-molten-red spirit came crashing down at her, reversing her mass-driver maneuver.

"Move back!" she told her troops, pumping some mana into her Levitation to move back.

Lucretia's Incarnate crashed into the ground in a three-point landing, then unleashed a gout of flame, burning Ree's nearby troops, including one of the war elephants.

Ree raised a shield while her troops repositioned, tapping out her mana pool once more and finally filling her Incarnate pool.

But just as she was about to begin the ritual that would summon her Incarnate, Lucretia melted the ground beneath Ree, sending her dropping into an end-of-the-world crevasse.

"Shit!" she said, activating her levitation spell. But with no mana left, and no ground to stand on to cast the spell, she was stuck floating toward cover.

Lucretia's Incarnate stomped to the crevasse and filled it with flame.

"Two–one, girl!" the Strega yelled, haughty.

Ree blanked out after another moment of burning pain.

"Shit," Ree said as she reappeared at her side's base camp. NPCs sat and stood, wounded—these were filler characters; they'd never actually been combatants, just added to make the battle seem more epic, more real. What she wouldn't give to be able to stuff spears in these soldiers' hands and send them out to battle.

She shook the burning pain off for a moment, the fictional strain of the battle seeming uncomfortably real. Much more of this and she'd need to sleep the fight off for a weekend. And if she lost, then Lucretia would walk free for everything she'd done.

And that would just not fucking do.

Ree's Incarnate spell was ready. She had her own personal War God coming.

The Guardian wasn't the toughest spirit, or the most damaging. But it was adaptable, and more maneuverable than the Doombringer.

Lapis-blue light formed around her as she chanted, lifting her high into the air as the spirit form coalesced around her. She felt her awareness expand to fill the three-story-tall being, the soldiers before her now as small as toddlers in her eyes.

"A girl could get used to this," Ree said, reveling in the sensation of power—of power and will creating form. If only the PC version of the game came with sensation kicks like this, gamers wouldn't ever log out. Maybe it was better that the VR systems had never really taken off.

Ree tromped forward, resisting the urge to make Mechwarrior piston sounds. With the Guardian, she moved at four times her caster pace, so she booked it toward the fissure with the lava armor. She knew more than a hundred minions had bought it by now, so it was time to turn the tables. Guardians could outmaneuver Doombringers in a one-on-one fight, but Ree wanted every advantage, especially since Lucretia seemed like she had Incarnates coming out of her ass.

She cut her way through a unit of infantry on the way down into the crevasse, then caught a single confused troll that seemed to have lost its sisters and brothers.

Ree batted the troll into the lava, then saw her prize on the far side of the pit. The rocks between were sized for casters, not Incarnates, so Ree cast Haste on the Incarnate, then with a whoop she jumped the lava in a single bound. She raised dust as she landed, which settled to reveal the chest. Her Incarnate reached out, and the breastplate of the armor rose into the sky, spinning. The icon dissolved, and the armor straps wrapped around her Incarnate, body wreathing in blue flame.

"Sweet."

Ree made her way up out of the crevasse, then over to the highest peak, where lava bubbled over, covering everything on the mountainside in molten death. Except for her. Ree waded through the lava like it was water and turned to face Lucretia, who was scaling the mountain.

Ree shouted, launching into *The Simpsons'* "See My Vest" as Lucretia approached, her Doombringer lumbering along slowly, made slower by avoiding the lava flows.

Ree charged another round of fireballs. Looking at the one clear path through the lava, she was able to predict the Strega's path, and lead the Incarnate, hoping she remembered how quickly the Fireball spell's blast flew at longer distances.

Both hands thrusting forward, she released the spell, which shot out a trio of spiraling fireballs, burning white-hot, thanks to her armor upgrade. Lucretia's Incarnate stopped, then tried to reverse, but the spell still caught it in a glancing blow, burning torso-size chunks off her magical titan.

And now for the encore. Ree cast her arms wide and used the Guardian's signature spell, summoning a giant fuck-off great sword that filled the Incarnate's hands. Ree charged down the mountain, splashing through lava like the shallows of the beach, then leaped up, drawing the sword over her head. Lucretia raised a shimmering shield in defense, but Ree's flaming great sword shattered the shield and cleaved Lucretia's Incarnate in two.

2–2. The next point would determine the winner and prove Lucretia's guilt or innocence.

"Boom, baby!" Ree pressed her advantage, mowing through Lucretia's minions, which also charged Ree's mana pool. She rallied her troops just beyond a break in the lava flow, since her armor's resistance didn't extend to her minions. The artifact was boss-tastic, but it wasn't god mode.

Speaking of bosses, a trio of Volcanic Rock Constructs crested the hill, steps crushing and cracking the stone beneath them. And behind them came Lucretia, again in her Incarnate form.

"Are you fragging kidding me?" Ree shouted at the air, half out of frustration, the other half hoping that maybe the Auctioneer would step in and call the game on the obviously-cheating Lucretia.

But the world didn't bother answering, so Ree was stuck with a whole lotta angry coming her way. She ordered her troops into formation, the pikemen in front, Elephant riders on the side to flank, and archers standing by, for all the good they'd do. She'd need the hammer-wielding berserkers to have a chance of denting the Constructs' armor, and they weren't anywhere to be seen.

"You're fucking cheating, I know it!" Ree shouted across the battlefield, betting that Lucretia's Incarnate could hear her just fine.

"It only looks like cheating because you have no clue what you're doing, child."

"Bullshit! I know this game just fine. The first one, I'll give you. Maybe even the second. But there's no way you built up the mana for those Incarnate spells that fast this time. How are you doing it? Some kind of artifact you brought with you? Sorcerous cheat codes?"

"That's for me to know, and you to resent. That armor doesn't make you invincible, and my friends here are eager to prove it."

The Constructs plowed through the pikemen, shattering shafts and crushing bodies beneath beach-ball-size fists. The Elephants charged into their flanks, knocking the Constructs over. But then they got right back up. Lucretia's Incarnate disintegrated one of the Elephants with a wave of its hand, then stepped through its space in formation, making her way toward Ree.

Ree brought her great sword around, still confident that her Guardian form could win in a one-on-one against the

Doombringer at close range. Ree strafed around to the side, moving as fast as she could, boosting the Incarnate with another enchantment. Lucretia lashed out with a red energy whip but missed Ree once, twice, before the third strike cracked across her Incarnate's chest, sliding off the armor.

In return, Ree chopped down with a swing of her great sword, cutting off one of the Incarnate's arms. Lucretia screamed, then pushed her Incarnate forward, wrapping its remaining arm around Ree's Incarnate, bringing the two into a tired-boxer clinch. But with no ref to pull them apart, Ree pulled the sword up to slice the Doombringer off her.

But instead Ree felt the power, the scale of the Incarnate, disappear. She shot up and back as if launched from a catapult. She kept her eyes on the Incarnates, which dissolved in each other's arms.

Martyr.

Fucker. One of the Doombringer's alternate powers was to sacrifice itself to destroy another Incarnate. The casters survived, however.

So they'd be finishing this on foot, with a straight-up magical duel or a race to fill their mana pools.

Ree had no interest in waiting again, and poured mana into her Levitation spell, flying forward as fast as she could. She had to end this soon, before Lucretia could pull another trick out of her voluminous sleeve.

CHAPTER FOUR

Finish Her!

Lucretia's Constructs tore up Ree's forces; the pikemen were gone, the Elephants routed. Now the Constructs were King Kong–ing their way through a group of Ree's infantry, tossing soldiers left and right. Lucretia had rejoined the fight, shooting lightning bolts from the back of one of the Constructs in order to stay out of the way of Ree's ground forces.

Which conveniently put her into easy line of sight for Ree's own attacks. Ree flew low, coasting just a yard above the rough terrain. She hid behind a ruined pillar, charging a Fireball spell. She popped out and fired, hoping they would slow Lucretia and maybe even bring down the Constructs so she could focus on Lucretia alone, with the minions left to pound it out on their own.

The fireballs shot with less heat, now that her armor was gone, its timer reset. One sheared a leg off the Construct that Lucretia was riding, but the Strega saw the spell coming and flew off, leaving the construct to crash into infantry like a shattered mountain.

Lucretia flew forward, her staff gathering energy for a spell. Ree started weaving a Mana Sink, and threw it forward to cancel out Lucretia's fire burst, jumping out from cover and making her way across the ruined plane toward Lucretia. It took a lot of mana to cancel out spells, but if Ree could just get close . . .

Another blast shot forward, and Ree flew over the blast, switching back to the free levitation for a controlled fall. She zipped left and right, the searing air whipping her hair into an unruly mane.

But with each blast dodged, Ree got closer and closer. When she was within fifty feet, Lucretia responded to Ree's aerial charge by backpedaling, flying up and back. But that required going over the battlefield, where Ree's archers had just respawned. Lucretia took a volley of arrows, swatting most out of the air, but not all.

A pair of arrows stuck out from the Strega's leg and waist as Ree approached.

"Converge on the caster!" she shouted, her orders carrying to her force's armies, what few were left after the Constructs' rampage. The Constructs would catch up and crush her minions soon, but Ree didn't need longevity, just this one last push.

She maxed out her levitation spell, closing the distance to Lucretia as she came in from above at an angle. The Strega filled the air with another burst of fire, and Ree emptied her mana pool on a Shield. More than a bit singed, she soared through the fire and smoke, turning left to adjust as Lucretia fled.

Ree cut off her levitation and dove straight at Lucretia, leaning into her staff like a lance. The staff caught the Strega beside her wounded hip, and the women tumbled to the ground. Ree's impact was cushioned by the other woman, but not so much that the sharp rock didn't tear through her robes, opening scores of cuts along the way.

Lucretia unleashed a burst of fire as the women got to their feet. Ree dove to the side, rolling and collecting more cuts for her dodginess, but cuts were better than becoming barbecue, hands down.

Ree swung her staff in both hands, the weapon slamming into Lucretia's free arm with a satisfying crack. Ree twisted her grip around like she was working a longsword, and hacked again at the Strega as she backpedaled across the rough terrain.

Moving backward when you couldn't see where you were going? Not a great idea. Ree hopped to the side and thrust forward with the staff, shooting a weak burst of fire with her sliver of mana. Lucretia canceled it out with Shield, but that left the Strega with no mana to fly. So when she stepped back onto a distinct lack of rock, she was screwed. Lucretia kicked on her levitation to avoid the fall, but without more mana to move quickly, she was a floating duck. Ree tackled the Strega and wrapped her staff around the woman's neck, grappling the weapon and the woman's arms up and putting her into a modified half nelson.

Lucretia screamed, trying to fight back. But they were themselves enough in this world that Ree had the strength advantage. Ree's grip slipped, the staff falling away.

Shit. There went her easy win.

Ree pushed the pair toward the ground to recover the staff, but Lucretia pushed up with her flight, sending the two women spinning in midair. Ree grabbed the straps of the Strega's dress with one arm, then wrapped her other around Lucretia's neck. She tightened the choke and held on for dear life.

Spinning and twisting, the world moving too quickly to keep her bearings, Ree felt like she was going to hurl sprites.

Just. Hold. On.

And after an indeterminate nauseating forever, Lucretia went limp.

With her spell gone, the pair fell. A lava plume burned her for all her remaining life, but Lucretia's death logged first.

3–2.

Ree snapped back to the real world amid a chorus of cheers. She looked left to Lucretia, whose face was beet red with anger. Behind her, Ree saw the stats scroll for the battle light up the massive screen, with video replays of the kills.

Note to self: Get the replay video on that to run on loop with a digital picture frame. Hot damn.

Ree knew that she should step over and offer Lucretia a "good game" handshake. That's what a good sport would do. But Lucretia's hat trick of Incarnate summons had Ree in a decidedly unsportswomanlike mood.

Instead, she looked back toward the Auctioneer, who looked on with a champion poker face. Accusing Lucretia of cheating wouldn't help now; it'd just make her seem like a bad sport. Ree just needed the result to stick so this whole thing could be over and done with. Preferably with a random pot of gold in Lucretia's skirts that could pay for all of the repairs at Grognard's.

The Auctioneer raised her arms and spoke over the crowd. "Quiet!"

A few more whoops and a little bit of applause later, the crowd quieted down. Grognard wrapped Ree into a rib cage–crushing bear hug, picking her up off the ground. Ree gasped, then wobbled as the brewmaster set her back on her feet.

"Way to go," Grognard said.

Eastwood stood and offered a hand, green gills not doing anything to wipe the smile from his face.

"Couldn't have played it better myself," he said.

"If they'd been playing *Goldeneye*, you'd have cleared her out three to zero, flu or no," Ree said.

"True, but this was nearly as good." Eastwood blew his nose, blinked, and then seemed to summon as much dignity as possible to say, "Thank you, Ree."

"Cut this shit out; you're going to make me cry," Ree answered.

Eastwood wrapped her up into a hug, whispering in her ear,

"Lucretia cheated. She won't leave well enough alone. This isn't over."

At that, Ree stiffened, then looked over her shoulder at Lucretia, who stormed back and forth, fuming. If she were like Ye-jun the Manwha specialist, she'd have clouds of steam-anger attached to her forehead.

"Be seated, everyone!" the Auctioneer said, and Ree took her seat once more, facing the front of the room.

"Lucretia d'Fete has been convicted in trial by combat and will be subject to the community's highest penalty: banishment. But first, Lucretia will pay all damages for Grognard's store, totaling fifty thousand dollars, to be delivered by the Autumn Equinox." Lucretia thrashed in her seat, livid.

"And to ensure that she does not strike out again, she will submit to another giese to not curse, assault, or otherwise harass any members of the Pearson Underground. She will be allowed to use her magic only for self-defense and to benefit Grognard's Grog and Games until such time as the damages have been paid. After that, she will leave Pearson and never return, under penalty of death.

"So say we all," the Auctioneer pronounced.

"So say we all," the crowd repeated.

Lucretia spat out a long string of Latin, gesticulating at Eastwood and Ree. But there was no power behind it, no crackling of energy. It wasn't Hexomancy, it was just trash-talking in Latin and rude gestures.

"Let's get out of here, before Lucretia blows her top," Grognard said.

"What about the giese?" Ree asked.

Grognard nodded back at the Auctioneer. "She's got it. Drinks are on me."

Never one to turn down celebratory booze, Ree led the group away from the trial floor. Pumped fists, applause, and handshakes of congratulation were waiting for her from the crowd. Patricia Talon picked Ree up into a bear hug,

Chandra gave her a fist bump, Uncle Joe presented her with a limited-edition *Magic: the Gathering* championship card, and Shade gave her a pair of his Spirit Shades, which could peek across to the Spirit realm, on top of being totally rad-looking '80s sunglasses. She'd bought a pair back during the shoot of *Awakenings,* and then promptly lost them in the sewers.

After they made their way through the crowd, Grognard led the trio back to his regular booth spot. He stepped over to the side, nodding at Reyna, who ran a Geekomancer's dream of a costuming shop. If she ever had the money, Ree would gladly drop several grand there, putting together outfits to go along with some of her favorite movies, seeing if she could borrow a page from Talon and use costuming to enhance her Geekomantic antics. Mostly, she just wanted the Jedi robes, because duh.

Grognard pulled fabric off a boxy shape, revealing a black cooler. Sliding it over into his spot, he cracked the lid, revealing four growlers with Grognard's label on the side. He handed one each to Eastwood and Ree, then took the third for himself.

"To justice," Grognard said.

"I wish Drake had been here to see the look on Lucretia's face," Ree said.

"Well, he isn't, so that means more beer for us," Eastwood said, raising his growler to toast. "To Justice."

Ree clinked her growler against the others, and repeated the toast.

They drank and talked for another hour, a receiving line of congratulations interrupting the privacy of the moment. With the store closed, there wasn't a better place to accept the well wishes, so the three of them stood around as what seemed like the entire Pearson community came by to offer their thanks, including Tomas's gaming buddies, Alexi's sister, and Siobhan's twin, Maeve.

Ree hadn't known any of the fallen well, aside from their preferred drink order and their taste in card game factions.

But this wasn't about Ree, it was about the fallen, and so she was as gracious as she could be, letting the friends and family get the closure they needed by thanking the woman who had ensured justice for their loved ones.

"You're a hero," Maeve said, teary-eyed. "I'm so glad that you joined us."

A hero. Ree didn't feel like a hero, but heroism wasn't for yourself. That was kind of the point, wasn't it?

They finished off the growlers, splitting the fourth among them. They left with an entourage when the Market closed down, trusting in the safety of numbers.

"You done good, kid," Grognard said as he split off from the group.

"When are you going to stop calling me 'kid'?" Ree asked.

Grognard harumphed. "When you're older than I am."

"See ya, old man," she countered.

"Don't you get started." Grognard nodded and pulled the door of the bar closed. The brewmaster never talked about his house/apartment/lair; it was always the bar. Just another thing he kept close to the chest.

The honor guard escorted Ree back to the U-District, where Eastwood bade her a sniffly good night.

"I'll call in the morning."

"Must you? Can't I have one nice Sunday hangover without supernatural bullshit dominating my life?"

"Maybe next week," Eastwood said.

This is my life, Ree thought as she tromped home to collapse, not interested in throwing a Shake of Victory over a liter and a half of beer. That way lay doom.

True to his word, Eastwood woke Ree at 7:45 the next morning. Ree had to be up for a temp job at 9, so it was only a minor sin against slumber.

She snatched the buzzing phone from her bedside table, seeing Eastwood's picture and info on the screen. "What?" Ree asked, still groggy.

"Good morning to you, too," Eastwood said, far too peppy for the hour.

"You're just saying that because you haven't been to bed yet."

"Yeah, so? I was up, checking on that Latin that Lucretia spouted there at the end. The translation is about as ominous as you'd expect."

"A curse upon your nads and seven generations of your descendants, or something like that?"

That got a chuckle. "More or less. It reads like prophecy. And the thing that's got me worried is the line about the three fates and their shears, each coming for their due."

"So you're due for some bad haircuts? They can't be much worse than the shaggy antihero mullet you're rocking now."

"I really shouldn't bother calling you before your first coffee."

"No, you shouldn't. See what happens when you do? You get ninety percent snark, ten percent coherence."

"Come and see me when your shift is done. We need to make plans."

"Fuck. Got it. Try not to get dead while I answer phones, okay?"

"No promises."

⨂

Nine hours later, after several hundred conversations' worth of helping people get onto Oregon's no-call list, Ree's brain was oozing out of her ears from banality. She skipped dinner, catching the crosstown bus from the financial district back toward the Fortress of Dorkitude.

She walked down the steps and buzzed at the door, a recent concession Eastwood had made to civilization, or at least to Ree not having to pound on the door or text him to be let in.

Eastwood buzzed her in, and Ree stepped down into the mini–*Warehouse 13* of Eastwood's lair, metallic shelves stacked twenty feet high, running the length of the fifty-yard-long room. The shelves were chock-full of memorabilia, signed first editions, movie props, and more. As far as Ree could tell, it was the most complete Geekomantic arsenal this side of San Diego Comic-Con. But it was also Eastwood's business, the storeroom for his online merchandise store, which kept the very high lights on and maintained Eastwood's brooding renegade hero lifestyle (aka pizza and beer).

"Sup," Ree said, rubbing her temples. Her old prescription was too weak now, and since she couldn't spend eight hours doing data entry with her eyes six inches from the screen, she'd given herself a headache by staring through prescription lenses at an old LCD screen the whole day.

"Can you order dinner? With a side of migraine medicine?" she asked as she approached Eastwood's *Person of Interest* wall, with a dozen flat-screen TVs hooked up to the wall to form a giant viewscreen. Below it was a table overflowing with laptops, desktops, video game consoles, and media devices older than she was.

"Also, what's with the Betamax player?" she asked.

"I was doing research," Eastwood answered.

That was answer enough. Ree prided herself on her genre emulation skills, but when it came to magical ritual and research, Eastwood ran circles around her.

Eastwood's fingers ran like quicksilver over a keyboard, and a single screen loaded an image of an aged manuscript. "So, when I ran the recording . . ."

Ree's stomach grumbled. "Dinner?"

"Didn't you eat on the way?"

"No. I'm at friends-with-detriments levels of familiarity with broke. Why else would I be working minimum-wage temp jobs on a Sunday?"

"A sense of civic duty?"

"I think being a superhero exempts me from that," Ree said.

"No tights, not a superhero."

"Except for the time that wearing tights saved your ass."

"I had the Duke right where I wanted him."

"Kicking your ass?" Ree asked.

"How does Turbo's sound?" Eastwood said, changing the subject.

Ree made a most unladylike moan of pleased hunger.

"I'll take that as a yes."

"Always."

"You going to be okay to work before food, or do I have to banter with your hangry self until the food is ready?"

"I'll be good," Ree said, crossing her heart.

"So, I recorded the whole trial, just in case."

"Of course," Ree said. "That's not paranoid or intrusive at all."

"Paranoid and right," Eastwood said. "When I ran Lucretia's rant through the translator, here's what I got."

The river runs astray, plagued water seeping into the bedrock.
Sisters three come as the seasons turn,
shears in hand, they will cut apart the rotten knot.

"So you're plagued water now? What's up with that?"

"Yeah, I don't know. Poetic crap. But when I went back to my sources on the Strega, it started to make a bit more sense.

"When a Strega fails in her assignment, three more are dispatched to correct the error. One comes each season, striking when their powers are at their strongest." Another run on the keyboard, and three more screens popped up with calendars.

"The Autumnal Equinox, Winter Solstice, and the Spring Equinox."

"Well, the equinox is, like, three months off. Plenty of time to figure out how to take out the Strega. What do the books say about the others? Are they all like Lucretia?"

"Each Strega has their own M.O. Some are up-close-and-physical; others use cat's-paws and traps. We've got time, but just because the Strega's powers are at their apex at the changing of the seasons doesn't mean they can't take swipes at us ahead of time to put us off our game or the like. We need to be ready every single day."

"*You* need to be ready," Ree said. "You're the plagued water here."

"And you were never supposed to become a Geekomancer."

Well, there was that. Unless that part was a line of bull. But why would Lucretia lie about that part, and not others?

"So what? We're in constant danger anyway."

"It means we need to stick together until we can get the Strega to call off the hit squad or we get through the next year."

"I changed my mind. I do need that food first." Ree resumed rubbing her temples. "If we're going to be *Tonight You're Mine*'d for the next nine months, I'm going to need a better stream of income, unless you want to start working crap temp jobs and hanging out at Zombie Café."

"Frak that. You're working for me."

"I thought you said you could pay 'a little.' I can't live on 'a little.'"

"We'll make it work. I've got some ideas on how to turn a better profit on the business here."

"If we're going to talk business, I am definitely going to need that pizza first," Ree said, picking up her phone.

It picked up on the first ring. It was Cole, sounding hurried. "Pearson's best, Turbo's Pizzeria?"

"Hey, Cole, it's Ree. I've got a long night in front of me, so I'm going to need you to pull out all the stops."

"Hit me," Cole said.

Ree laid out a massive food order, sat for a while to rest her eyes, and then went to retrieve the pizza and prepare for an all-nighter.

CHAPTER FIVE

You Can Be My Long-Lost Pal

FALL

Being a bodyguard was turning out to be not all that bad. In some ways, it was a simpler life. Ree didn't have to run here and there doing crap temp jobs nearly as much and even got to pick up the odd swing shift at Zombie Café. But the long hours wreaked havoc on her social life.

Three months passed almost without Ree's notice, and before long, school was back in session, the U-District flooded with even more students than last year, which had seen record attendance.

Ree clicked through to the next episode of *Community* when a velociraptor stirred in the room beyond. In reality, it was Eastwood, but thinking of his stirring sounds as a velociraptor was funnier, and Ree could use all the excitement she could get. Bodyguarding turned out to be four parts waiting around to one part playing big sister to a dude nearly fifteen years her senior.

Ree checked her phone: 4:31. Eastwood was getting up later and later, like a grizzly bear easing into hibernation.

He was about that hairy, too. Ree'd basically lived at the Dorkcave these last few months, with all of the TMI revelations that came with the territory. Twelve hours of covering Eastwood while he slept and did errands, then home for some blissful alone time and tiny snatches of socialization before crashing out and getting ready to do it all again.

If she were a real bodyguard, for some teen idol or politician, she'd at least be putting away some serious money. As it was, Eastwood's business tricks hadn't done jack squat, and she was getting by on minimum wage, which only worked because Eastwood had media feeds that aggregated everything in the world of pop culture, bringing down Ree's entertainment fees to basically nothing. She'd watched the entire run of *The West Wing*, *Star Trek: The Next Generation*, *M*A*S*H*, and a half-dozen other shows, deepening her love of choice properties to round out her Geekomantic skills.

She found that being strategic was actually counterproductive. She could pick a show for its useful abilities, but she had to like it on its own in order to get any useful power out of it. She tried to give a new superhero show another chance to expand her power range, but it just didn't work for her—too much clunk and not enough zoom, character- and plot-wise.

But several runs through the *Clone Wars* cartoon and *Avatar: The Last Airbender* had led to some respectively Jedi-and-bender-tastic outings with Eastwood, so it was definitely paying off.

Eastwood emerged from his bedroom, toweling off his hair. "Morning."

"That's a very generous interpretation of the word."

"I just woke up, it's morning."

"How solipsistic of you," Ree said.

"I don't taunt you when you've just woken up." Eastwood zombie-shuffled toward the coffeemaker, where a fresh pot sat waiting for him.

That was another part of bodyguarding—it was also like being a personal assistant with a much higher risk of grievous bodily harm. Unless you were comparing it to being a PA in Celebromantic Hollywood. Then the risk was probably about the same.

Eastwood poured himself some coffee in a House Targaryen mug and fished out a doughnut from the mini-fridge. Eastwood ate like a teenager with scurvy but never seemed to get any heavier, constantly carrying around a small spare tire that never inflated any further.

Whereas Ree's infrequent patrolling sessions with Eastwood, and more rarely, Drake, were barely enough to keep her in fighting form. She'd tried doing yoga in the Dorkcave for a couple of weeks but got bored and quit. She tried to get Eastwood to buy a treadmill desk, but that had gone nowhere, and Ree wasn't about to lay out money to get one for her "workplace." And Eastwood was up for sparring only once a month or so. Which left her with running boring circuits around the Dorkcave while listening to podcasts.

"What's the news from the world?" Eastwood asked.

"Life goes on. No alerts, a few flame wars about fall TV, and a lot of buzz about the latest *Iron Man*." Ree waved toward the TV screens, each turned to a different news site: CNN, *Ain't It Cool News*, io9.com, and more.

"You've got cabin fever," Eastwood said. "Let's go out for breakfast."

Ree was on her feet, donning her jacket. "Burger Bin has happy hour starting at five." So did Bites, but Eastwood's tastes ran to the pedestrian.

Eastwood retrieved his lighter trench coat, donning it like a member of the Kingsguard wears his cape, throwing it behind him and putting his arms through the holes all in one smooth motion.

Ree had to admit that it looked pretty cool.

"We're two days away from the equinox. You still think

the Strega are going to come a-knocking?" Ree asked.

"Definitely. If we get through the end of the week with no sign, then I'll do more research. Plus, you don't want to be out of a job, do you?"

Ree made for the door, Eastwood following. He wasn't quite as spry without his coffee. He called it "lubricating the servos." "Out of a job? I could get a real job. I would kill for a real job. Grognard says that he's on track to reopen in November. We get this wrapped up by the end of the month and maybe things can go back to whatever passes as normal in this town."

That got a chuckle. "Strange life, where running around on rooftops and drinking magic beer in a bar in the sewer is normal."

"What can I say, I'm a creature of habit."

⋅✕ˣ◈ˣ✕⋅

The line at Burger Bin was already out the door, but not yet down the street.

As they walked over, Ree texted Drake,

On the town with Baby Bird. You up for some 2nd story action tonight?

Ree and Eastwood chatted about *Leverage* while waiting in line. The Doubt would likely wipe away any magical discussion they had, but Eastwood believed, reasonably, that it was better not to press their luck.

"Plus, you never know when you're being watched," Eastwood said, his paranoia comfortably familiar.

To which Ree said, "I just assume I'm always being watched." An inheritance of Millennial upbringing.

Not expecting to hear back from Drake for several minutes, Ree slipped the phone back into her jacket and continued on.

"After season two, the formula-breaking episodes become even more important. They've got the team dynamic down, but the formula starts to wear thin on even the best episodic show, which is why you need to innovate like *Leverage* did. Without smart writers willing to take risks, you end up with *Law and Order*."

"You take that back," Eastwood said, stalwart *L & O* fan that he was.

"Nope. Show is the background radiation of the cable universe. It's always there, but it doesn't seem to do much more than tell us that something interesting happened once upon a time. Not my scene."

"But Falling Skies is?"

"Can't help it," Ree said. "I was raised on Spielberg. The family focus plays my heartstrings like a puppeteer."

"But it's such bad science fiction," Eastwood grumbled, taking another sip of his coffee. He never seemed to think it odd that he, a grown man, would wander around the neighborhood with mugs of coffee from home, even when standing in line for a restaurant that served its own (passable) coffee. But that was waaay down on Ree's battle-picking list with Eastwood.

Ree peeked ahead in line. There were only two cashiers working. Someone must have called off. At this point, Ree was a regular at Burger Bin. It was one of three places Eastwood liked enough to go out to eat, which meant she'd been coming twice a week for months, and that was on top of her occasional 3 AM milkshake run with Drake after patrolling.

Her phone buzzed, and Ree pulled up the text message.

Dear Ree,

Unfortunately, I am engaged for the evening. I wish you the best with Baby Bird, and do try to find some time for yourself.

I remain,

Drake Winters

One day, that boy would learn to be casual, but he still treated text messages like letters that were best hand-delivered by servants in order to inquire whether a gentleman could call upon a household of acquaintances.

Five bucks said he was going out with Priya. They had been going strong for five months, maybe six, depending on when you started counting.

That hadn't been a nightmare at all. Definitely not. She was simultaneously very happy that Priya finally found a good guy, after several years of rolling critical failures on the Random Dating Encounter charts of OKCupid and Shaadi. com. But on the other hand there was the fluttering in her stomach and uncontrollable grin she got whenever Drake walked in the room.

It was almost intolerable keeping a lid on her libido when he was around. In her real life, friends came first, but in the Underground, Drake was her patrol buddy and outlet for getting away from and venting about Eastwood. Talon didn't patrol anymore, and no one else was up for the high intensity.

Ree texted back,

Got it. Have fun, loverboy.

Twenty minutes later, they got to the front of the line. Eastwood ordered enough food for a basketball starting five, while Ree resisted the urge to have a milkshake for dinner/breakfast and went with their spinach salad, a concession to the crunchiness of the Pacific Northwest. It was a travesty to pass up the amazeballs burgers, but bodyguarding was too sessile, and she'd already had two Burger Bin burgers this week. The law of diminishing returns was seriously undermining her yen for dead cow.

Ree escorted Eastwood back to the Dorkcave, then triple-checked the wards and security and made her way home. She'd been up for going on eighteen hours, playing watchdog since late last evening.

She texted Sandra on the way home, hoping to get some aggressive normalcy on before crashing out for the night.

When Ree arrived back at the Shithole, she discovered a note left on the dinner table in Sandra's precise script, explaining the lack of response via text.

Staying over at Darren's for the weekend. There's chow mein in the fridge!

Miss you,

Sandra

Without a social outlet, Ree didn't have anything more useful to do than catch up on some shut-eye, so she crashed, lightsaber on her bedside table, just in case.

She dreamed about rooftop duels and long shifts staring at the door, nodding off, then being torn apart by razor-sharp tarot cards.

✕◈✕

Buzzing woke Ree from a stone-dead sleep. She clawed for her phone, then jumped several steps toward awake when she saw a text from Priya. It was a group MMS to the Rhyming Ladies.

It was 3:25 AM, and the text was brand-new.

EMERGENCY MEETING, my place. Bring booze.

CHAPTER SIX

The Friend Signal

Ree messaged back as fast as her fingers could type, muscle memory leveraged hard enough that she avoided the typos.

Whoa, what's going on?

The response from Priya came within seconds.

Just come over, please?

A minute later, as Ree was dressing, Anya piped in.

I'm on my way. ETA 30 min. Have Jager, will travel.

Ree threw on last night's clothes, stuffed the lightsaber back into her jacket, and flew out the door with a bottle of Pinnacle whipped-cream vodka.

She wasn't unfamiliar with 4 AM, thanks to her magical superhero lifestyle, but that was usually at the end of her day, not halfway through her night, stumbling with bed-head and a bottle of liquor stuffed into her coat.

There were only a few things that would prompt emergency meetings of the Rhyming Ladies at 3:45 AM without explanation, and very few of them were good.

Priya lived far enough crosstown that Ree had to either jog for a half hour or take a cab, which she knew would be plentiful if she went deeper into the U-District.

An entirely unaffordable $13 cab ride later, Ree buzzed at the front door to Priya's apartment, a fourth-floor walkup in a shadier part of town, three blocks from a park that was largely ceded to drug dealers after nightfall.

Priya buzzed her up, and after a far-too-tiring tromp up the stairs, Ree found herself at Priya's door. Her friend had a shawl drawn around her shoulders. Her makeup was smeared—she'd been crying. The seamstress-engineer was dressed for a night on the town, her brown-black hair tied up and back with gear-bedecked pins, several locks loose as if she'd been . . . well, as if she'd been in a fight, frankly.

Ree's defensive instincts went into overdrive. She'd been out with Drake. What the hell would have gotten her into a fight?

"Thanks for coming," Priya said, sniffing back tears. Ree stepped inside, set the bottle on the foyer table, and grabbed her friend to deploy her most comforting hug.

"Pri, what happened?"

Priya closed the door and stepped back. Priya's studio apartment was two-thirds workshop, one-third actual apartment. Couch and table were mounded over with machinery, bolts of cloth, and several types of sewing machines. She was a perfect complement to Drake in the Steampunk world, her head as much in the clouds about projects as he was.

Ree handed over the bottle, and Priya filled glasses with ice and poured the vodka three fingers to the glass. This was serious fucking business, if Priya was in heavy-pour mode.

"Drake and I were out at a Steampunk maker-space for a meet-up, art show, performances, all that stuff," Priya said, perching on one of her worktables, leaving Ree the uncovered seat. "It was a full schedule, so we didn't get out until after three."

Ree took a long swig of the sweet vodka, resigned to the fact that her whole day was going to be triage mode, even more than she'd expected. This was a breakup story or she was Elmer Fudd.

"We were walking back from Fane and Douglas and a trio of guys in hats and coats blocked us off on the sidewalk and pushed us into the alley." Priya took a slug from her drink. "The bigger two had knives, but the little guy in the middle had a gun, probably a .22."

Priya hugged herself with one hand, defensive body language telling Ree just how scary the encounter must have been. Priya's focus waned; her eyes glossed over. "The lead guy said, 'Give us all your money, and we'll let you go.'"

Priya continued. "I went for my wallet, but Drake stepped forward and tried to defuse the situation."

Ree's bullshit sensors started going off, but she let her friend finish, already suspecting she knew the story behind the story.

"He said, 'Are you quite convinced of the rightfulness and propriety of accosting a young couple in the middle of the night, when there is a police station not three city blocks from this location?'

"And the little guy said, 'Shut your trap, Gov'ner, and give us your money.' The guys with the knives moved forward, and Drake tried to disarm them. He got one's knife away from him, but then the other one came in. They both grabbed him and threw him against the sidewall.

"I yelled for help, and the two guys started beating him. He fought back, and the whole time, the guy with the gun was just looking at me, with the most terrifying look on his face, like the Cheshire cat on meth. The thugs went for him again, so I jumped in and sprayed one with my mace. He yelled, then swung at me. I ducked under that, but the other one grabbed my arm and threw me into the wall, too."

Priya pulled her hair back, revealing the hastily-bandaged wound at her eyebrow, face still crusted in blood. "Drake got back up and clocked one of them over the head, then pulled a knife of his own. The guy with the gun shot Drake in the chest, and he went down."

Fuck. Ree was already suspecting that this story came from the Doubt and not from what really happened, but if Priya was reinterpreting it as a shooting, Drake must be truly hurt.

Ree looked at her glass as she finished a sip. It was already empty. Priya continued. "Then a police siren started, and the muggers ran down the far end of the alley. I grabbed Drake and pulled him up to his feet. But where he'd been shot, there wasn't much blood, just a hole in the shirt. He was wearing a chain mail shirt. 'I've been thinking of taking up historical combat; wanted to see how much these things really weighed.'

"It didn't really make sense, since I didn't hear it. . . ." Priya's eyes glazed over again, and she leaped back into the story.

"But he was okay, and we walked back here." Priya's glass was empty, too, and she topped off both women's booze.

"We patched up," Priya said. "But when that was done, he was all closed off, looking over his shoulder, nervous. He apologized fifteen times in that way only someone like he could, this long litany of his failures and deficiencies all the way back here, about how he should have been able to protect me, that he shouldn't have tried to fight and that they should have run.

"He said that if he couldn't protect me, then he didn't deserve my attentions, like it was his fault that those guys came after us." She stopped, looking down at her glass. She held it in both hands, squeezing hard like she was trying to crush the thing.

"He fucking dumped me twenty minutes after we got mugged in the middle of the warehouse district, then he just left, still apologizing, and told me that I should call you and the others, that he would do what he could to, I don't even know, something. And then he just left."

Ree's internal monologue ran a string of curses, her heartbeat stepping up with sympathy and anger.

"Who the fuck does that? What the hell, Ree? He was all Prince Charming perfect, more than a bit weird, sure. Maybe too into the scene. But one mugging and he completely flips, when he got hurt worse than I did? You know him, right? Through that catering job? Has he pulled something like this before?"

Ree reeled at all the different angles of this clusterfuck unfolding before her. Fifty bucks she didn't have said that the "mugging" was the result of the Doubt, so she needed to get the story from Drake to see if something magical had been the cause, but looking after friends came first.

"I don't know, Pri. You're the first person I know he's dated in town, so I don't know if this is how he does stuff. And I bet he was scared, if he got shot, but that doesn't excuse a goddamned bit of this."

Ree's drink was empty again, and her ears were hot.

The door buzzed.

Priya leaned forward, but Ree raised a hand. "I got it," she said, trying to be calming even when her own emotions were scaling up toward super-storm levels of lividity.

"Sup?" Ree said, pressing the button.

"Ree? It's Anya."

Ree buzzed in Priya, and took the entrance time to walk over and give her friend another hug.

"I'm so sorry, Pri. I didn't know he was an asshole."

"This is the only asshole thing he's done, though. It just doesn't make any sense. Unless all that adventurer bluster was enough of an act that as soon as something real happened, he freaked and ran, tail between his legs."

Ree did some quick calculations. Priya could relay the story to Anya while Ree made a call to get the real scoop. Anya already knew the real deal about magic, ever since Halloween, and had been epic levels of cagey with keeping it all under wraps. "The

Jimmy Olsen to your Superman," she called it. Anya wanted to tell the others, but Ree had wanted to minimize exposure, try to keep the Ladies free of her magical bullshit.

Too late now. The time for full disclosure had come and gone months ago, and the only thing that could be done now was to get it over and done with, come clean and circle the friend wagons.

They opened the door for Anya, who was dressed even more "Oh crap, midsleep emergency" than Ree was, her hair wild, jacket thrown over yoga pants and a sleep shirt. Anya had her keys held in her left hand, Wolverine-style, relaxing as the door opened. She stuffed the keys back into her jacket and said, "Are you okay?"

Anya Rustova (Strength 7, Dexterity 12, Stamina 15, Will 15, IQ 16, Charisma 15—Musician 5 / Geek 2 / Scholar 4 / Opera Diva 3) was built like a classic Russian spy, all curves and vivacity in a compact frame with Brazilian-blowout hair. She was usually a bargain-finding style icon, all cashmere scarves and designer clothes, but she dressed up because she wanted to look good, not because she *needed* to look good. Not offstage at least. And when the Friend-signal went up, looking fancy didn't mean jack.

Ree stepped forward, "You take over for a sec. I need to make a call."

"What?" Anya said. Priya echoed the question.

"It's about Steve," Ree said, using the code they'd adopted to say, "Something magic is up," when they were around friends not in the know. Ree was hoping that pretty soon, Steve would leave town, no longer needed.

"Sure," Anya said, stepping into the apartment.

Ree anger-stomped down the stairs, remembering a flight and a half down that it was the middle of the night and she'd doubtless woken people up on a Monday morning.

She pulled up Drake's number on her Favorites list and called. She got to the front door before he picked up.

"Ahoy ahoy," he said, with the least enthusiasm she'd ever heard him muster over the phone.

Ree was outside, with no one around. But it was still 4 AM. *Fuck it.*

"What the goddamned fucking fuck were you thinking?" she asked, ears on fire like the time she'd tried a ghost chili pepper with nothing but water on hand to drink.

"Ah. You've spoken to Ms. Priya, then. First, let me—"

"No 'ah' bullshit. Tell me what happened, because I'm pretty sure it wasn't thugs with knives, and I want to know the truth before I roast you over the coals and feed your skinny ass to the gnomes."

He was silent for a beat. When he breathed in, she heard a wince of pain, which undercut her rage, but not enough. Full-on sisters-before-misters mode was on.

"On the journey back from the gathering, we were assaulted by a panther, or something close enough to the form of a panther as to be indistinguishable. If panthers could climb and hang on walls, which as I recall, they mostly cannot."

"Less taxonomy, more explain-y," Ree said.

The sound of ripping duct tape came over the phone, and then more wincing. "The panther crawled down the side of the building and leaped at me. I pulled Priya back into the alley and threatened the panther with my handgun, but it pressed the attack. I fought back, but the beast was terribly fast and quickly had me on the ropes, mauling me against the sidewall, my gun cast aside. I'd thought that we'd be safe; the crime reports for that neighborhood are consistently two orders of magnitude lower than others, and with monster attacks trending within three percent of those crime reports, given the Doubt—"

Ree cut him off again. "The parts about Priya, please," Ree said, anger at having to get Drake back on topic doing nothing to diffuse her rage, though it was entirely familiar. In better circumstances, this would be a gentle ribbing, not an interrogation.

"She sprayed the panther-thing with her mace—quite

bold, but it had little effect. The creature cut her face before returning to me. I managed to wound the creature with my knife after it gouged me, and then the beast thought better of the fight. It scaled the walls, disappearing onto the roofs.

"After that, I escorted Priya home. I told her that if I was so careless as to not be able to protect her from the dangers of the city, then it would be far better for her if I removed myself from her life, as I did not deserve her affections."

"Bullshit, Drake. This random-encounter shit happens to everyone. If you're embarrassed about being underprepared, then prepare better. And the only person who gets to decide if you're worthy of Priya's affections is Priya. If you asked for her to forgive you—did you even wait for her response, or did you just go gallivanting off into the night to take a page from Eastwood and get your brood on?"

"I thought to spare her the shattering of her worldview that would come from sustained activities in contravention of the Doubt. Better to think poorly of me and be safe."

"Nope, nope, and a whole lot more nope. You can't just turn tail and leave her friends, including me, to clean this up. I'm telling her what really happened, and then you're going to apologize again, this time so she'll remember for real. What happens after that is up to her. You hear me?"

"Yes, ma'am," Drake said, cowed.

"Good. Now get yourself patched up and wait for my next call." Ree took a breath.

"And Drake?"

"Yes?"

"I'm glad you're both okay. If she was on her own, she might not have made it. You fucked up, but not all the way."

"Thank you, Ms. Ree," Drake said, reverting to the more formal address.

"Night," she said, and hung up.

Ree dropped her phone back into her jacket and stared at the midnight street. Lights buzzed sodium light onto the ground, joining only two lit windows on the block of apartments stacked on top of bodegas, cell phone/TTY/SIM shops, Thai restaurants, and the one trendy boutique stuffed between the working-class businesses, a single sprout that promised more gentrification to come.

That dork. Her heart had a knife through it and a seeping bullet wound besides, then it had been tossed in a fail blender, thanks to her protectiveness of her friend and her unresolved feelings for the foolhardy, self-righteous jackass she'd just dressed down like he was an army recruit who'd shit his pants.

Ree buzzed Priya's apartment again and walked back up the stairs when the door opened.

Scaling the steps, Ree remembered to be quiet again, which gave her the time to try to tamp down her rage into something slightly more manageable. If she was going to break the masquerade for Priya, this was going to be a very long night, and Drake wouldn't be the only one coming off like an asshole.

She'd considered telling all three of the Rhyming Ladies about the turn for the weird her life had taken back during Halloween, but she'd ended up telling only Anya. Then, every adventure, bizarre attack, or weird development in her life became another brick in the wall she'd never meant to build up between her magical life and her real life, with Anya her begrudging partner in the construction job. The time to come clean had passed months ago, so the only thing left was to just put all her cards on the table.

Which was a fucking fantastic thing to do when she was a half-dozen shots into drunk on an empty stomach and had months of accumulated exhaustion. But you played the hand you were dealt—life wasn't in the habit of handing out Mulligans.

The door was open, and so Ree stepped back inside to dance the Exposition Tango.

CHAPTER SEVEN

The Exposition Tango

Closing the door behind her, Ree walked over to pour herself another glass full of vodka, inadvisable though it may be. She nodded to Anya, and said, "First off, I'm sorry. I should have come clean to you and Sandra a long time ago. I'm a jerk, and I hope you'll forgive me. But what happened tonight was more than enough of a giant neon sign that I can't pretend holding back is doing anything but hurting you."

"What's going on?" Priya asked, back on her perch. Anya stood to the side, her own glass half-empty.

"Back around Halloween, when I got scarce all of a sudden after Jay dumped me, that wasn't the only thing that was happening. . . ."

Ree laid out that whole week's worth of zaniness, including telling Anya, then gave a summary version of what her life had become since that week: patrols, Geekomancy, the Dorkcave, Grognard's, Midnight Market, and more. She left out the real identity of Eastwood's lost love, lest the news get back to her dad. Dad was far away from all of this bullshit, and Ree could spare him from the heartache. That at least was still true.

Then she moved on to explain what had really happened that night, relaying Drake's account, hoping he hadn't been whitewashing the situation to make himself look better. Not likely, given what she knew about Drake, but it was all Ree had to work with, barring mind-reading magic, and that was a Costco-size can of worms she was hoping to avoid, especially involving Drake. There might be . . . side effects.

Priya listened attentively, and after one or two bouts of glassy eyes as the Doubt tried to wipe her memory, the reality of the situation stuck with the woman, who grew livid, her cheeks reddening.

"What the ever-loving fuck, Ree?"

Setting the glass down between several piles of gears and a glue gun, Ree raised her hands in the universal sign of "Hold on; please don't punch me." "I'm sorry. I'm sorry. I'm sorry, I'm so sorry. I was a selfish jackass for keeping this to myself, just like Drake was selfish for not telling you. We didn't want you to get hurt, which is what happens when you're in this world. It's just as scary as it is exciting, and neither of us wanted that for you."

"I'm a godsdamned adult, Ree. I can make decisions for myself." Priya turned to Anya. "And you kept this from us the whole time?"

Anya shrank before Priya's accusation, looking down. "I'm sorry. But Ree's right. After Halloween, I've been carrying a .358 in my purse everywhere I go, and I'm still terrified any time I'm away from crowds."

"But how is that different from real life?" Priya asked. "Monster or meth-head, getting jumped in an alley is getting jumped in an alley."

"It is and it isn't. When monsters and shit know you can see them, they tend to get a hell of a lot more aggressive. But that's no excuse. Now you know. It doesn't make what Drake did any better, but now you know the truth, and you can decide what you want to do."

Priya took another sip, wobbling ever so slightly. "Thank you for finally telling me the truth," she said, the emphasis on *finally* stabbing like a misericorde straight through Ree's heart. "And what I want to do now is be alone."

Anya went over to give Priya a hug, but she brushed the diva off, making her way toward the kitchen.

Taking the cue, Ree and Anya left to the sounds of the triple locks on Priya's apartment door and walked in silence down to the street.

"That went awesome," Anya said.

"Could have gone worse," Ree answered. "She could have disowned us as friends right there."

"Who says she didn't?"

"Let's just go home." The pair walked to the cross street, Ree keeping a hand on the hilt of her lightsaber even as her vision blurred, lagging behind the movement of her head.

Anger-drinking while explaining magical bullshit was, in reality, a terrible idea. She'd need a good liter or so of water and several hours before she'd be worth anything to anyone.

After a few minutes' wait, a cab turned the corner, and they flagged it down.

Anya dozed with her head on Ree's shoulder as the cab headed toward Anya's side of town to drop her off first.

All the while, Ree beat herself up mentally, pulling no punches. Months of omissions and deceptions all spilled out at once. It was like ripping a bandage off all at once, only this bandage was one of fifteen, each covering a different psychic wound. The melange of mental bullshit in her life, between Drake and Priya, Eastwood's paranoia, the ruins of Grognard's, and the maybe-threat of the Strega was just too much for her emotional RAM to handle.

The cab finally arrived at her street, and Ree forked over half of her remaining money.

Note to self: Invoice Drake for the booze and that cab ride. When you're done being too mad to talk to him.

She took the stairs up to the Shithole very, very slowly, now that the enormity of her binge-drinking had hit her like a backpack full of bricks.

Step one was water.

Step two was food.

Steps three through six were more water.

Step seven, if she made it that far, was more sleep.

Ree got as far as step three when her phone lit up again.

"No," she said, staring at her cell as it displayed Eastwood's name and picture. "Nope."

The call went to voicemail, and was quickly followed by a text message.

Come quick. I just got jumped.

"Fuuuck," Ree said, reading the message.

Myh hoem hlife just blewq up. totally drnkg rught nnw.

She pressed send before seeing how typo-tastic her message was, but she let it slide, since it was an accurate representation of her not-fit-for-duty-ness.

Shit. Get over here as fast as you can, then. I'm going into lockdown. Email when you're at the door, everything else will be shut off.

The headstrong part of her wanted to stomp back downstairs and go to war, but Ree had, in this case, enough self-awareness to know that doing so might just get her killed. And while that might resolve the love triangle that had just jumped in a bucket of gasoline and then started playing with a butane torch, it wouldn't do Ree any good. Self-immolation solved so few problems, in reality.

Returning to steps three through seven, Ree topped off her oversized plastic cup with more water and tiptoed to her room as best as she could for the sake of her neighbors, only causing two different crashing thumps as she knocked books and a stack of bills to the floor.

Shitshitshitshit, Ree thought on a loop, sneaking into the bedroom and closing the door behind her.

Ree took up her laptop and earphones and settled into a drunken meditative stupor, guided by last week's episodes of a daily news show, downing water as quickly as her stomach could handle.

Five episodes, four refills, and three trips to the bathroom later, Ree felt like she had her shit together enough to go over to Eastwood's, though she gave herself only even odds as to whether she'd puke if she had to get into a fight anytime before she could sleep again.

×ׁ×⬡ׁ×ׁ×

The sun was rising as she walked up to the Dorkcave and thumb-typed an email to Eastwood, announcing her arrival.

She thought 6:15 was a reasonable time to pronounce "getting up early," so she'd showered and changed into fresh, combat-ready clothes. She felt approximately 67.4 percent human, which was a good 30 percent more than she'd been expecting.

A minute after her email had winged its way through the Internets, the door swung open with its Foley Artist 101 creaking sound.

Ree stomped down the stairs, taking still-a-bit-tipsy joy in the thunderstorm sound.

Crossing through the stacks revealed a bandaged Eastwood and an empty health potion amid the forest of empty soda cans.

"You okay?" she asked.

Eastwood rubbed the back of his neck. "I've been better. Was my own fault; I shouldn't have gone out without backup."

"No, you shouldn'tvead. Should not have," Ree said, catching her slurred speech and auto-correcting herself.

"Are you okay?" Eastwood asked back.

"Drake and Priya's relationship just blew up because magic and condescension, so Anya and I have been in triage mode, with bonus exposition. I can't keep my friends in the dark about this shit anymore. This is my life, and I want them in my life. Ergo . . ."

"Bad idea, kid," Eastwood said, arms crossed. "That just puts more people into the crosshairs."

"I am not having the Peter Parker secret identity talk right now. Priority here is getting you to a not-in-imminent-danger place. What happened?"

"Got hit-and-run by a derby girl. But, like, an armored, paramilitary derby girl. Her pads were all metal, and her gloves and skates had razors on them."

Eastwood waited a beat, for effect. "We've got a Strega on our hands. Right on time. I don't know if this was a planned ambush, string-tugging and all, or if she just caught me unaware and made the most of the situation. Hard to tell with Fate Witches. She got me but good. Would have punched my ticket if I hadn't BAMF-ed back here with a Nightcrawler card I've been carrying around since Lucretia's trial."

"What did she look like? You get a picture?"

A shake of the head said not only no, but hell no. "I mostly saw her from the back, after she plowed me over and opened me up like a filet. Her uniform was green and silver, the skates were black with the metal cops, and she had black hair tied up into a bun under the helmet. Middle Eastern, bigger, probably five eleven, two hundred pounds. I'd know her if I saw her again, I think. Definitely would if she's in her gear."

"Not a lot of derby girls with steel-plated pads, last time I checked," Ree said. Though armored roller derby did sound like an awesome, terrible idea. Definitely not a lethal, insurance-nightmare-inducing idea. Maybe something for the directors of *Bloodsport* to rally around and use to try to make a triumphant return. "So, you want to go after her now, or try to do some tracking mojo? What's the plan?" she asked.

"A quick check to make sure she isn't laying C4 in the outside wall of the building wouldn't go unappreciated. Short patrol, maybe, with one earbud plugged into my security systems here, in case she wanted to draw us out in order to trap the place up."

"That'd be pretty unwise, though. If she's heard about you from Lucretia, what with the Wile E. Coyote setup here." Ree gestured to the half-dozen traps, loaded crossbows, trip wires, and other security systems Eastwood had laid in over the last several months as he spiraled deeper into paranoia.

"Yes, but Lucretia doesn't know about this," Eastwood answered, patting his trap master (a modded Xbox 360 wireless controller).

Ree picked up the Wonder Woman bracers she'd used during the fight last Halloween. She should just ask him to keep these. But that'd be a month's worth of wages, and she couldn't deflect bills with them, just bullets. "Or we could hang out here and let her try to make a run at the base. Home field advantage and all."

"I doubt she's that bold."

"So bold enough to try to shiv you on the street, but not so bold she'd break into your house? How's that again?"

"One is bold and slightly ridiculous. The other is very bold and incredibly ridiculous."

"So out we go," Ree said. "Power-up first?"

"Go for it. The con is yours."

And by "the con," Eastwood meant his ten-petabyte media database of films, TV, cartoons, and odd video clips from all around the world. It was the closest thing Ree had ever seen to a complete media library, which made it the Geekomantic equivalent of the Library of Alexandria. Minus the burning.

Ree kicked off her mental algorithm, brainstorming the most appropriate power and source for the situation.

The Strega was on wheels, so she'd be fast, but somewhat bound by momentum, and not as good over rough ground. Spider powers would be a good counter—speed, three-dimensional movement abilities, webbing would gum up skates pretty damned well. But if Lucretia's been informing, they'll expect that.

What else?

Ree ran a search query and saw that Eastwood had the short-lived '90s *Flash* TV show, so that was an option. Meet speed with super-speed. But that level of power would burn through her charge really damned fast. For Ree, the Geekomantic sweet spot was the the perfect middle ground between:

1) Properties she loved

2) Versatile but not ginormous powers

3) Abilities that combined well with the props and tools she had on hand

Which at that moment were her lightsaber, the phaser, and her standard sideboard. However, she was standing in the middle of a Geekomantic Fort Knox.

"You got some cards or props for glue traps or grease spells?" Ree asked.

Eastwood grunted in the affirmative, and made his way to the stacks.

"What are you thinking of, power-wise?" he asked, his voice bouncing off the far wall and echoing back, hollow.

"Spider-Man's the obvious choice, but probably too obvious, since twenty bucks says Lucretia was keeping tabs on us during the fights at Grognard's."

"Fair bet. What about Static Shock? Close, but sufficiently distinct . . ."

"To be just different enough. You got an appropriate flying-thingie board?"

"That might be the rub."

Tumblers in her brain still spinning, she turned back to the media library.

"If you don't have a good flyer, I've got a fun alternative." She called up *Captain America: The First Avenger*, and selected forward to Cap's first mission, rescuing the POWs, which was quickly followed by a montage of awesome. Plenty to get excited about (and not just Chris Evans's abs, Hayley Atwell's lips, or Sebastian Stan's brooding brows). And the Captain America power suite overlapped with Spidey's just enough—speed, strength enough to overpower a woman who outmassed her by no small margin.

"You got a decent Cap shield?" she yelled over her shoulder.

"I have a half-decent one. Won't those bracers do?"

"Better resonance with the movie if I can have the actual shield. At least, that's what Talon says."

"She'd know," Eastwood said. He rustled around through a couple of boxes, then said, "Ha! Canceled order. Never shipped, then I forgot to put it back in the right place."

"If you would let me handle all of the mail orders . . ." Ree said.

"Later," Eastwood said. "Here, catch!" Eastwood tossed the shield like a Frisbee. Ree caught it with both hands. It was a cheaper prop, less than two feet across, and made of plastic.

"This is a kid's toy."

"It's what I've got."

"I'll give it a shot." Ree turned back to the screen and cued up the film, letting the massive wall-mounted speakers go to work.

The film popped up on nine synced flat-screen TVs, the standard media consumption mode in the Dorkcave. They'd tried playing films on the full five-by-five, but you had to sit so far back to get the full effect that the stacks cut off a third of the screen on either side.

Ree wheeled the gaming chair back into her preferred spot and dialed into the film, focusing on Steve Rogers's earnest compassion and selfless bravery, his devotion to his friend, and his desire to be more than just a curiosity, and hoping the magical power-up would sweep the rest of her inebriation and exhaustion off the table.

Ree watched the set of scenes twice through, and by the end of the montage, had the film's Captain America theme buzzing in her ears, all bright brass and retro enthusiasm. She wasn't a huge American Exceptionalism fan, but this Cap, at least, came off like America Trying To Get Things Right. Nazis were a slam-dunk of a bad guy, and so Hydra, as super-Nazis, were all the better. You couldn't go wrong in fighting bad guys that disintegrated people at the drop of a hat. Worked for Leia and Han; it'd work for Cap and Ree.

Wishing she'd started working with Priya to get some cosplay action going so she could have the corresponding outfit, Ree strapped on the shield, which felt not much heavier, but far sturdier in her grip. It might not last too long, being a low-grade prop, but it'd have to do. Plus, she had her own crossover action going on with the Wonder Woman bracers.

They wouldn't cancel each other out, right? She'd crossed the copyright streams before, and it had been fine. But Geekomancy wasn't anything resembling an exact science. Like the films, comics, and games they came from, the rules of Geekomancy seemed to be relative, based on more factors than remotely made sense. It was as if a set of rules lawyers occasionally broke down the GM of the universe to institute house rules, or got the GM to update to a new rules set.

But the music was strong, the Super-Soldier Serum was with her, and she had double defense action between the shield and the bracers, a good match for the Strega's blades, especially when paired with her standard melee and ranged weapons.

She did, however, look kind of ridiculous, walking around with a kid's plastic prop. But she'd survived middle school; she could survive some odd stares from the people of Pearson.

"Ready, Sergeant?" she asked, her voice coming out broad and earnest. She laughed at herself, wondering how much she must be sticking out her chest, both metaphorically and literally.

As long as she didn't look like Rob Liefeld's Cap, she'd be fine.

"Sergeant?" Eastwood said, eyebrow raised. He had his trusty *Star Wars* blaster, his own lightsaber (green to Ree's blue), and a set of bagged-and-boarded comics stuffed into the outer pocket of his well-worn (and bloodied, and muddied, and so on) trench coat. He wasn't Hollywood's vision of a hero, but he'd proven his grit more than often enough.

"Onward!" Ree pointed toward the door, reveling in the cheesiness of it all. Usually her Snarky Good inclinations ran counter to such uncomplicatedly earnest goody-two-shoesness, but it was fun to play the part, live a little while in a world that wasn't so many shades of gray all the time.

Eastwood opened the door, and they went on the hunt.

CHAPTER EIGHT

Sk8er Girl vs. G33k Girl

The pair started with a quick whiz around the neighborhood but expanded their search, Ree very much aware of the ticking clock on her Geekomantic charge. If she didn't use any power, it'd stay for a while, but if they were stomping around for thirty minutes with no contact, she'd need a re-up, which would leave them vulnerable.

"Any ideas of where to search next?" Ree asked.

"Skate park?"

"Good call."

The Sandusky Park had been assembled between several skater clubs, teaming up with an Indiegogo to buy the abandoned lot and turn it into a skate park.

Some local grumpy gray-hairs and yuppie parents complained but seemingly only out of a sense of propriety. Several of the skater kids' grandparents would hang out in the park, playing checkers on the tables at the edge.

The park had a half-dozen skaters spread around, rolling up, jumping off, and standing around on the various apparati. Most looked under twenty, with an older cluster in one corner, rotating through being filmed as they tried (and often failed at) complex tricks, earning scrapes and bruises at a rapid pace.

"Any sign?" Ree asked, scanning the park.

"Nope. Not that easy."

Feeling bold and a half, she started toward the nearest group of skaters. "Let's ask the locals. Maybe one of them has seen her."

"Nice shield. You steal it from a kindergartner?" one of the skater kids asked, an African American girl with a Blink-182 shirt and red athletic shorts.

Ree's natural inclination was to bite back with something like, "Yeah, I stole it from your room. No dust on it, though. Weird." But what came out was "Very funny."

Being square-jawed and forthright is kind of boring.

Eastwood stepped in, drawing attention. "Any of you seen a derby girl, around yay tall, muscled, wears metal elbow and knee gear?"

Half of the park was watching them now, the sounds of rubber wheels on concrete faded to just the far trio with their flip camera.

"Pretty simple question, folks," Ree said.

"Take a hike, Comic-Con," said another skater, a lanky kid with a splash of acne across his face as bad as Ree'd ever had as a teen. He was tall already but looked like he had more to grow, his hands and feet still a size too big for his body, like a puppy.

"Well, actually, I have seen someone who fits that description," said a female voice from behind them.

Ree pivoted in place, her shoes scrunching on the concrete.

Behind them, ten paces back, a redhead in a coat. As she ditched the raincoat, her whole image shifted from a bland middle-aged white redhead to a thickly-muscled Middle Eastern woman, six feet tall with skates, and shimmering metallic armor in the form of skating gear, elbows and knees, a polished metal helmet with the blocker stretch-cap on the top.

Also, blades on the gloves and skates. Don't forget the blades.

"That her?" Ree asked.

Eastwood sighed, reaching for his weapons.

"No ambush this time?" he asked.

"What do you think this is?" the Strega responded, hands open.

I really, really don't want to look behind me, do I? Ree asked herself, but she did anyway, not one to invite a sucker punch.

Back at the skate park, illusions wavered and dropped, revealing a ten-woman derby squad, from petite, lithe women to larger bruisers like the Strega, with a half-dozen between them, muscled women in their twenties through their fifties. Their aggregate stocking display could make a strip-mall witch blush, but all wore the black and red jerseys.

"You brought your team," Ree said, embarrassed at how obvious her dialogue was coming out. Ol' stars-and-stripes had a knack for stating the obvious. Next time, she was going with Brubaker Cap. He was subtler.

The Derby Strega grinned, showing a cracked incisor. "Yep. Name's Connie Clothos-Line, and these are the Fighting Fates."

"We seem to have forgotten the rest of our team back at home. Can I interest you in a rain check on the bout?" Eastwood asked.

"No chance. My sister should have punched your ticket months back, and I'm here to do what she couldn't." Connie pulled up a whistle and blew.

And we're off.

Ree had seen only a handful of derby matches, unless you counted *Whip It.* (She didn't. Maybe if she were a Cinemancer.) But these women were all athletic and ranged from tiny and fast to three nearly as big as Connie—powerful women crackling knuckles as they took formation.

First things first—spool up her props. Ree focused on the shield, which became heavier, more solid, in her grip. She wound up and hurled the shield softball-style at Connie's knee level, hoping to take the Strega off her feet. She bet that the prop would do what the real shield was supposed to do, as long as she hurled it right. She'd heard through the Geekomantic grapevine that Cap shields were useless, otherwise.

She hoped.

Jack and Joe were with her this time, and the shield hurled forward in proper fashion. Connie pushed off, skating to one side. Her hands contorted in a Ditko-fingers fashion reminiscent of Lucretia's Hexomancy. In addition, the woman shouted, "Foul!"

The shield wobbled, glowing with energy the same green as Connie's helmet, and then the prop went wide—way wide, bouncing off the ramp behind the Strega.

Hexomancy. Her least favorite thing. As long as the Strega could do the gestures and speak the curses, Hexomancers were nearly untouchable. You'd slip, fall, get a Charlie horse, or any of a hundred bits of bad luck, all adding up to a one-way ride on the failboat.

Ree ran forward at a diagonal, building up a buffer between her and the Strega. First step would be getting her shield back, second was to down Connie's backup. Then she and Eastwood could double-team Connie. But where Lucretia was weak sauce in hand-to-hand combat, Connie looked like she could tank with the best of them.

Dozens of wheels made a solid droning on the concrete as the women moved forward in formations. At least it looked like the other Derby girls weren't Hexomancers, too. Then they'd be properly fucked. Eastwood had his blaster out and was stunning the skaters left and right, until Connie called another foul, gesturing like a derby judge. Eastwood's blaster slipped from his hands, dropping to the floor with a lifeless clunk.

"Crap!" Eastwood shouted, diving for the prop as the skaters closed in on him, throwing elbows.

A pair of derby girls closed in on Ree, but what they didn't know was that she was filled with righteousness and the resulting super-strength. With Connie's attention on Eastwood,

Ree threw a roundhouse that picked one woman up off the ground, then punched the other one in the sternum, sending her sputtering to the ground. She'd automatically calibrated her super-strength for KO and not kill, which was a blessing.

Those two down, Ree dropped and slid down the skate park ramp, letting the buff coat take the abrasion. She came out running and bent down to pick up the shield when she heard another foul called, and instead of snatching the prop up with a slick smooth motion, her gait changed last second and she kicked the shield, sending it skipping across the concrete and slamming into the wrong side of a ramp.

Ree opened her mouth to say, "Screw you!" but all that came out was "Dangit!"

It took her another seemingly interminable thirty seconds or so to retrieve the shield. She was finally far enough out that Connie ignored her, leaving her to the four skaters bearing down on her, using ramps to gather speed.

Ree picked up the shield just as a thickset blocker leaned into a shoulder check. Ree planted a foot on the rear ramp out of the park and pushed on the shield.

Magic and body mechanics met mass and momentum, a not-quite-as-momentous immovable object versus irresistible force. The end result? A massive clang as the skater deflected off the shield. The derby blocker went out of control, taking a header into the ramp and cracking her helmet. Ree suppressed the sympathetic wince and took the initiative to drop into a crouch to trip the next skater behind the knees. The skater fell defensively, landing on her pads, but hard, thanks to the head of steam she'd built up.

Ree copied the skaters and built up speed, running up a ramp and jump-slamming into the next two, leading with the shield. She landed on the shield, which ate up the impact, Vibranium proving its awesomeness once again. But the shield wasn't a high-end prop, and it would only be good for another couple of hits in all likelihood.

Looking back, she saw that none of the skaters were getting up, but all were still breathing. Just how she liked it.

Back around Connie, Eastwood was getting the full cartoon mob treatment, pinballing between beatings as he scrambled to recover a weapon, any weapon.

Skaters took turns buzzing him, throwing elbows as they passed by. And behind them, the other team members kicked the weapons away, separating the Geekomancer from his tools—blasters, lightsabers, playing cards, dice. The floor of the skate park was as messy as Grognard's had been when Connie's "sister" had trashed the place.

Eastwood wasn't taking it lying down, for sure. He threw elbows and knees, getting in good shots here and there. But with Connie bearing down on him and being outnumbered six to one, he couldn't hold his own without weapons.

"Get out of the park!" she shouted to Eastwood, who had gotten to his feet, a trio of smaller women closing in on him, probably regular jammers. Connie had her focus trained on Eastwood, so Ree had the time to get off a throw. Probably.

Ree chucked the shield at the trio, aiming high and hoping for one of Cap's patented ricochet shots. Connie called out a warning, but it was too late.

The shield bounced off of one, two, and then three helmets, cracking the first two with Vibranium might.

But between the second and third helmet, the shield reverted to a plastic disk, and clattered off the third woman's helmet with no effect.

Which meant it was time for another tool. The lightsaber was out, since she wasn't going to turn the skate park into a bloody soup if she could avoid it. Eastwood's lightsaber could do this weird thing where it only stunned, but hers was all or nothing.

The Captain America power would fade soon, but Ree'd earned black belts in Taekwondo and Hapkido before she thought of her Force FX lightsaber as anything other than a cool way to signal her geekdom and something to have fun waving around in the dark privacy of her own room.

Ree proceeded to jump-kick, roundhouse, and shoulder-toss her way through the derby team, stronger and faster than any of them, thanks to the magic. Or that was the plan.

But the plan didn't account for Connie. The Strega's Hexomantic curses thwarted Ree at nearly every step. Her jumps were too big or too small, her footing was terrible, and her shoelaces came undone.

And every time Ree went for Connie directly, she would trip, slip, or just end up running the other direction—she was like a super-magnet with the same charge as Ree, or they were like a lead pair of detectives in a buddy show who were not going to get together anytime soon.

Several of the women clearly had martial arts skills in addition to their derby chops, though a few got in lucky shots.

Too lucky. Strega cheater lucky.

Ree launched herself into a sliding sidekick that should have folded the woman in two, but she slipped on the concrete, catching herself in a safe fall that still burned all along her thigh, side, and forearm.

The Cap magic kept the impact from opening her leg or arm, but the theme music was dwindling fast.

Ree decided to expedite things, pulling out her phaser (which was set to stun by default). She'd been hoping to save it for Connie, but Eastwood didn't have much more time. He was about as tenderized as hamburger meat, definitely the same shade of red-pink.

Dropping the closest two skaters, Ree rolled under the clothesline thrown by another of the thick blockers. She zapped the woman as she tried to turn, then jumped into a back-kick to clothesline a woman who'd come up behind Ree.

"Your team isn't doing so hot, Connie," Ree called out to the Strega, who was going one-on-one with Eastwood.

Four on one, really, as a trio of skaters kicked and punched at Eastwood's flanks.

As Eastwood swung his holdout knife, trying to keep the other women off him, Connie caught him across the jaw with a shredder-claw-enhanced cross.

"Shnikes!" Ree said, getting a bit tired of Cap's language filter. But the power was fading, the patriotic brass distant in her mind.

Ree unloaded a burst of stunning phaserocity into Connie, who turned the ray aside on her reflective armor, sending the beam up and into the clouds.

Nice armor, Ree said to herself. Chances were, that'd apply to the lightsaber as well. So instead, she pulled out her butterfly knife. She could do a lot of damage with a knife without killing, though she wouldn't get nearly the reach advantage.

Connie made another Ditko-as-referee gesture and called, "Foreign object!" and Ree's knife slipped right out of her hands in the middle of her figure-eight opening.

Well, that's that. It was time for some good old-fashioned infighting.

And that meant infighting. And clearing out the rest of the team. Two more derby girls advanced on Ree, and she used up the last of her Captain America mojo to thump one on the head and crescent-kick the other across the jaw, putting them both down. The music was gone, leaving Ree as only herself.

"If you swear off this hunt and GTFO now, with your team, this can all be over," Ree said, hands open but ready.

"No can do, twiggy. Sacred duty and all. My sister calls, and I answer. Scruffy here isn't part of the Plan anymore," Connie said, rancor capitalizing the *P* quite effectively. While the Strega talked, Eastwood circled around, so that he and Ree were flanking the woman.

"You sure?" she asked. "Your team looks like they could stand a week of recovery time, so now it's two on one, with no refs to save your bacon. Discretion, valor, all that crap."

Connie spread her stance and put up her dukes, turning to keep both Eastwood and Ree in her peripheral vision. "Bring it."

"Gladly," Ree said, shuffling forward as she drew another knife, cutting herself a path in to striking distance.

Connie pushed off and came at Ree, hunkering down into a metal-capped battering ram. Ree dodged to the side, her jumps no longer backed by super-soldier strength. Connie's knee bashed and cut Ree's shin, but Ree got in a slash across the woman's back in exchange. From the other side, Eastwood closed and swung with brass knuckles, each finger styled with a ward. Looked like a prop out of *Supernatural*, or maybe *Dylan Dog*.

Ree was hoping for *Supernatural*.

Fighting two on one, they should have been able to keep Connie on the defensive. But the Derby Strega was used to power plays and made offense her best defense, wheeling and turning to keep Ree and her sometimes mentor closer together so she could parry both of their strikes in the same motion.

Ree's knife made sparks on the Strega's armored cops as the Strega blocked, dodged, and weaved. The Strega got in a solid jab to Ree's head, blowing through Ree's block with her mass advantage but landing only her fist, not the blade.

As Ree stumbled back, Connie grunted, arcing over in pain. Eastwood jumped back, then charged ahead immediately, opening up to draw Connie's attention.

But it was no good. There was blood in the water, and Connie pressed her advantage, rolling forward and grabbing Ree from waist to shoulders. Connie grabbed and squeezed the woman in a destructive bear hug, locking down Ree's knife hand along the way. She fought back but lost her grip on the blade as she tried to flip it around into a reverse grip.

She was too short for a proper headbutt, so Ree opted for the second-best option, which was a stiff knee to the groin.

Her knee found only hard plastic. *And a jill, too? Fucker.*

Connie laughed, squeezing harder.

Eastwood pounded at the woman's back, but her grip held strong. Ree fought, puffing herself up as best as she could, then, taking Eastwood's timing into mind, deflated and dropped a half beat after Eastwood's brass-knuckled rabbit punch.

She didn't get all of the way out but slipped down to Connie's waist level. Ree dropped into the splits, scuffing one knee along the way, but it got her under the derby Strega's grip. Ree threw an elbow into the side of Connie's knee, above and just behind the armored knee guard. At the same time, she knuckle-punched the woman's upper thigh, all notions of clean fighting thrown out the window.

Connie grunted again, and Ree rolled back and up to her knees, the world spinning. She stood slowly, guard locked down tight.

Times like this, I really wish I was Chaotic Neutral. A Chaotic Neutral Ree would have just blastered and lightsabered the woman into ribbons and walked away for a hot dog.

Connie caught Eastwood with an uppercut that hit like a ton of bricks, and Eastwood stumbled back.

Ree jumped up on the woman's back with her best "little kid with enough grappling skills to be dangerous" grip, trying to snake her way around to a half nelson.

She held on as tightly as possible, wrapping the woman up into a triangle choke hold. Unsurprisingly, the woman dropped straight back, hoping to crush Ree under her substantial bulk. But Ms. Smith didn't train no chump.

Ree unlocked her legs and swung back, landing on her belly instead of becoming the squishy middle of a Strega-concrete sandwich.

"Now!" Ree said, wincing with the force of the impact. Connie rolled over to try to keep Ree on the ground, but Ree scuttled back to her knees, getting clear.

Giving her a great view of Eastwood landing the coup d'grace, clocking Connie in the back of the neck, below her chromed helmet.

Eastwood's blow made a meaty thud, supplemented by the slap of metal on flesh. Connie grunted once more, then collapsed to the concrete. Ree held her guard, in case she pushed on, but the woman seemed out for the count.

"Holy crap," Ree said, massaging her jaw, which would soon be blooming into impressive shades of purple bruising.

Eastwood had found time to take a minor healing potion or the like during the fight; his cheek was no longer slashed open like the cover of *Wolverine* #50.

"That could have been a bit easier," Eastwood said. "I'd take an easier fight next time, yep."

"What do we do with the team here?" Ree asked.

"Well, I sure as hell don't want to burn through the cards it'd take to BAMF them all back to the Dorkcave, and I definitely don't have the space or equipment to lock them all up long enough to do anything useful. I say we leave them and just take Connie here. I've got an idea."

"That's never good news," Ree said, scanning the edges of the park to look for reinforcements, further ambushes, or stray velociraptors. "This doesn't involve sacrificing puppies, right?" She went over to where the shield had fallen and retrieved the child's toy. She'd be better off with a full-size prop, but magic was magic.

By way of response, Eastwood's face scrunched up into a pucker of disapproval. "Just get over here, and grab an arm."

Eastwood grabbed one of Connie's muscled arms, and fished a collectible card out of his jacket. He held up a card, showing a Fleer Nightcrawler from the early '90s. Ree held on to the wave of nostalgia and lifted the woman's other hand with both of hers, counteracting the extreme gravity compliance of bludgeoning-related unconsciousness.

The older geek took the card between his teeth. With the sound of tearing paper, the world.

Went.

BAMF!

CHAPTER NINE

BAMF!

With the familiar sound of teleportation, Ree, Eastwood, and Connie popped back into the world, through several scary dimensions that Ree wished she'd not read the comics issues about, believing very firmly in blissful ignorance when it came to hell dimensions, and popped back into the Dorkcave, Connie between them, now lying on the floor in front of Eastwood's media wall.

"Tie her to the stacks while I get the ritual ready." Dropping the woman's arm, his focus went back into the rows and rows of merch.

"Sure, Eastwood," Ree said as she tried to move the woman, "I'll just drag the burly unconscious derby girl with fifty pounds of gear on. No problem!" Adrenaline from the fight bleeding off, her efforts to drag the woman on her own added up to an express ticket to nowhere. Without the magical superpowers, she was back to being small, sleep-deprived, and hungover, none of which were helping.

Harumphing, Ree let the woman's arms drop back to the floor. She turned around to Eastwood's media setup and cued up "Chosen" from *Buffy the Vampire Slayer*, watched for five minutes, then ten minutes, temporarily forgetting why, then pulled herself away from the show and tapped into Buffy-level super-strength to haul Connie over to the stacks.

Once she was in place, magical yellow handcuffs from Green Lantern went over a basic plastic zip-tie. The most important thing with Stregas was cutting off their ability to do all the gestural bullshit that Hexomancy required to make people slip on bananas that didn't exist and to get jams with guns that had just been cleaned and inspected.

Ree kept an eye on Connie, imagining that a tough witch would come to fairly soon.

Which reminded her of another thing. She grabbed a roll of duct tape and ripped off a five-inch chunk, pressing it over the woman's mouth, making sure to avoid the nose. She wanted the woman unable to do magic, not unable to breathe.

"Okay, here we are," Eastwood said, hauling a cardboard box through the stacks, moving with labored effort.

"What you got in there, a pile of bricks?"

"Better. Oracles." Eastwood set the box down with a thud, then slid it over to Ree with a not-at-all-smooth push with his leg.

"How does this help us?"

"I did some research. Eriko, an old friend of mine from the Astral Cowboy days, who still works Spirit-side, got me a tip. She heard that you can mute a Strega's power; there's a way to cut off their connection to their patron, Fate. Poof, no more Hexomancy. Best bet from that source is that if you take a Strega's favorite oracle, burn a copy, and make them breathe in the ashes, the sympathetic tie between them and the destroyed incarnation of the oracle causes them to lose their ability to control fate." Eastwood looked like a kid talking about the PS4, not a grown man talking about stripping someone of their power.

"That's your big plan? Rob these women of their powers entirely? No 'make them swear to never come after us,' no 'convince them that you deserve to live and I should get to be a magical girl if I want to be'? You're going straight to Fridging them via de-powering?"

Eastwood leaned back, hands crossing. He hadn't been expecting that, had he?

"She tried to kill us. Lucretia broke the spirit, if not the letter, of her judgment in giving out information about us. Lucretia beating Grognard's giese proved that. The Strega will keep on coming, and if we just beat them and try to lock them up, we'll have ourselves an Arkham Jailbreak's worth of trouble by next summer. This solves the problem without having to spill any more blood. This is the humane solution, Ree. It's just not the nice one."

"Don't you think taking her power away from her will just make her hate us more? What's to stop her from assembling another team and running us down when we aren't prepared?" Ree asked.

Eastwood's face darkened. "You have a better idea, then?"

She didn't. But robbing someone of their power, especially a guy doing it to a woman, rubbed her several of the wrong ways.

"I don't, but I don't like it. We should call Grognard, maybe see about getting her run through a trial, too."

"Lucretia stacked the deck in that trial; who says Connie wouldn't do the same? Can you keep on counting on luck?"

"Who said it was luck that I won?" Ree realized she was yelling. She took a long breath and spoke again. "How would you even figure out which oracle is hers?"

"That's not very difficult. Dab a drop of blood on one card from each deck, see which one resonates with a magical signature, using these." Eastwood pulled out a set of Shade-designed glasses, undeniably '80s. They matched the set she'd been given after the trail.

"I'm still not happy about this. Is there a way of making it less permanent, or making it just so she can't use the power against us?" Ree asked.

"Not that I know of. And the Strega aren't exactly forthcoming about how to help defeat them or slag their power. This solution cost me several favors, plus my original hero glaive from *Krull*."

"Aw, I love that thing." She'd found better tools since, but it was too ridiculous to not love.

"I want to make some calls before I sign off on something like this," Ree said.

Eastwood held a hand out, inviting her to go.

Quick-drawing her phone, Ree headed toward a corner of the room, calling Grognard.

"Yeah," he answered.

"It's Ree. Got a question. Another Strega came after Eastwood, nearly took him out. We posse-ed up and now we've got her tied up in the Dorkcave. Go team," she said, with little enthusiasm, her positivity batteries running red.

"But now Eastwood has this ritual that he says will take out her magic, permanently. And I'm not on board. These Strega think they're doing Good Work, and Eastwood's hardly squeaky clean. . . ."

"Mm hmm," Grognard said.

"That it?"

"This is your call, Ree. Either you're on board, or you try to stop him. This Strega tried to kill you, right?"

"Yeah, but people do that pretty often now. Doesn't mean I'm excited to return the favor or cut away their magic. Alex Walters, sure, I'd have done it in an instant. Wouldn't mind doing it to Lucretia. But this woman was getting her sister's back; they think they're Righteous."

"Most villains do, though, right?"

"And Eastwood thinks he's Righteous here, leaving my Chaotic Good ass in the middle."

Ree sniffed smoke, and turned to see Eastwood lighting a deck of cards on fire.

"What the fucking fuck!" Ree said, running back toward the scruffy geek and the unconscious Strega. Eastwood dropped the deck in front of Connie as the cards caught fire at unnatural speed, fire leaping a yard high, coruscating through a million colors.

The deck burned by the time Ree made it back to Eastwood, diving shoulder-first and knocking him over, the two sliding along the concrete floor.

Eastwood grunted. "Frakking hell, Ree. It had to be done." The older geek shoved Ree off to the side as he scrambled to his feet.

"No. Fucking. Way," Ree said, crab-walking over to Connie as the ashes wafted up to her nose.

The woman breathed in deep through her nose, head snapping to attention, her eyes going wide, shot through with bloody veins that went from red to purple. Then her whole eyes went white. Ree felt the air grow heavy, then crack and shatter all at once.

Connie screamed.

Ree turned and hauled off on Eastwood, laying him out with a roundhouse. He came back up, blaster in hand, giving her a threatening view down the barrel.

"Cut that shit out, now. It's done. Let's see if it worked."

"You cocky, self-righteous asshole!" Ree said, her voice filling the Dorkcave. Her hands were vibrating, her ears on fire.

"I just saved our lives from someone trying to kill us. Try to be a little grateful." Eastwood plucked a Green Lantern ring out of his coat and slipped it on with his left hand.

Connie's muffled speech turned both their heads.

She was struggling against her bonds, her eyes back to normal. Eastwood leaned forward with the shades.

"Her aura is gone. The magic, at least. She's just a pissed-off derby blocker now."

"Your definition of *just* leaves something to be desired," Ree said, remembering the power of the woman's blows.

Ree stepped over with care, prepped for random slips, muscle spasms, or falling pieces of roof. She ripped the duct tape from Connie's mouth, not above taking a little pleasure in the woman's pain. Light sadism was fine. The woman had tried to kill her, after all. And the pain of the duct tape wasn't permanent.

"You arrogant, selfish asshole!" Connie's voice was strained by fear. "You don't know me, don't know the people I've helped, the wrongs I've set right. My sister will come for you upon the solstice, and she makes me look like a rank newbie. What are you going to do next, slit my throat and offer up my blood to your dice bag?"

"I don't want anything associated with you anywhere near my dice," Eastwood said. "You have two options. You leave Pearson and never come back, or your story ends here."

"I'm not letting you murder her in cold blood," Ree said.

"Because you did a great job of stopping me before."

"Motherfucker," Ree said.

"We've established that," Eastwood said.

Ree saw red, the murder cue from *Kill Bill* playing in her mind.

"Maybe I should just sit here and wait for you two to kill each other, and then I can just skate away, scot-free," Connie said.

"Shut up!" Ree and Eastwood said in unison.

"I'm staying until I'm sure you're not going to kill her, but then we're done, Eastwood. Fucking done. No more bodyguard, no more Geek Girl Friday. ¡Estoy harta de bregar contigo!

"You were doing good for a while there, pulling off the whole Thunderbolt thing. But this is too fucking much. You couldn't wait ten minutes for me to consider, try to convince me, instead of steamrolling right over a grown-up discussion by making a huge fucking decision without your partner?"

"That what you think you are, a partner?" Eastwood asked. "Because I've never seen anything to make me believe you're anything more than a sidekick. You're Robin, not Nightwing. Not even Red Robin."

"Label me however you want. You're still a callous asshole." Ree dialed Grognard again, stepping back, but keeping both the geek and the Strega in her view.

"Me again. He did it. He fucking did it. I need you to come over and help me escort Derby Strega out of town so that Darth Geek here doesn't decide to just off her."

"Okay. I'll be over in a half hour."

"Any chance you could put a rush on that? Things aren't exactly comfortable here, what with the betrayal, the assault, and the burning rancor of a woman in armor."

"I'll see what I can do. Try to keep the body count to a minimum, okay?"

"That's the plan. Thanks, man."

Grognard grunted in assent, then hung up. "He's coming in a half hour. The three of us are going to escort Ms. Clothos-Line here out of town."

Ree turned to the Strega. "When we drop you off, you're going to do yourself a favor and never set foot in this town again. You won't inform on us to any of your sisters except to tell them to stay away, and you're going to be a good person, helping babies and shit."

Ree realized she was rambling but leaned into it. "You say you're a white hat, then prove it. Go forth and be awesome, bringing light and shooting rainbows out of your butt. Then we can feel bad for taking away your power, and you can be all smug about it and we'll brood, pondering our slow, incremental descent into villainy. Or at least, Eastwood here will do that, and I'll be busy having nothing to do with him. ¿Tu me entiendes?"

Connie's voice was cool. "Got it. You won't see me again. You going to take these cuffs off, or what?"

Ree looked to Eastwood. "Hell no," he said.

"Not yet," Ree answered.

"Can I at least get some water, then? Fights leave me thirsty as hell."

"I wonder why that is. Maybe the part where you almost killed me?" Eastwood asked while Ree went over to pour water from Eastwood's water cooler. It was probably the most innocuous office-y thing he had, the standard plastic setup with two spares waiting.

Ree helped the woman drink, her hands still bound.

And the following twenty-nine minutes passed without words, without anything resembling comfort or relaxation for any of the three in the room.

When the door buzzed, Ree jumped in place, the awkward equilibrium disturbed.

After quick pleasantries between Grognard and Eastwood, the ex–Console Cowboy released Connie's manacles, reattached them once she was on her feet, and the three of them walked her to the door.

Eastwood stuffed his psychic paper in his front coat pocket, all of the excuse or justification they'd need if anyone stopped them.

⨯✖⬡✖⨯

An hour later, Grognard dropped Ree off at the Shithole, and awkwardness shloughed off her like squamous scales falling from her eyes. But no way was she changing her name to Paul. Being a saint would be nice and all, but she was never any good at being a Catholic, which made her an outcast to both sides of her family. Luckily, her dad didn't give a crap about any of that and kept her shielded from most of the familial censure.

Ree walked into the apartment to see Sandra, Priya, and Anya sitting around the couch, several bottles of liquor open between them. Her roommate, Sandra Wilson (Strength 15, Dexterity 13, Stamina 13, Will 12, IQ 12, Charisma 13—Geek 3 / Scholar 3 / Professional 2 / Dancer 1 / Teacher 1 / Waitress 1 / Chef 1), was a Greek-American Amazon, just over six feet tall, with perfectly-formed ringlets of hair. Normally dressed business casual like it was her second skin, today she had on a T-shirt and worn pajamas, making the most of her Funemployment.

"Hey," Ree said, dropping her keys into the Bowl of Unlost Keys.

"Hey," Anya said. "I figured it was time to close the circle of knowledge."

"Thank God. Where are you?"

Sandra piped up. "I'll tell you where I am. I am confused, befuddled, a bit impressed that you kept this from me, and more than a little angry that you told Priya and Anya before you told your frakking roommate."

Ree tossed her coat into the closet and went to join the crammed couch. She poured herself some rum, drank, then poured some more.

"I'm sorry. It seemed safer, and it was unfair, and I'm so glad that you know now. I don't want to keep anything from you three. Never wanted to, won't ever again."

"Except weird sex stuff. You keep that shit to yourself," Anya said.

The laughter was stilted, a bit forced. *This is going to take more booze.*

"So, what do we say? I think this calls for dinner. A big, fuck-off amazeballs dinner, just the four of us, get shit back where it's supposed to be, no magic crap," Ree said.

"You going to cook?" Sandra asked.

Ree smiled, this one coming more easily. "I just said it was a good idea. If only we had a trained chef among us."

Sandra raised a hand of correction. "Partially trained."

"And the three of us put together are at least good enough to be one sous-chef," Priya said. "Let's see how ridiculously we can mess up the kitchen and leave it for Ree to clean up."

"I take it all back," Ree said, chuckling.

Sandra added, "And we're telling Darren when he gets back from his conference. I won't be able to keep the secret, so you should just go ahead and explain it to him, too."

"And the Scooby gang grows," Ree said, resigned.

"We're no Scoobies," Anya said. "I have no intention of gallivanting around the town with you trying to get ourselves killed, thank you very much."

Priya nodded. She wasn't her usually-animated self, still reeling from last night's drama.

Holy crap, that was only last night. The reality of it hit Ree like a dodgeball to the face.

Ree threw herself into routine, trying to wrap Priya up in the chatter, the energy of the group, to help throw out a life preserver of love and appreciation.

As someone who'd spent more than her fair share of time treading water in the oceans of Post-Breakup Depression, she knew the look well. Priya would recover in her own time frame, and she didn't want to push. This amount of time after getting dumped by Jay, Ree had been hurling in the bathroom, so compared to that Priya was doing great. Though who knew what the evening would bring?

Which reminded her that she should call Drake, both to yell at him some more and to tell him what Eastwood had done. Drake could make his own decision about the Geekomancer, but he deserved to know the truth about what had just gone down.

A general truthiness and freedom of information policy seemed like the way to go. Like freely informing him that she was still pissed off at him for how he'd treated Priya. But that freedom didn't extend to telling him how she'd felt about him right up until he'd dumped Priya. Really she still felt that way, but she was too busy being angry at just that moment. Angry hooking up wasn't a good idea for either of them, so that would need to be avoided at all costs.

Ree was pretty sure that the impropriety of such an occurrence would lead Drake to spontaneously combust, which helped. Sort of. Not really.

A half hour later, the kitchen was in full-on Chaotic Joyful mode. Three women tried to scramble around one another, moving between the small dinner table and the kitchen, making a salad, braised chicken, cous-cous, lamb saag, and—Ree's contribution—take-out hero fries from Turbo's.

On the way back from Turbo's, she'd called Drake but got no answer. She left a rambling voicemail:

"Hey, this is Ree. It's fine if you don't pick up, though why would you, because this is a voicemail and things don't work like that anymore. Did you ever have an answering machine? Anyway, Eastwood and I ran across the first of the Promised Strega. Yeah, with capital letters. So anyway, she was a derby girl and had a whole team, and she nearly killed Eastwood, but we won, and then he was all 'I know how to solve this, I just have to do some creepy magic ritual; that's fine, right?' and I was all 'No, that's unacceptable!' and then I went to call Grognard to get my back, and the fucker did it anyway. So then I punched him and said I was done with him, for realz. Grognard came over and then we kicked Connie Clothos-Line out of town, and so here we are.

"Also, I'm still mad at you. But be careful."

Ree kept the voicemail to herself when she got back to the house, though it was kind of directly counter to the self-congratulatory truthiness she'd just been thinking about.

Fuck off, self. Life is complicated. Plus, she was sparing Priya's feelings. No one needed to hear about their ex right after a breakup, unless it was along the lines of "Yeah, screw that guy! We never liked him," which Ree couldn't muster, even if she was perfectly livid enough to do so.

Too much of her last twenty-four hours had been spent in mortal peril or so angry she could vibrate out of her shoes.

But now she had hero fries, Cole Lutz's imported and adapted version of a Midwestern locavore's divine recipe for duck-fat fries with Parmesan, red pepper flakes, cilantro, and something else that Cole wouldn't say. Not even to Ree, the most beloved of Cole's broke-ass customers.

Ree offered the fries first to Priya, meaning them to be an olive branch. After all, knowing Drake was all Ree's fault in the first place.

Priya took a handful of fries and nibbled at them, less zestfully than usual.

But it was a start.

CHAPTER TEN

Food Means Family

S andra took a break between bites of hero fries to ask, "How did you, Ms. Can't Keep Her Mouth Shut About Spoilers of a Show that Aired Twelve Hours Ago, keep all of this from me for a whole year?"

Ree took a sip of her margarita. "It was a sacred duty, or something. I didn't want you to have to deal with any more of my bullshit than you do already."

"Appreciated," Sandra said. Then she raised a finger for a point of correction. "But just because you have to fight monsters doesn't mean you can get out of cleaning the bathroom or paying your half of the rent."

Laughter filled the room. Anya held a high C "Buuuurn," deploying her opera diva powers to drive the point home. *This. More of this, please,* Ree thought, taking mental snapshots of the evening to keep with her through the crappier times.

The four of them sat crammed around the Shithole's dinner table, which was positively overflowing with food. When Sandra got nervous, she cooked. And discovering that magic was real and that her best friend could do it was cause enough for an early Thanksgiving. Greek salad (a Wilson family recipe), braised chicken, Ree's contribution of Turbo's hero fries, a carefully-tended curry from Priya, and heavy pours of alcohol, both vodka and tequila, courtesy of Anya and her seemingly-bottomless pantry of booze.

"It's all the opera people, I swear," she said. Anya had been dubbed the hostess for all cast parties, and as a result had a collection of two-thirds-empty bottles that would make a great archaeology or anthropology project someday.

Ree was on her third margarita, relying on booze to help her mitigate the awkwardness of a personal confession and the dropping of the masquerade and turn it into an impromptu party. Not that she wasn't happy to see everyone, but it was a lot of spotlight on not nearly enough sleep.

"So when you took that catering job, what were you really doing?" Sandra asked.

"Ah, that. There's a Geekomancer and general magician hangout bar-slash-store underground run by a dude named Grognard. I've been working for him. That is, until the place got totaled this summer by the first of what appears to be a quartet of homicidal Fate Witches."

"So is that why you show up to breakfast looking like you've been through a war zone?" Sandra asked.

Ree nodded, taking another sip. "It's true. Now everyone can stop thinking I'm a raging alcoholic with a propensity for getting into fights at bars."

Crickets.

"Yeah, I didn't have much faith in that one, either," Ree said. That got some laughter. Ree offered a toast, clinking glasses around before she drank again.

"So, are you going to show us some magic, or what?" Anya asked, cheeks red from vodka.

Then a beat. "But don't, like, burn the place down."

"It'll take a minute. I don't want to go waving a lightsaber around when I've had three margaritas."

Priya, without speaking, held up four fingers.

"No," Ree said, counting.

"It's four," Sandra said.

Ree extricated herself from the table and very intentionally climbed over the couch to the Media Corner, aware of her drunkenness. "My point exactly."

She loaded *Spider-Man* into the Blu-ray player and skipped forward to the scene where Peter uses his spider-powers to climb up the wall.

Her friends watched, mostly silent, only occasionally interrupting with the sounds of ice against glass as they drank. Ree zoomed in on the feeling of adulation, the sheer joy of discovery as Peter explored his powers. When she felt the rush of energy, she kicked off her shoes and started climbing, hands and feet sticking to the wall. She took three short steps up the wall, then hung from the ceiling by her fingertips and knees.

Her friends whooped and cheered and applauded. Ree's stomach churned, and she scrambled back down the wall and dropped to the couch, the power fizzing out between the short exposure and her booze-undermined focus.

"Ta da!" Ree said, taking a bow in her seat.

More applause.

Her stomach rumbled. "Next time, I'm not doing that after three . . . okay, four margaritas."

As they settled back into their food, Anya asked, "How you doing, Pri?"

Priya raised her glass and drank again by way of response. "Shitty, but I've had way worse. I think you're the next one scheduled for heartbreak, though."

"As the keeper of the chart, I'm afraid that is so. But you know what?" Anya said. "Fuck the chart. I'm declaring a moratorium on shitty relationships. Only good ones from here on in."

"If only I knew the magic to make that happen," Ree said.

"Enough of that crap," Priya said, wobbling to her feet.

"Another round?"

All of the women raised their hands. Even drunk, the women had years of experience making drinks for one another, though as the evening went on, the drinks tended more and more to just be booze on the rocks or straight up.

And so the evening went, with laughter, stories, and food. Oh so much food. Eventually, the group collapsed on the chairs and couches, settling in for a viewing of *The Avengers*.

"I don't understand how people don't understand that Black Widow is the most effective character in this entire movie," Sandra said. "She outsmarts Trickster God, outfights her better-armed colleague without hurting him when he was going for the kill, takes down dozens of Chitauri using nothing more than handguns and a cool taser, and then brings the whole invasion to a close."

"I think people just got distracted by all the abs," Ree said.

"True that," Priya said. "But you've got to give it up for the girl, she kicked some major ass. When are we getting her movie?"

Ree grumbled.

Priya chuckled. "I take that as a 'not scheduled,' then?"

"Yep," Sandra said.

Twenty minutes later, as the Avengers headed into NYC, Priya nodded off, and Anya volunteered to take her home after the group emerged from their post-prandial-cinematic coma around 1 AM.

After a round of hugs for the departing duo—vigorous with Anya, awkward with Priya—Ree saluted Sandra and plodded off to bed. Her world was three kinds of messed up, but, at last, her home life was not one of those kinds. Things would be awkward with Priya for a while, but they'd been friends years before Ree knew anything about Geekomancy and had come through worse situations.

She had three text messages from Eastwood, one angry, one apologetic, and one saying just "Be careful." Which was really Eastwood in a nutshell.

But he wasn't her problem anymore. Grognard's would be up and running soon, and her life could go back to its weird version of normal until the solstice brought another Strega and another round of Hexomancy Cage Match.

But for now, bed.

CHAPTER ELEVEN

Grognard's Returns

WINTER

Grognard's Grog and Games held its Grand Reopening on the last Friday in October, with tournaments, giveaways, and the christening of the Wall of Heroes.

The brewmaster and host had taken the opportunity afforded by the total gutting and renovation to add in a few new features.

For one, the new wards were triple-layered, carved, painted, and woven into the front and back doors. Grognard had laid in a backup generator, extra emergency rations, and had seeded weapons into the tables, some of the chairs, and into the bar itself.

Ree thought he was going a bit overboard, but this was the man's home, for all intents and purposes. And when someone fucks with your home, it is reasonable to arm the fuck up. Most patrons didn't know the extent of the retrofit, but Ree had helped him put most of this together, back to working after they'd kicked Derby Strega out of town.

A cheer rose up from the new modular tournament table, three tables latched together for extra stability. Ree knew that they also had handles on the bottom, and could be detached from their bases to become shields.

Dude had gone all out. When one had being out of a job for six months and the violation of his safe space to get angry about, the mind could go to interesting lengths.

But for now, the table was filled with a gigantic game of *Warmachine*, five players and their armies arrayed across the handmade terrain, a gift from miniatures specialist Chandra for the reopening.

Uncle Joe had donated several thousand dollars' worth of singles (arranged alphabetically by artist, as was the man's fashion). Eastwood had sent over a set of *Star Wars* rebel soldier blasters, which adorned the Wall of Heroes, alongside Talon's set of matching seaxes and targe shields, one for each of the group Grognard had pronounced "Grognard's Heroes," the six who had stood up with him that summer against Lucretia's assault:

Ree, Eastwood, Drake Winters, Chandra, Uncle Joe, and Talon. Ree had asked to be omitted, since she'd been on the clock. That had gotten a round of laughter and a scowl, which was basically as praise-y as Grognard could get. Shade had turned down the offer of being named among them, since he was embarrassed to have been unconscious basically the whole time. And "Lieutenant" Abigail Wickham had been disqualified on account of betrayal, natch.

Each of the Heroes had a special-ordered stein from a friend of Grognard's. The steins displayed the hero's name in painted script, along with an art nouveau–style portrait of the hero in their element. Ree's showed her in her Grognard's server garb, wielding both her lightsaber and a tray full of drinks.

The whole thing was an embarrassingly kind gesture, but Ree knew that it was as much for Grognard as it was for anyone else. The sanctity of this place had been violated, and now he was arraying tradition against the ghosts of fear and failure.

Also, beer. *So much beer*. The steins came with a lifetime supply of Grognard's home brew (the nonmagical variety. Dude still had to make a living).

Ree swung by the *Warmachine* table, grabbed up empty glasses, retrieved Chandra and Talon's steins for refills, and cleared off a plate of mozzarella sticks that had sat forgotten for two hours, solidifying into a fried mass.

Grognard cleared his throat, and stepped out from the bar. The crowd went silent.

"Everyone, get your drinks ready. We've got some toasting to do."

Ree went into overdrive to prepare the room for the toast. She'd gotten herself back into bartender practice over the last week, which had helped Grognard with his "Oh God, will anyone come back?" nerves. She'd never known Grognard to be one for nervousness, but people could surprise you.

After she'd poured six beers, mixed three different drinks, and opened yet another bottle of wine, everyone had their drinks ready, Ree included, her personal stein loaded with the Critical Hit Ale.

Grognard stepped over to the Wall of Heroes and put a hand on the portraits of Tomas, Alexi, and Siobhan, all three in black and white, beneath a hand-calligraphed poster (courtesy of Drake) that said "The Fallen."

"First, we raise a glass to those who died while within my hospitality. They were part of us, and they will not be forgotten."

"To the victorious dead!" he shouted, filling the room.

As one, they echoed, "To the victorious dead!" then drank.

Grognard waited a moment. "I want to thank you all for coming. It means a lot to me. Grognard's Grog and Games is safer and stronger than ever, and so are the drinks."

Pause for laughter.

"*Warmachine* now, *Magic* next, and there will be an all-night tabletop D&D for anyone who wants to stick around. We get more than seven, and Ree will run a second game.

Dark Sun, right?" he asked.

"Hell yeah. High adventure on the steamy sands of Athas, unlike this Hoth bullshit upstairs."

Where Pearson usually got a snowfall over the course of winter, maybe four to eight inches, this year there'd been a freak blizzard, dumping more than a foot on the city in the last week, confounding everyone who wasn't a magician preparing for the arrival of another Strega with a blood feud on their mind.

"But for now, keep playing, keep drinking, and welcome back." Another round of cheers.

Grognard was in better spirits than she'd seen in months. Everything was right again in his world.

Ree's? Not so much. She hadn't said, emailed, or texted a word to Eastwood since the throwdown with Connie Clothos-Line. She'd talked with Drake, but it was more awkward and stilted than it'd ever been. They'd gotten on better the first time they ever met than since he and Priya had broken up. Priya was doing fine, throwing herself into her role as the props and costume mistress for a local film that had been overfunded by 75 percent on Kickstarter.

Drake, on the other hand, was still moping. Hence why he was sitting in the corner rather than partaking of the festivities.

Ree wandered over, seeing that his stein was empty.

"Need another drink, Hero?"

Drake Winters (Strength 12, Dexterity 15, Stamina 13, Will 15, IQ 16, Charisma 15—Inventor 5 / Gentleman 2 / Steampunk 7 / Fae-Touched 3) looked up from his notebook. His dishwater-blond hair had grown out to the point where he looked like a K-pop bad boy. It constantly needed to be brushed back from covering his vision, until Drake had used his goggles as a headband to tie it back.

He wore his standard Man Out of Time uniform: brown duster over Victorian-esque pants and collared shirt, belt and bandolier adorned with gadgets and weapons. He'd been getting a good sulk on for a few hours now, and it was depressing even Ree. Her rage had faded as she saw Priya move on, and now Drake was just beating himself up, stuck in a loop of guilt. With the weather, he had an extra vest on over the shirt, and a fur cloak shoved in the corner of the booth.

Drake looked up and forced a polite smile. "I am fine as is, Ms. Ree. I would not be here if it weren't for Grognard's strict insistence."

"You don't need to keep yourself in jail forever, you know," Ree said, the two beers she'd allowed herself loosening her lips.

Drake winced as much as he smiled at the comment. "What I need to do and what I wish to do needn't be the same. How is Ms. Tharakan?"

"She's doing great. New projects, conventions, the whole deal. You screwed up, you apologized, you parted ways. One decision like that doesn't have to define your whole life."

"Not three months ago, you were berating me for the high-handed arrogance of my actions. Has that changed?"

"You were an ass. Everyone's an ass, sometimes. Sulking just means you keep yourself from doing anything new, and get to keep remembering how you've been an ass. Think about it," Ree said, then headed back to the kitchen.

Grognard's new chef, Ji-min, was whirring over the stoves, hair tied back as she managed the fryers and grill, both working at capacity. Grognard offered to get her help for the opening, but she refused on a point of pride.

"How you doing?" Ree asked.

"Just fine. Burgers up in one minute. New mozz is there." The woman indicated the plate with a sideways jut of the head, hands a whirlwind of seasoning and stirring.

Ree was not entirely certain that Ji-min was baseline human, given how fast she worked. But the woman knew her way around a kitchen, and that was all that mattered. Ree dropped the dishes into the basin, where Habib scrubbed away, his hands prunier than a retirement colony. Habib sighed as the sudsy water overflowed with the additions.

"Shit, sorry," Ree said.

"Not your fault. They keep eating, I keep working. I'm fine, okay?"

Ree grabbed the new plates, took a breath, and then hip-checked her way back into the bar.

Three hours later, the crowd had thinned out by a third, most settling down into the *Magic* tournament or a few tables nearby. A pair played a pickup game of *Warmachine* over in the store section. Drake had emerged from his funk enough to sit at the bar, chatting with Grognard and Talon.

Still no sign of Eastwood, which suited Ree just fine.

"Anyone heard from Eastwood?" Talon looked to Grognard. "Thought you threatened him with gross bodily harm if he skipped out on tonight."

As if in response, the front door opened without issue, indicating it was being opened by someone who bore an invitation poker chip. The chips were all-new, with the bar's logo on one side, INVITED on the other.

Eastwood burst through, his face reddened. But for a change, he looked unharmed. Just pissed.

"There he is!" Grognard said, throwing his arms open, his mood unassailable.

Dutifully, Ree pulled down Eastwood's stein and set it in front of him at the bar. "Drink?" she asked as he settled onto a bar stool.

"Jack. By the fistful."

Ree backed off as if struck, Eastwood's negativity as thick as a tidal wave.

"Not it," Ree said, sliding behind Grognard. She got a squint of disapproval, but the big man slid over, grabbing the bottle of Gentleman Jack in one smooth motion.

"Glad you could make it," Grognard said. "Everything okay at the Dorkcave?"

"The hell it is. I just got stiffed on three more orders. The payments went through, I shipped the goods, then when I do my end-of-week numbers, the money's gone, the charges reversed. That's the fifth time this month. Five thousand dollars' worth of gear. And when I ping the accounts to collect, they bounce.

"Someone is fucking with me."

"You sure it isn't just holiday orders going awry?" asked Talon, who operated her own sword smithy and mail-order shop. Patricia Talon (Strength 16, Dexterity 15, Stamina 13, Will 16, IQ 13, Charisma 10—Geek 3 / Blacksmith 5 / Swordswoman 5) was the kind of woman you almost never saw on film or television, only in weirdo movies like *A Knight's Tale*—muscled, beautiful, and constantly covered in soot. She came from SCA people, and had been fighting with swords since before she was potty-trained, to hear her tell it.

"No way," Eastwood said. "This has scam written all over it. I just haven't managed to backtrack any of the IP addresses or POP servers. Whoever's doing this, they're good. Had to call a few of my old Wild Wild Web buddies to get some in some help tracking them down." Eastwood looked to Grognard. "That's why I was late. No offense intended. Congrats on the reopening." Eastwood raised a toast, which Grognard met with his own stein of beer. It was his enchanted Nocturnalist Coffee Stout, which had all of the taste and none of the alcohol.

"Think this is the next Strega?" Grognard asked.

"Maybe. Weird way of coming at me, though. These lost sales are going to add up, but it's a big change from waves of gnomes or a squad of homicidal derby girls."

Drake approached the bar, stein in hand. "In my travels, each of the Strega had their own methodologies, more different than the same. When I was traveling with the Contessa—"

"Yeah, I get that," Eastwood said, cutting Drake off before he could dive into another story about the Contessa of the Lapis Galleon, his Faerie kidnapper-turned-patron/lover from the days when he was adventuring around in the Deep realms of Spirit, science fantasy–style.

Talon asked, "So you've got people on it, and in the meantime, what? Drink?"

"Not a bad plan. No, in the meantime, I'm buffing up my stock and quintuple-checking my traps. Sooner or later, she's going to make a run at me, and I'll be a Cylon's uncle if I'm going to get caught flat-footed this time."

Ree left the conversation and returned to service, buzzing around the store to pick up empties, take orders, and give encouragement to the various gamers, taking care to not offer anything that amounted to scale-tipping advice. It didn't take much to clue in a player who'd gone astray, but she had no skin in this tournament game, quite intentionally. Didn't do for anyone associated with the House to be seen playing favorites.

It also did her good to step away from Drake. After weeks of minimal contact, he was almost new again, like her resistance to his dimples, that accent, and his pleasantly annoying habits had tanked.

And that wouldn't be fair to Priya. Friends' exes were off the table, barring incredibly extenuating circumstances.

So, temporally displaced handsome inventor-heroes who you knew first counts as extenuating? asked a part of Ree's mind, sending her mindscape back into a hurricane of mixed feelings.

Down, girl, she told herself, heading into the kitchen for another round of drop-off-pick-up.

This was going to become a problem. Flipping out on Drake and then not seeing him had not, as she'd hoped, done a single fucking bit to spoil her feelings for him. She was still angry, but keeping a grudge when Priya had moved on seemed to be nothing more than spiteful.

Not that she wasn't down with a little spite here and there, but with Eastwood on her permanent shit list, she needed some adventuring buddies out and about the town. Shade and Talon didn't patrol, Uncle Joe was done with hero-ing, and Grognard had the store.

So if she was going to keep up her Urban Fantasy Vigilante act and have someone watching her back, it was basically going to come down to the man whose back she'd like to be watching, even if it made her feel guilty.

Hulk smash squishy feelings! Ree thought to herself, and got back to work.

At the stroke of midnight, the again-diminished crowd broke into the two RPG sessions, most of the patrons sticking with Grognard for *Pathfinder*, the other three heading off with Ree: Drake, Talon, and Uncle Joe.

After some lead-in and backstory catch up for the premade characters (Drake a Thri-Kreen Monk, Talon a Gladiator, and Uncle Joe a Preserver), they dove into the dirty streets of Tyr for a Noir-inspired bout of back-alley fights, twisted knots of alliances, a hidden stash of steel short swords (worth a fortune on the metal-starved Athas), and some intra-party conflict. Then the clock struck six, marking twelve hours of Grand Reopening awesomeness.

Ree and Grognard high-fived and toasted to a successful night, then Ree packed it in and made her way home.

Drake offered to walk with her through the unseasonable cold.

No ulterior motive there, not at all, Ree thought, layering up as the adventurer waited by the door.

Stay good, Ree, she told herself, then stepped out to the stairwell leading back up to the mundane office building.

The Tales of Baron Drakehousen

Outside, the coastal winds gusted, tossing dusted snow up and at their barely-uncovered faces. Ree'd lost her temperature tolerance after too long in the Northwest, leaving her wearing a balaclava, scarf, and three-quarter-length peacoat, with thermal underwear and four layers of shirts. She felt like a Stay Puft extra in a Bourne movie.

Drake, on the other hand, looked only marginally uncomfortable, extra layers on top and bottom, but still moving briskly like the sprightly punk he was.

"Thank you for allowing me to walk you home, Ms. Ree."

"Sure. Something you wanted to say that you couldn't say in the bar?" Ree asked, hoping to focus on the conversation and not on the fact that she was going to be a Geeksicle by the time she made it home in the cobalt-blue predawn, the world not yet awoken on Saturday morning.

He nodded. "I wished to express, once more, my most sincere apologies to Ms. Priya, and to yourself, for my unconscionable behavior. While I've acculturated to many aspects of this world, many of my notions about life and relationships are still firmly ingrained from my youth and life in

Avalon. Much responsibility fell on men there, more than was appropriate, as it came at the loss of self-determination for women.

"This is not meant as a complaint as to my being put-upon, but to indicate that my time here on Earth has shown me that there are no shortage of highly capable women, most of them not interdimensional travelers. I'd thought women such as yourself and the Mistress to be the exception, and I discovered myself sorely mistaken.

"Instead, I perceived my failure to protect my paramour as a moral failing, rather than as an unfortunate eventuality of life as an adventurer. But regardless of the cause, my behavior following that attack was ruled by, as you call it, Patriarchal Bullshit," Drake said, her words not fitting his mouth.

"I get it, man. We're all carrying around bullshit from the world around us. It's like the fucking Matrix sometimes. No one's immune, and for being raised in what might as well be the Victorian era, you're a damned sight better at being respectful than most of the guys I've dated."

That's not how she'd meant that to come out. *Too late, then! Moving on.*

"You've apologized to Priya, and you've apologized to me. But the only way to make it better is to do better, day by day."

"Understood. That is my most devoted intent. Disentangling the magical adventures of my life from that which intersects most directly with the unknowing public has proven increasingly difficult, given romantic endeavors."

"That's just romance, man," Ree said. "You date much before you gallivanted off with the Contessa?"

"I did not. A studious youth, I made few efforts to make the connections necessary for courting, and my family impressed upon me the need to elevate my station, thus eliminating the social propriety of courting women from the less-affluent working class.

"Sadly, few women were permitted to be inventors in my

day. The coming of the Kadel caused a great deal of disruption, but I was not present to see how the world must have changed in my absence. The Mistress was never able to track down Avalon's Aetherial Signature after our initial departure."

"She said that, did she?" Ree asked, thinking she had a pretty good handle on this woman. The Contessa sounded like a user. Take in a pretty boy to be her sidekick, get what she wants out of him, then kick him to the curb.

"Of course. She tried for weeks, but we repeatedly ran afoul of temporal eddies drawing us off course and back into another adventure."

"I'm sorry," Ree said. Though if he'd gone back home, he'd never have been around to help her, and the world would be less marvelously strange without Drake Winters.

"But you've done a lot of good here," Ree said. "Remember that. Everyone fucks up, even heroes. I'd say especially heroes, but I'm not one to talk about not beating myself up. If I'd told Priya and company about the magic crap before you two met, who knows what would have happened?"

They continued chatting on the walk home, trading stories to draw their attention away from snowfall and whorling gusts, courtesy of double-digit-MPH-or-something winds.

"Fuck you, Winter!" Ree shouted, her voice vanishing into the wind as they reached the front steps of the Shithouse.

"Patrol tomorrow?" she asked.

"I would like that. Sleep well, Ms. Ree."

"Just Ree is fine."

"As you wish," Drake said.

Unlike the last times he'd said it, this time Drake winked as he spoke. Or maybe that was just the snow in his eye.

Rather than dealing with that question, Ree charged up the stairs to the Shithole.

De-wintering took the better part of ten minutes, Ree trying very hard not to wake Sandra on a weekend. She'd been working long hours at her new gig as an assistant for a catering company. Ironically, she was doing the actual work that Ree had been pretending to be doing when she was covering for her job at Grognard's.

I should bring them by, sometime, Ree thought, though she'd tried to keep her worlds as separate as she could. Cross-pollinating all of your social circles could be really convenient, but it made taking refuge from one group's drama with another all but impossible.

She managed to set her alarm for 1, then collapsed into bed.

⚄

Her hateful, rage-inducing alarm snatched her from the warm embrace of slumber, and so Ree stumbled her way into wakefulness, going about the morning (afternoon) at a relaxed pace. She was on for Grognard's that night, so patrolling would need to be done by 6 so she could get to the bar for opening.

There were leftovers from Sandra's catering gig left on the communal shelf, so Ree helped herself to a breakfast of hors d'oeuvres and coffee, which only worked due to sheer force of will on Ree's part.

Sitting on the couch, she took a lap around the Internet while catching up on her daily news shows and making a note to herself of the TV she'd have to binge-watch in the future to get current: *Person of Interest, Grimm, Supernatural.*

Ree ran through her day to make sure she wouldn't need a time-turner. *Start patrolling at 3, done by 5:30, shower and down to Grognard's, done at 3.* She had Sunday off, thank God.

A quick scan of the weather showed that it was still below freezing out. She draped her coat and thermal underwear over the heater, preheating it so there'd be some extra juice to help her bony ass fight off the weather.

She texted Drake to confirm the time for their patrol.

3 PM at the Shithole, done by 5:30?

The response came a minute later.

Message received and confirmed. Until then, I remain your humble servant,

Drake Winters.

He couldn't be cuter or odder if he tried.

Ree spent the rest of her free time putting together her patrol gear and laying out that evening's work clothes, more black-on-black. Grognard wasn't formal, but server's wisdom dictated black for covering up various and sundry stains, discolorations, and other bullshit. She left her makeup pencil out on top of the pile, in case she had time for a Daily Design, a little affectation that she practiced whenever there was time, wearing a pattern or drawn-on tattoo for the shift, taken from whatever was inspiring her that day (or, just as often, what was cool or easy. The Eye of Horus was very popular, as was Death from Sandman's facial art).

Bundling herself up again, Ree kept her lightsaber, blaster, and sideboard handy, opting for thinner, capacitive-touch gloves so she could use her phone. She'd been using thicker mittens for patrolling in the winter wonderland Pearson had become. But with those, she'd have to take them off to use her phone, so the warmth would come with a notable Geekomantic delay.

A snowflake drifted into her eye, sneaking around her lashes.

If it turned out that the Strega had anything to do with this Capital-*W* Winter, she was going to punch that jackass so hard her ancestors would feel it.

When she came stomping down the steps in front of her building at 3:01, Drake stood at the ready, his rifle held over his shoulder like an umbrella, which is what his glamour was currently disguising it as. Most people didn't react kindly to weird people carting around rifles, even if they looked comically fake, as Drake's did, being a contraption of Avalonian Steampunkery.

Drake's oddity wasn't the least bit muted by his winter clothes, though Ree was convinced he had some kind of charm to ward off the cold. There was no way a boy that skinny could stay that warm. Then again, they'd be running and jumping their way across the city, so as long as she kept moving, she should be fine, too, right?

Keep wishing, kid, she told herself.

"Ready for a run?" Ree asked, winking.

Patrolling in winter was bullshit. Teeth-chattering, ear-burning bullshit. In real weather, she and Drake could make their way from rooftop to rooftop, boosted by Drake's new-fangled jump boots and Ree's genre emulation (*I heart you, Spider-Man*). But when the roofs were slick and stacked high with snow (no one shoveled the tops of buildings unless the owner was super-rich and/or fastidious) the whole thing got a bit too dangerous.

They gave up after the third time one or the other of them slipped trying to get up to a jog, and instead climbed their frozen asses back down to street level, wandering around the neighborhood, talking about everything and nothing, keeping far enough away from other bystanders so that they could talk mostly freely.

"So Anya's got the lead in *La Traviata*, and no matter what Madame Wesselman pulls, Anya just rolls with it. I snuck into a rehearsal last week, and Anya's killing it. You should come to a show when it goes up. I'll make sure we can alternate nights so Priya won't have to worry."

Drake's expression darkened at that.

"Just ex-boyfriend protocol, man. No offense."

"Of course. But I would be delighted to partake. *La Traviata* is not unlike a drama we have in Avalon, known in the lingua franca as 'The Revelation.' I had the fortune of seeing it once during a break from classes at the Institute. . . ."

And so Drake launched into another one of his stories about Avalon, which she preferred vastly to the admittedly wild but always enraging stories about the Contessa, his Mistress. It was very clear that she had worn the adventurer's pants in that relationship, as well as the whip, and not in a healthy way. Woman sounded like the pulp adventure poster child for selfishness and abusive personalities if ever there was one.

But whenever Ree even poked at the edges of criticizing the Contessa on account of the dozens of times that she had abandoned Drake in order to go do something insane and impossible to save the day, or her countless dalliances with other men (and women, and agender beings) during their adventures, or any of her other ridiculous shit, Drake would leap straight to her defense.

Most everyone had that One Ex that still had their claws in them. For Ree, it was Jay, who seemed to have been happy with his petit bourgeois lifestyle upgrade, since Ree had never heard back from him. But when her heart skipped several beats just looking at his Facebook updates, she'd let Sandra unfriend the bastard so Ree could try to move on with her life.

It mostly worked, except for Facebook's friend-of-a-friend update bullcrap, which dropped Jay into Ree's feed again and again. *Thanks, Zuck.*

Drake wrapped up his story, leaving room for Ree to respond. Over the year and change she'd known Drake, she'd learned to apply her server's ability to partition her brain, listening and processing Drake's stories while letting her mind wander. Which was particularly handy on patrols.

And for seeing monsters.

She reached out and grabbed Drake's shoulder.

"You see that?" she asked, deathly still. Something black and purple had flashed around the corner, catching on the setting winter sun.

"I'm afraid not. Shall we?" he asked, hefting his not-umbrella.

"We shall."

They moved carefully into the alley, walking shoulder-to-shoulder. Ree had one hand on her blaster, the other wrapped around her sideboard of cards.

As they crossed into the alley, a purple-black panther looked down at them from the wall, three claws buried in the concrete. It hissed, then jumped.

The two split apart, a practiced motion constrained by the limited size of the alley and by Ree's extra layers of poof. She drew the blaster and shot, missing on the quick-draw. Drake backed off and brought his rifle up to a firing position.

The panther hit the ground where they'd been standing not a second ago, and whirled in place, realizing that all of a sudden, it was flanked at ten and two. A true 180-degree flank was no good when firearms were involved, because Friendly Fire Isn't.

Ree unloaded another burst from her phaser, aiming down so a miss didn't have the chance of randomly vaporizing a bystander across the street. The time it took to adjust the shot let the panther dodge, leaping at Drake. The adventurer tucked and rolled under the panther, the beast's claws scraping along his reinforced coat without gaining purchase.

Dropping the phaser, Ree pulled out her lightsaber and thumbed it on. In an instant, the metal-and-plastic prop hilt sprung to life, blue blade almost white in the weak light of winter. Ree cut forward in a figure-eight pattern, drawing the panther's attention away from Drake. The monster leaped, sinking its claws into the wall. It turned in place and climbed horizontally. The creature bound across the ten-foot alleyway to the opposite side, then leaped over Ree's head, twisting in the air, as if to land with all four paws in her back.

Ree bet that most magical panther-monsters could pull off that attack against normal mortals.

But most mortals were not lifelong *Star Wars* fans with impossible laser swords. Ree spun in place, crunching as snow packed beneath her boots. She sliced through both a fore and hind paw. The monster hit the ground, as ungraceful as she'd ever seen a feline be. It scrambled back into a fighting posture, snarling and baring its fangs.

"Smile," Ree said, ducking to the side.

As she cleared the line of fire, Drake's rifle lit up with green energy, exactly as they'd practiced six months ago.

The sound of *zot* filled her ears. It was a risk to jump right in with a move like that, but Ree still had the lightsaber to dissuade the panther from jumping her shit if Drake missed the beat. When the burst of light cleared, the panther was nothing more than a pile of ichor.

Part of the reason why most people didn't believe in monsters anymore was the fact that they didn't leave any remains. Dead creature = sticky ichor, which dissolved within an hour. Unless you got it on you, which Ree often did. Theoretically, this meant that she had valuable materials for thaumo-biologists or whatever, but no one had come asking about her stained, tattered-ass clothes, so she tended to just burn them if she couldn't get the stains out.

She'd been going through a lot of clothes this last year. Even her geeky T-shirt collection was running low, a feat that would have been unthinkable before last Halloween. Many brave shirts had given their lives to protect the people of Pearson.

Ree offered a high five to Drake as she turned. "Nice. Knew that practicing that would pay off."

Drake met her gesture. Despite the practice, he was still the whitest boy in White Town when he high-fived. Dude could tussle with monstrosities the size of an SUV without losing his cool, but try to get him to give a smooth high five, and all of a sudden he was as square as they came.

It was kind of cute, to be honest.

Checking on the street, Ree saw that they hadn't attracted any rubberneckers. The Doubt had the tendency to make people just walk on by, interpreting monster attacks as muggings, or just erase them from people's memories entirely. A backhanded fuck-you to the magical world from a bunch of Enlightenment Technomancers that had caught on like a viral video, then set itself up as the global cultural default everywhere it could get purchase.

"Looks like we're clear," Ree said, extinguishing her lightsaber, the blade retracting into the hilt, which returned to its cold metal and plastic form.

"So it seems. I do believe that that creature was the same one that assaulted Priya and I this autumn. Good to be rid of it."

"Oh yeah? I was wondering. You come through okay?" she asked, replacing the lightsaber in her coat pocket.

"Once again, the jacket has served its purpose well enough." Drake pulled out his pocket watch and clicked the face open. Half-four. Shall we adjourn for milkshakes?"

"You read my mind." They might be able to scare up something else in the next half hour, but doing so would take them farther away from Grognard's, so this was as good a time as any to call it. And she was not one to turn down a post-fight milkshake.

⋅✕⸰✕⊛⸰✕✕⋅

The Burger Bin was relatively quiet, which was to say that the line was only ten minutes long, mostly families brave enough to venture forth into the ridiculous wintery weather in search of glorious sweets and juicy burgers. Ree ordered a small of her might-as-well-be-patented Milkshake of Victory, which had chocolate, peanut butter, caramel, and nearly everything else included, with whipped cream on top because reasons.

As always, Drake had vanilla.

The low flow of traffic meant that they were easily able to find a table in the corner, away from prying ears.

Ree shed several of her outer layers, and Drake followed suit. Their coats and gloves and Drake's not-umbrella bulked up so much that it looked like their booth was seating four rather than two.

Drake combed back his sweat-slicked hair and set his goggles aside.

"You need a haircut, hippie," Ree said.

"I rather think that I lack the tie-dye required for that accusation to bear any weight."

"Informed comeback burn." Ree usually got those pop culture digs across like fastballs over home base. But Drake had been studying up.

"You've made it to the sixties and seventies in your history, then?" Ree asked, mixing her shake with the spoon provided. She scooped herself a heaping bite with whipped cream on top. The taste of sugar and fat hit her taxed system like a drug. Sugar addiction was no joke, but it was way more fun to feed than heroin or anything involving needles.

"Enough to fake a greater degree of cultural knowledge than I actually have."

"Welcome to the club. That's all any of us ever do. Except when it comes to nerdy shit. Then you better know your crap."

"Fortunately, I am still granted a pass on that by the Underground. The doorkeeper gave up on me after the third straight month of asking me to name the dwarves in *The Hobbit*."

"It's all about clusters of assonance." Ree set the spoon down and started counting off names with fingers. "Bifur, Bofur, Bombur. Balin and Dwalin. Oin and Gloin, Fili and Kili. Ori, Nori, Dori. And Thorin, who doesn't rhyme because he's the king."

Drake chuckled. "I know Professor Tolkien was a philologist, but it just sounded like you were speaking an entirely different language then. And not even the one that I imagine the good professor was intending. These stories are powerful, that much is clear given how important they are to you and your friends. I can see that power, but it does not speak to me in the same way that the call of steam and aether do."

Ree sipped her milkshake, then returned to spooning it out. It had been mixed thick today, and a chunk of something was stuck in the straw. "No reason it has to. For all the talk about 'universal storytelling,' when push comes to shove, you are from a different universe."

"Strange, then, to consider the tall stack of variables that led us to the same place," he said, face bright, though he was mussed and scuffed. It was how she liked him best, truth be told. Pristine and shiny Drake was a bit too put-together. She wanted him down in the dirt, with her.

Smooch him, her libido cried, bringing back the chorus from another visit to the Burger Bin.

Down, girl, Ree repeated, imagining a miniature version of herself next to a pressure cooker of libido, trying to hold down the lid.

There were two ways forward from here. Take the road open before her, or run the other way and follow the Rhyming Ladies' code.

No dating friends' exes echoed in her mind, and she sat back, feeling like she was pulling her way through molasses and pushing against a magnet's draw at the same time. She reached for her milkshake, standing, and due to extreme distraction, knocked the shake over, plastic lid splitting and spilling the rest of her confection all over the table.

"Shit. Shit, sorry," Ree said, her server's instincts taking over as she launched herself toward the napkins.

"Is everything quite all right?" Drake asked, standing as well.

"Just me being a klutz. I swear, it's like I've never been through a winter before," Ree said, speaking mostly to herself, avoiding looking into Drake's molten honey eyes as a form of self-defense.

And she was doing that self-effacing crap again, too. Feel nervous, minimize self.

Bullshit.

"I better head home and get ready for work. Nice job today," she said, running through a conversational closing formula as fast as she could to veer the conversation away from places she wanted desperately to go but couldn't.

Ree tossed the massed pile of soiled paper towels and the ruined shake, and grabbed her pile of coat and gloves, nearly falling over herself as she made her way to the door.

Better a dork than a traitor, she told herself, bracing for the outside.

For once, she looked forward to the cold. It brought clarity. Well, clarity, hypothermia, and eventual death, but she had a short walk home.

CHAPTER THIRTEEN

Caveat Venditor

Ree had the time and a pressing need to get her mind off dashing blond men with easy smiles and strong hands, so she arrived at Grognard's with the left side of her face covered in complex, interconnecting wards straight out of an epic fantasy. She'd add some to her knuckles, but they'd just smear over the course of the evening and get all over the drinking glasses. Not worth the bother.

Eastwood was already stationed at the bar when she arrived, sucking the life out of the room. She could practically feel it as she stepped out of the kitchen.

There were any number of places she wanted to be at that moment that were not where she was:

1) At home, taking a cold shower

2) Anywhere, talking to her dad

3) ~~Smooching Drake~~

3) Talking to Priya

But in reality, she needed to be:

4) Exactly where she was, earning money to pay the bills and shovel away some of her renewed hillock of debt (downgraded from a mountain, but building its way back up damned quick since the summer)

Rather than facing Eastwood right away, she took a survey of the bar. Uncle Joe sat in a corner booth with a stack of freshly-opened boosters, arranging and sleeving his new cards. A bald and bearded hipster couple sat at a table, holding hands and sipping lagers. She made a note to ask about them, since she hadn't seen the pair before. Grognard's was an invite-only establishment, so walk-in traffic was pretty well nonexistent.

A trio including Chandra were setting up a large game of *Warhammer 40K* in the store section, Chandra arranging ruined city terrain, doubtless to provide lanes of fire for her mighty Orks.

Ree did her best to keep busy, never staying still for more than a moment between refilling drinks, unpacking boxes with inventory restock, cleaning tables, and more.

Around eight, Grognard followed her into the office.

"Go see your friend," he said.

"Shubba-what?" Ree asked.

"That friend. Priya. The one that dated Drake. You're too twisted up about her and him and Eastwood. I'm surprised you haven't asked to take off already. Go sort the shit out. Eastwood's safe enough here for now; the Strega can wait a day, but not more. You may not like Eastwood, and if you think letting the Strega get him is proper payback for what he's done, that's your call. But he's my friend, too."

Some of the tension bled out of Ree's shoulders, more of her neck reappearing after an evening where her pauldrons had been rubbing her earlobes. Over the last months, Grognard had opened up more, talked in complete paragraphs more often. But it was still weird.

"How do you know all of this?" Ree asked.

"Bartender. It's my superpower."

"Point. Thanks, boss. I'll get things sorted out and keep the CW drama away from the store."

The brewmaster grinned. "Too late for that. You should have seen the looks Inspector Gadget gave you when you weren't looking. He'd give the puppy pound a run for its money."

And so Ree cashed out her tips, said good night to Chandra and the gang (and pointedly not Eastwood), then headed out.

Once she hit the surface, she tapped out a text message to Priya with her gloves, getting ready to head out into the winter wonderland once more, the night cast in yellows and whites by the streetlights and headlights, accenting the neon and the dim moonlight.

Got off work early. You free for a chat tonight?

Then she cued up something suitably angsty for her walk home. *Go go gadget Civil Wars.* From Grognard's, Priya's apartment was more or less the same direction, so she wouldn't be walking fifteen minutes and then need to turn around.

It was late enough into the evening that she wasn't going to count on the buses, and it seemed like half of the city's cabbies had fled south to the Bay Area, migrating like birds when the weather rolled in.

She moved through mostly-empty streets, the business district fairly empty on weekends, the businesswomen and office dwellers not around to fill up the neighborhood restaurants and bars.

Two blocks later, her phone buzzed in her coat. Ree pulled it out, snow whirling around fast enough to melt on her screen as she read Priya's response.

Sure. Come on over. Shall I call the Ladies?

Can this be just us? Ree answered, not wanting to tip her

conversational hand, but also not interested in having this conversation with the others around.

Ree stepped up the pace, crunching through the snow, watching for patches of ice in the packed-down snow, melted and refrozen into a Trojan Horse of catastrophic gravity compliance.

She'd need a plan for what to actually say, how to parse the situation without coming off like a heartless jackass.

So, Priya. I've kind of been sort of infatuated with your exboyfriend since at least this spring. Yes, I know you started dating in the summer. Nothing happened, though we have been gallivanting around the town fighting monsters for about fifteen months, so there's that.

Ree sighed. *Yeah, that'd go over great.*

If she'd been better at grokking her own feelings, or hadn't just been coming off an epic breakup, maybe the situation could have been avoided. But Drake was so old-fashioned that he'd never made the first move, having strangely run right over the level of acquaintance when a gentleman could call on a lady and straight into the place where they were crossing dimensions together, and she could have done something about it but didn't want to do anything untoward and cross his boundaries or make his head explode, and there they were.

And now he was Priya's ex. And given that Ree had insisted on the "no dating exes" rule back with her first college boyfriend Vinay, it'd be pretty shitty of her to beg out of the rule now.

Nope. Still fucked up, she acknowledged, and went back to square one while the tragic "just bang already" not-lovers of The Civil Wars crooned at each other, the moon eyes and maudlin sexual tension screaming from every note.

Ree arrived at Priya's just around nine. Which meant that there could be drinking. This was good. As long as she could get through the conversation before getting to plastered. She hadn't touched anything at work, despite a powerful hankering for wine to calm her shit down.

Priya opened her door wearing her crafting belt and goggles, magnifying glasses in place so she could see the detail work. No one was actually likely to lean in and see the background gears she painted onto the base-plate level of her Steampunk Ghostbusters proton packs, but she'd know they were there. And Priya's art had to satisfy her before it was allowed to even think about satisfying anyone else.

The third proton pack sat on her work desk, paints, glue gun, and a stack of gears surrounding the work in progress. Abney Park played in the background.

"Hey," Ree said as she stepped into the apartment, Priya closing the door behind her. "Glad you were free."

Priya shrugged. "Not really free, but nothing that couldn't wait. Drink?"

"Yes, please."

Priya mixed up a pair of White Russians in no time flat, handing one to Ree.

"So, what's up?" she asked.

A mental gun went off, and Ree's heart started racing.

"Okay, this is going to be awkward no matter how I do it, but if I don't, it's going to be even worse."

Priya gave the "go on" nod.

"And I know this isn't kosher, and it's kind of shitty for me to do after Vinay, but that was a long time ago, and maybe that makes it slightly less shitty, but I have to ask."

The world closed in, and Ree went into full-on monologuing.

"This whole thing is seven shades of weird, because it's all wrapped up in the magical world crap and the Geekomancy, and Spirit realms and Faerie realms, and cross-cultural weirdness and friends dating friends, and for a while I let not knowing what to do lead to not doing anything, and then there was the pilot and Jane Konrad, and then you and Drake, and then you and not Drake, and now I'm working with him on the magic hero thing again, and it's just totally messed up in this maddeningly exciting and juvenile way, and I just had to tell you and say I'm sorry."

"That wasn't a question," Priya said, as Ree checked back into the world around her, her ears hotter than when she had to duck her head into the oven to pull out the full racks of cinnamon rolls at Zombie Café.

Woman up, she told herself. "I want to ask Drake out. Is that okay?"

"Of course it is," Priya said, not missing a beat.

"I'm sorry for even asking, but every time he says, 'As you . . .'" Ree stopped.

"Wait, what did you say?" She'd barreled right over Priya's inevitable response, so busy continuing to bargain and apologize that she thought maybe she'd missed the actual answer.

Priya took a long sip of her drink. "Do it, Ree. I knew he had a thing for you from the beginning, but I didn't know you felt the same way. I get the superhero, 'protect the ones you love' thing, even though it's bullshit." Priya's eyes were red at the edges. "I'd be a liar if I wasn't sad that it couldn't be me, but Drake's something else. He's not the kind of guy you take home to Mom. He's a 'run around and have adventures, crack wise, and fight monsters' kind of guy. Plus my parents would flip if they found out I was getting serious with a white boy."

The gadgeteer-costumer smiled. "He's your kind of guy. Always was. I just didn't realize it until too late. I thought he was a little too into the scene, a late bloomer who had a bit more passion than sense. But he's exactly as weird as you are.

"Go get him, sis," Priya finished, toasting with tears in her eyes.

"You're not just saying this because you think it's the right thing to do and are being all self-sacrificing and noble?" Ree asked, sniffling.

"At no point did I say it was that," Priya said, making it very clear that was exactly what she was doing. "I'm fine. I'm no superhero. I want to live my life with a minimum of chances of random monster encounters, and you go running toward them. Drake doesn't want to endanger someone, but you go after danger yourself. He thought I was someone he had to protect, but you, you'll keep his ass out of the fire. You two just have to get over your respective bullshit and figure out how to be together."

"When did you get Yoda levels of wise?" Ree asked, putting her drink down.

"I've watched every season of *The Bachelor* and *The Bachelorette*, so I know exactly what *not* to do."

Ree wanted to hug her friend but also wanted to respect the fact that doing this was taking a big honking act of will on her part, and godsdamnit why did feelings have to be made out of squishy gut-wrenching complicated crap?

"Now get out there and call him before my heroic self-sacrificing demeanor crumbles and I have to buy stock in Kleenex," Priya said, taking a long slug from her drink.

Ree thought better of it, then wrapped Priya in a hug anyway.

"Those proton packs look amazing. You're a badass," she said, trying to take the conversation anywhere, literally anywhere else.

"Get," Priya said with the best smile she could muster, her eyes still red.

And so she went, wrapping herself up again and heading to the street.

She pulled out her phone in the building foyer, not interested in trying to have a sensitive phone call over the howling winds.

First, she checked in with Sandra, who was, in fact, staying over with Darren that night as Ree'd remembered.

That settled, she considered calling her dad, just to push things off a little more. But while she was sure he'd be as cheerleader-y as ever, she needed to shit or get off the pot, as the saying went.

"Here goes something," Ree said.

Drake picked up after the second ring.

"Ahoy ahoy?"

Hearing his voice sloughed five pounds of worry off her shoulders. *You got it bad, girl*, she told herself.

"Hey, it's me. You free? I got off early from work and was hoping we could chat."

"Oh, certainly. I was just recalibrating the Aetherial Breakthrough Actuator. It's been inconsistent to a degree that's approaching dangerous, but given that it is currently without power, my apartment will not implode if it's left for the evening."

"What's great is that you actually have to make stuff like that clear," Ree said, an unconscious smile on her face.

She continued, "Can you meet me at the Shithole in forty-five minutes? I need to do some errands." It would only take her twenty minutes to get home in this weather, but she wanted the chance to change and primp at least a little.

"Certainly. Until then," Drake said.

"See ya." Ree hung up and exhaled the rest of her breath.

Someone upstairs was looking out for her, and sent a bus around the corner for Ree to catch a quick ride home in just ten minutes instead of twenty. The buses were slow, too, since most of their drivers had never had to work their routes with snow, but it also meant she didn't need to make tea just to warm herself up.

She dumped all of her coats and work stuff in her room, checked the clock, then activated a nonmagical Preening Whirlwind. This involved taking a lightning-quick shower to wash off the smell of beer, then changing into fresh clothes. She considered wearing a date outfit, but thought that most of her more "modern" date outfits might magnify what was already likely to be a very shocking course of action for the temporally-displaced old-school Drake.

Instead of a "date" outfit, she changed into the next set of work and adventuring clothes, with well-worn jeans that fit like tights and her Inigo Montoya T-shirt. She futzed with her hair, then decided to leave it as is, slightly curled and still wet from the shower, not short enough to dry instantly, but not really long enough to fully tie back to keep from getting wet. The perils of in-between-length hair.

She reapplied a quick base of makeup and resisted the urge to wear her vampy red lipstick. She didn't need to vamp out with Drake, which was kind of the point. When she was out with the Rhyming Ladies, she found that she often wanted to play up the "I am actually a woman and want to find someone to date" card, or the other single men and women at the clubs and concerts would gloss right over her and fixate on her more outwardly-sexy friends, whether their tastes ran toward the Amazonian, the voluptuous, or the "exotic." (In racist objectification land, Indian seemed to trump half–Puerto Rican for the title of Most Exotic. Feh.)

Calm down, she told herself. *Come on too strong and you might explode the poor man's mind. It'll be weird enough for you to come on to him, let alone if you tackle the boy as soon as he steps in the door.*

Though that would be hilarious, she realized.

So as to avoid compulsive nervousness, she picked up her phone and caught up on the Internets.

She had a good half-dozen DMs from Charlie with various links about geeky gossip (*Star Trek: Into Darkness* rumors, mostly. Did anyone believe that Benedict Cumberbatch *wasn't* going to be playing Khan? Whitewashing aside, it seemed like a slam dunk).

She was tapping out a response to Charlie's link about a rumored Easter egg that fixed the ending to *Dragon Age II* when the buzzer rang.

The Shithole had its failings, mostly the walk-up, but it did have a working buzzer system with video. Someone buzzed your apartment, and a black-and-white screen at the door showed video. Drake looked like he had, in fact, just dropped whatever he was working on and come over. Smudges on his face, hair unkempt, and wearing the leather overalls that, as far as she could tell, came out only when he wasn't certain that things weren't going to explode on him.

Ree buzzed Drake into the building, then proceeded to fidget for a while. She unlocked the bolt and slide locks, waiting. Ree swore she could hear every step he took, her urge to flip out, run, and/or hurl escalating moment by moment.

With Jane, she'd had prepostrous circumstances and the short time frame to keep her shit together. Relatively. Plus, since Jane had been a mess because of the curse, Ree had reacted by being the stable one. With Drake, it was all about forcing the question that had been sitting at the edge of her vision since the end of the Halloween origin story to their acquaintance. The friend-to-lover jump was a risky, risky move, but she had verification from basically everyone in the universe that this was a match waiting to happen.

None of that kept her from jumping when Drake knocked on the door.

CHAPTER FOURTEEN

Here Goes Nothing

Ree held in the *Eep*, and stepped forward to open the door.

Drake lit up as he entered, running a gloved hand through his hair.

"Good evening," he said, moving forward with familiarity to put his coat away. Ree pivoted to give him room but felt his warmth as he passed by.

"Can I get you something to drink?" she asked out of habit, though she really didn't want him to have a drink in hand that he might drop, or worse, use as a body language shield.

"Yes, please. My superintendent believes that the proper response to this spate of weather is to consign the building to the climate of the Sahara. It reminds me of—"

"Drink coming right up," Ree said, trying to head off the story without just shutting him down.

She removed the already-poured glass of water, as well as the also-already-poured glass of tequila she'd made for herself. Making sure she wasn't transposing them, she returned and handed the water to Drake, who had shed his coat. He was down to his working chaps and a soot-and-grease-stained collared shirt. The smudges and dirt were gone from his face, though.

He took a long, long, impossibly long drink, and Ree joined him, cutting herself off at two shots' worth. She wanted to be loosened up, not sloppy.

"So," she said, not sure what else to say. "There's no way for this to not be awkward. I should know, because I've been running scenarios for months like I was planning a heist, and all signs point to awkward. So it's just going to have to be awkward."

Drake arched an eyebrow, the move so isolated and precise and so archetypically Drake that she couldn't help but laugh, the nervousness bubbling over.

"Are you quite all right? Is there something amiss? With Eastwood, perhaps?"

"No, none of that," Ree said. *Beat around the bush some more, why don't you?* taunted an inner voice

"We've been friends for a while and have faced down more weird-ass shit together in fifteen months than is probably best for our mental health to recount all at once. And we get along great, but we come at life from such different worlds that I don't have a flying fuck's idea what that really means above and beyond the friend angle."

Several thoughts passed over Drake's face, reacting and considering.

Ree set her glass down, seeing that Drake had done the same.

SHIT OR GET OFF THE POT! yelled a voice in her head.

"Oh, fuck it," Ree said, stepping forward, grabbing him around the ears with both hands, and going in for a big, Roger Rabbit–scale kiss.

Ree pulled back, watching every nanosecond for a response. The infinitesimal moment before Drake moved stretched on to forever, letting Ree's brain churn through every possible negative reaction and rejection possible in a blatant contravention of the ordinary flow of time because screw you, emotions.

Drake blinked, a hilariously cartoonish motion.

"I'm sorry, I didn't—" Ree was cut off by Drake plunging forward, restarting the kiss with vigor.

Drake wrapped his hands around Ree's lower back and pulled her up into his embrace.

FUCKING FINALLY! said her brain, high-fiving itself while victory GIFs played in her mind, lighting off fireworks of sensation and arousal and fiero.

As the moment stretched into infinity, twin buzzing sounds crashed the party.

"Ignore," Ree declared, returning to the kiss.

A moment later, the buzzing was replaced by twin "Hey! Pick up, gorrammit!" in Eastwood's voice.

The pair disentangled. Ree asked, "What the hell?" in the direction of her phone, which sat on the lip of the couch. From behind her, she bet that Drake's phone was the other source of Eastwood's weird phone-hack.

Ree woman-handled Drake as she stepped over to retrieve her phone, unwilling to let go now that she'd gotten her hands on him. She stared murderating daggers at her phone, which continued to make the "Hey! Pick up, gorrammit!" sound despite being on silent.

"This had better be fucking good," Ree said, putting the call on speakerphone.

Eastwood's voice answered—but not live, as a recording.

"Ree. If you're hearing this, then I haven't checked in with the specialty app I made. What follows is the GPS information for the tracking chip I've had embedded subcutaneously. I'm in trouble. Please, I need your help."

She hung up and called Eastwood right back, ready to give him a large, cannon-shaped piece of her mind.

Rational Ree knew that this was probably a big deal, and that they should get moving.

But Libido Ree was not going to stand for the universe so blatantly and unfairly cock-blocking her in such spectacular fashion, and someone was getting chewed out, that was *for fucking certain.*

The call rang through to voicemail, and Ree hung up, wishing for a moment for the return of old telephones where you could slam down the receiver to express anger. If she slammed her phone like that, the gorilla glass would shatter into a million foot-shredding pieces. Instead, both phones beeped again, Ree's displaying a destination point on her maps app.

"We shouldn't ignore that, should we?" Ree asked, one hand still wrapped around Drake. As long as they were still touching, that moment wouldn't vanish, wouldn't escape back into impossibility. It would stay real.

Drake ran a hand through Ree's hair. She leaned into the touch, wishing for the universe to have better timing.

"I'm afraid not. As conflicted a figure as he may be, he is a friend, and a fixture of the community. And I for one have no interest in letting Lucretia get the last laugh."

"Damnit. But when we're done with that, I move for an immediate resumption of smooching."

"Seconded," Drake said, his face flush. "I was rather hoping that I knew the reason why you asked me to come calling, but even an imagination spurned on by visits to countless impossible realms of Faerie could not predict how ravishing that kiss would be."

Ree rolled a save vs. melting in her shoes.

"Put a pin in that beautiful mushy stuff. I won't do any good to you as a puddle and needing to be carried around in a bucket. We can do better than the Wonder Twins. Also, not related."

Drake smiled the smile of missed pop culture references, and moved for his coat. Ree let him go, heading back into her bedroom to retrieve her own coat.

You are going to owe me so damned bad, she thought in Eastwood's direction as they bundled back up and headed into the night.

⚬✕⟐✕⚬

The GPS signal led them to an overpriced parking lot in the center of town, the kind of place where event pricing topped $30, and somehow, every single day in the week seemed to be an "event."

In reality, the only time that Thursday was that kind of event was when it was trying to take your money.

"So, where's Clint?" Ree asked, looking around the building. The structure had room for several hundred cars, and if Eastwood was stuffed into someone's trunk, this would take a while.

Drake asked, "May I inspect your mapping program?"

Ree handed over the phone, feeling a jolt of not-actual electricity when their gloved hands met again.

They made their way into the ground level of the parking garage, walking by an empty guard station with snow piled around it like it was the peak of a mountain.

It was all she could do to not just pop the locks to an SUV and head to Makeout Town, though making out in cars had never actually managed to be that comfortable.

Focus, Ree. Nookie later.

"And how accurate are these signals, usually?"

"GPS? Usually within a hundred feet or so, if you're using the good ones."

"But it does not indicate elevation, does it?"

"Why would it . . ." Ree asked, then stopped in place. "Shit. He's at Wells's, isn't he?"

"That does seem likely. I thought that her laboratory was located farther south."

"She had to move after the attack on Grognard's. Too

many gnomes in the neighborhood. She moved uptown, right around here. Sadly, that means it's sewer time."

Drake's nose wrinkled in autonomic disgust.

Ree made her way toward an alley. "Not exactly the kind of getting dirty I was hoping for tonight."

Now, where is that going to be? Ree did mental math and started sweeping snow aside, revealing a manhole cover.

Drake helped her clear off the rest of the snow, and then Ree pulled out her switchblade to jimmy loose the cover.

"Actually. You got a crowbar in that coat of yours?" she asked.

"Alas, no. I left my breaking-and-entering kit in my semi-formal jacket."

Ree took a break to apply another smooch, which caused Drake to wobble, nearly losing his crouched footing.

"And what was that for?" Drake asked.

"Your sense of humor."

"Then I shall endeavor to not be as humorous during our melees, as I rather think a battlefield kiss is inadvisable, despite its prevalence in films."

"I just need to channel an action movie and we'll be fine."

"Very well. How long will you need?" Drake asked, working to pry open the manhole.

"I mean, in general," Ree said, pulling on the other side. They got the manhole cover free of its slot, and hauled it off, depositing it by the edge of the street. Drake draped his feet into the hole.

"It's cool. I got point," Ree said, wagging the lightsaber.

Drake removed his feet. "After you."

Ree gave Drake her best flirty wink and held the hilt down into the sewer, thumbing on the blade.

The blue light illuminated the sewer, a thick stream of sewer water flowing thanks to melt from the epic snowfall.

"Looks wet down there. Watch your feet." Ree dropped into the sewer, landing into a crouch, holding the light-saber tight as she looked both ways, checking for gnomes, alligators, or whatever the Pearson sewer might have in store for them that week.

"All clear," Ree announced, stepping to the side and holding her lightsaber parallel to the flow of the sewer, keeping the blade away from Drake as he dropped into the tunnel. His landing made a splash that flowed over her thankfully-waterproof boots.

Uggs, in addition to being the stinkiest kind of boot, were also *not* waterproof. Instead, Ree went for the ugly but functional pig leather, purchased secondhand for lessened ethical wooginess.

"Okay, here we go. Watch my back?" Ree asked.

"And I will also keep an eye on our flank." Ree could hear his smirk without having to hear it.

"Cheeky."

"I find that the intimacy of a passionate kiss leaves me rather less inhibited about making such comments. Though I will, of course, cease to do so should you wish."

"No, no. Game on."

Drake lit the directional light he'd re-created off a snake light design, Steampunk-ifying it with gears and copper. "Pardon my presumption, but does this mean that we are courting now?"

They reached a T-junction, bearing left after Ree checked both directions. If she was remembering right, Dr. Wells's new location was just down on the right.

"That's the idea. Though maybe it's not the smartest thing to sort out our relationship status in a sewer. How will we update Facebook from down here? 'Ree Reyes and Drake Winters are in a relationship and it's complicated by the fact that they're constantly in mortal danger' is strangely not an option."

"Unfortunate. That would encompass the situation rather effectively. I remember your friend Charlie saying something about the importance of Facebook officiality at one point or another."

"Charlie's very much a pics-or-it-didn't-happen kind of guy. Validity through confirmation and public knowledge and all that."

"Is that your preference as well?" Drake stopped for a moment, focusing as if listening for a distant sound.

Ree pointed back down the hall past where they'd turned, asking the question with her facial expression.

Drake shrugged as if to say *Uncertain, but I heard something*.

They'd spent a lot of time in sewers together.

Is that what their relationship was going to be? It better not. It'd just take a concerted effort to not make it all about the work. She had plenty of ideas of other aspects she'd like to see involved, and not just the ones that involved beds and no clothes.

After waiting for a minute, they continued onward, moving slowly.

Ree's mapping app showed the beacon right on top of their position. She pointed her lightsaber at the various doors and holes, trying to remember Wells's new clinic location from the one time she'd visited. Blunt force trauma didn't tend to help this part of her memory, strangely enough.

She waved the blade at one of the doors, and they moved, almost shoulder-to-shoulder. Almost, though, so it wasn't quite as distracting.

Ree gave Dr. Wells's code knock, which was the Morse for S.O.S.

Something moved in the distance, back where Drake had stopped.

Yep, something's out there. Let's just hope it decides to bugger off by the time we're done.

A few moments later, the sound of metal on metal, and then the door swung open, revealing Dr. Wells, Pearson's resident Aesclepiomancer.

Dr. Wells was a short woman, constantly wearing a lab coat as a badge of office. The space was lit, framing her from the back and in blue-scale from the front.

She kept her hair long, locs tied back.

"There you are. Come in," she said, voice flat.

Ree shut off her lighstsaber, saving its nostalgia battery for their trip out, if needed. Drake stepped inside, still covering them, and then Dr. Wells closed and relocked the door. She pressed a palm to the door and spoke some Latin, and Ree felt something intangible slide into place.

Magic senses tingling. She couldn't always feel magic, but when she knew to expect the working, it was much easier.

Dr. Wells's new location lacked the painting of the derby girl on the roof, but this one had its own mural, a graffiti-as-art-history of medicine. "The real history of medicine" as Wells said.

The mural started with the original followers of Aesclepius and Thoth, the keepers of sacred medicine in antiquity in Saqqara and Thebes. Next were several pictures of Aesclepiomancers through the ages, passing down the mundane aspects of their art across the western world with pictures of traders on the Silk Road, mixing and trading secrets with other traditions, and then going into hiding during the Enlightenment with the rise of Technomancers.

And now, Dr. Wells: A Geekomancer's best friend after nine rounds with the monsters (human and magical) of Pearson.

"He said you'd be coming." Dr. Wells strode at Resident-on-Rounds speed back to one of her rooms. The new locale was much bigger than her older digs, big enough for a dozen beds in the front room, plus three private rooms.

The doctor opened the door onto an ICU room, tubes and wires, the whole nine yards. And at its center, a beaten and broken Eastwood.

"Holy shit," Ree said, hand going to her mouth.

The bearded geek was wrapped up from head to toe, one eye and his mouth uncovered.

"You made it," Eastwood croaked.

"How are you awake? And what the hell happened to you?"

"Strega Number Two. Turns out she wasn't satisfied with just bleeding me dry. I stepped out of the Dorkcave tonight right into some art deco mousetrap. Pressure plate at the base of the stairs. As soon as it clicked down, a grate wrapped with barbed wire dropped down on the stairs, putting a roof on top of me. I couldn't move the mesh, so I tried to get back inside, but she'd installed a super-magnet, which must have been activated by the pressure plate. I saw the marbles make their way down and around, gears and levers dancing together."

A coughing fit stopped him, shaking the full-body rig. Dr. Wells glided straight by to the display instruments.

"Gently, Anthony. Shallow breaths."

He took a slow, wheezing breath, and continued. "Then the grate came up and steel bowling balls started falling on me like monster-size hail. I tried to make a run for it, but all that got me was a face-first introduction to the concrete of the steps."

"My goodness," Drake said, his face gone white. Well, whiter.

"I couldn't get out. There must have been eight or ten of the things on me, crushing my ribs, legs. One hand was already in my pocket, so I pulled out the sideboard. I couldn't even see the cards, so I just started tearing. I knew the Nightcrawler was in there somewhere. But first I managed to half suffocate myself with a circle of protection, and then make my problem even worse by casting giant growth and shredding my back with the barbed wire. But I made it, and the Doc can pick up from there."

"He had a shattered patella, ulna, and radius, a cracked jaw, broken ribs, and severe trauma pretty much everywhere else.

"If this weren't the solstice, he would have died. But while the Strega's powers are at their height now, so are mine. But it took every bit of skill to keep him from death's door. The rest, he has to do on his own."

"So you can't heal him anymore?" Ree asked.

"Not with magic. The rest is up to mundane medicine and luck."

"Shiiit. You get a good look at her?"

"That's the good thing. She stood at the top of the stairs and gloated for a while. Couldn't see the cards in time to stop me, which is why I managed to get away. Gotta love monologuers."

"Takes one to know one," Ree said, the tide of her anger rising again now that she knew Eastwood wasn't in immediate likelihood of kicking off. Drake's cough was quite clearly a tut of disapproval.

"You want to know what she looks like or what?"

"Yeah. Can't let her walk around like she owns the town."

"That's what I thought. I'd peg her at five-six, Scandinavian."

"A little short for a Scandinavian," Ree said.

"They're not all giants."

"Says you," Ree said, remembering her school trip to Amsterdam, where she'd felt like a ten-year-old at a basketball game.

Eastwood carried on. "Athletic figure. Runner's gear, but designer, silvers and golds, with a big-ass art deco hairpiece, all silver triumphalist architecture-like."

"So we went from gothic lolita to derby to art deco?" Ree asked.

"Everyone's got a hobby."

"Did she give a name?" Drake asked.

"Lachesis," Eastwood said.

"They do like their flashy names, don't they?"

"You get anything from her we can use to backtrack her?"

Eastood tried to nod, then winced and slumped back into the bed. "Wells has it. Just a bit of one of the levers of her traps. You'll need to use magical methods, I figure. But if you set the sting right, you should be able to snare her. If she's going to try to finish the job."

"She would be making her way here," Drake said.

"Nope. Wells made sure of that."

The doctor nodded. "I've never met anyone who could find me that I didn't want to. I moved because clients couldn't get to me, not because the gnomes could."

"So we go after Lachesis, then what? You want me to Incredible Nullifier her powers away, too? Then you try to convalesce and outpace the next season so we can do this whole thing again?"

"I'm in no condition to do it myself, kid. And you're the one who declared yourself Pearson's personal superhero."

"Damn my heroic code," Ree said, fully aware of how ridiculous she sounded. It was one thing to let Eastwood fend for himself when he was capable. Letting an attempted murderer run free and continue to endanger people in the city was something very different.

"You up for a game of cat and mouse?" Ree asked Drake.

"As long as this does not count as our first date. I'd rather preferred the notion of your traditional dinner and a movie."

"Done."

"Oh, good. That took long enough," Eastwood said.

Dr. Wells smiled.

"You, shut up," Ree said, pointing at Eastwood. "And you, back to bedside manner," she said, pointing at Dr. Wells. "The lever?"

Dr. Wells handed over a mangled lever covered with runes

She checked her phone. It was getting late. That was good for a break-and-enter, but less so for a stakeout. And she *really* wanted to get back to the smooching part of the evening.

But first, they'd need to get out of the sewer, which she guessed might prove to be tricky.

"Okay. I'm on it."

"The oracles are in the Dorkcave, if you can get back in. I remember you getting out easily enough last time you needed to."

"Got it," she said, not convinced in the least that the power-snuffing idea was remotely the best option. But she could cross that bridge when she came to it. Or just light it on fire, maybe.

"Thanks, Doc," Ree said.

"Do your best with Eastwood. I rather believe that Ree is not nearly done being angry with him," Drake said.

Dr. Wells nodded. "Try not to let whatever's banging around outside in when you open the door, will you?"

Ree sighed as she walked back into the main room.

"I was hoping I was wrong about that,"

Sure enough, the sounds of splashing and stomping outside signaled that something not-at-all tiny was lurking in the sewer passage.

Ree plopped down onto one of the cots and pulled out her phone.

"Time for a power-up. What did you bring today?"

Drake took the cot opposite, scooting it forward so he could put his boots on either side of hers. They were all disgusting, but she appreciated the touch even through the stink and the thick leather.

"My rifle, a bayonet for same, my kukri, and the handgun. What were you thinking for this situation?"

Ree thumbed back at the wall and the unknown beastie outside. "That sounds like something big. Which makes me think I'm going to want the brick power suite. Or I could do Spider-Man again and go three-dimensional."

"If that thing is truly as large as we're thinking, should we not merely use one of your teleportation cards to make a quick escape?"

"I'm fresh out of cards that could move us both. This year's been rough on my stash."

"So be it. I can provide fire support, but it seems prudent that you once again take point, dangerous though that may be."

"Just because there can be smooching after the Shake of Victory doesn't mean we do this any different. You start getting all white knight self-sacrifice-y, and we're going to have problems."

"I know that now. But that will not prevent me from worrying."

"Free country," she said with a wink. "I'm feeling Buffy on this one. You good to watch the door while I power up?"

"Certainly." Drake shifted around to face the door, rifle leveled. His left foot still pressed up against hers.

Ree cued up "Chosen," her go-to empowerment episode for the show, with Buffy at the height of her chops, the show at its most overt and potent with its girl-power message. Sure it was on the nose, but she hadn't met a Buffy fan who failed to shiver when they saw the beaten girl put her hand up and stop her abuser, who hadn't gotten a smile when they saw the little leaguer's look of *Oh, I* got *this.*

Diving into the episode, Ree imagined herself among them, remembering the scrawny, awkward girl she'd been, desperate to be one of those Chosen.

Twenty minutes later, a charge of badass sisterhood put spring in her step, and she hopped up, moving to the door.

"Ready?" she asked Drake. He joined her by the door, a hand on the thick metallic ring that stood in as the door handle. She was point; he was mark.

"This is still not a date, by the way," she said, flashing a hungry smile. "So we both have to get through this so there can be more smooching."

"Agreed. Lead on, my dear."

She nodded, and Drake hauled the door open. Ree thumbed on her lightsaber, and they bounded out into the sewer.

Oh, it's just a crocodile, Ree thought ironically.

A crocodile twenty feet long, with glowing green eyes and four-inch-tall demon birds with onyx wings and angry red eyes swarming around it.

No biggie, she thought, gulping.

CHAPTER FIFTEEN

Still Not a First Date

The crocodile's maw was a good five feet long and two feet wide. More than big enough to swallow her whole down to the calves.

Ree considered her plan, mental voice taking on a Buffy-esque patter:

Step one: Avoid getting eaten.

Step two: Take out a limb or two.

Step three: Wrasslin'.

Ree slid to the side, giving Drake room to open fire. Rifle-fire vaporized a few of the demon birds, sending the rest to the air in a cloud that was equal parts Hitchcock and *Pitch Black*.

The crocodile ran-swam forward, too big to just glide through the water, but getting a boost as it went, the winter melt leaving yard-deep water to work with.

"Stay up out of the water," Ree said, lightsaber dancing around in a defensive pattern, working like a bug zapper as the demon birds swarmed her. A couple of birds winged through her defenses, coming all at once. Beaks and claws carved through her coat and bit into her buff jacket, the best present Drake had ever given her.

"You could just turn around and go the other way, you know," Ree called out to the crocodile, which seemed to not be in the mood to respond.

This was the problem with nonsapient monsters. They didn't appreciate good banter. Peter Parker didn't have this problem, and Buffy's rank-and-file mooks could at least grunt aggressively in response.

But this time, she was wrong.

The crocodile spoke with a voice like an avalanche. "This is our kingdom, morsel. We are Scale, sovereign of the sewer." The crocodile bound forward, snapping at Ree.

"The fuck?" Ree cut at the croc's face, jumping back, training saving her ass despite the talking-monster surprise.

"This is quite unusual," Drake declared, still picking off the demon birds with deft, controlled shots. The swarm diminished, retreating to form a halo above the croc's head.

"These sewers are ours now, mortals. The price for trespassing is death."

"Dude, I've spent more time down here than just about anybody. I'm the Duchess of Pearson's sewers. Just ask Yelp."

Scale growled, "Yield, and we will do you the favor of killing you before we consume you."

"Thanks, but no thanks," Ree said, drawing her phaser and zapping the croc at the left shoulder.

The creature roared, anger muting out language. And then it charged.

Ree slashed at the creature's face, and the blade glanced off, raising sparks.

Ummm, that's not supposed to do that, Ree thought. The thing about lightsabers was that they were fucking *lightsabers,* and they cut through everything that wasn't another lightsaber or Cortosis-weaved thing-a-ma-whats-it.

And who the hell ever heard of Cortosis-weaved crocodile scales?

Plowing right through her attack, the crocodile bit down on Ree's arm. Jagged teeth eviscerated the arm of her coat, and pierced the enchanted buff jacket, drawing blood.

Ree dropped the lightsaber, pain blue-screening her vision.

Scale worried at her, shaking its snout back and forth, teeth tearing into her arm. Without the Buffy magic, the bite would have snapped her bones like twigs.

Screaming seemed like the thing to do.

Blue bolts soared over her shoulder, searing wounds into Scale's back. Drake dove past her with a kukri in one hand and his Hellboy gun in the other, rage in his eyes.

He landed hard on the creature's back, sliding the kukri between two clumps of armored scales at its neck. With purchase, he started unloading the über-revolver, the gun's report filling the sewer.

Thinking of Buffy and the Chosen, and maybe a little of smooches, Ree pushed through the pain, "Drake, get out of there!" She pulled her pocketknife out and chucked it at Scale's eye, grateful for the hours of throwing practice at every range, including "close enough that maybe you should just hold on to the knife and stab," which is what she would be doing save for the Cortosis-weave scales and the Ow-fuck-ow death grip on her other arm.

Thanks to Buffy magic, the blade struck true, burying itself to the hilt in Scale's right eye.

The creature roared, releasing Ree's arm. She dropped to her knees, blood flowing.

That's going to need medicine or magic, ASAP, she thought.

The demon birds pecked at Drake as he tried to ride Scale like a bucking bronco. But Drake was no cowboy, and the über-croc rolled, plunging the adventurer into the water.

"Shit!" Ree called, running through her mental inventory. The lightsaber did nothing, Drake's rifle did a little, the knife was fine, so was the gun.

If Ree'd learned one thing in nearly three decades of video gaming, it was that you spammed attacks on the weak points.

She dropped off the ledge into the water, plunging her head

down into the sewer water, searching for the glint of silver. The tainted water stung her arm, accelerating the onset of bacterial DoomCrap, on top of whatever nasty shit was in Scale's mouth already.

Coursing her good arm through the water like an oar, she cut her hand on an aluminum can lid, but then knocked something cylindrical farther ahead of her.

She kicked herself forward and reached, her breath already going short. It was more than a little hard to maintain breath control with a seeping arm wound. Her fingers found metal again, and she pulled it in, wrapping her hand around a familiar rubber handle. Ree tucked her legs up and stood up in the water, gasping. Drake was holding on to his kukri for dear life, his shoulder-mounted light strobing, mega-revolver silent. Downside to a revolver, even one that shot fifty-cal shells.

Ree spun the lightsaber and thumbed the blade back on, the weapon leaping to life and adding her blue light to his yellow-orange.

She dove forward, digging deep into the Buffy magic to guide her hand. She stabbed the lightsaber forward, leading Scale's movements. The lightsaber missed his eye by inches, glancing back and off the creature's neck.

Point control's for shit with this arm, Ree admitted.

Scale mauled at her with one arm. Ree ducked under the blow, face smacked by choppy water. The croc's claws ripped her coat in two but didn't break the buff jacket.

That coat was ruined anyway.

Ree stabbed at Scale's eyes again, missing as the creature dropped into the water, coming up for another massive chomp.

Time slowed, and Ree saw her opportunity jump out at her like a Quick Time Event. A dangerous, disgusting Quick Time Event. But she knew that despite the slowing of time, she couldn't get out of the way of this chomp. Knew with every inch of her sewer-sopped body.

But there was another way. A gross, possibly fatal way.

So she dove into Scale's massive maw, making herself as narrow as possible and tucking her knees up to her chest, leading with the lightsaber.

Focusing to keep her sense of up and down, she landed in Scale's gullet and twisted her wrist, the lightsaber slicing a hole in the crocodile's throat.

Teeth tore at her on both sides, but she kept going, using the lightsaber like a whisk, careful not to let it cut up toward where Drake would be.

Scale's roar deafened her, and the world rocked and rolled around her.

With a massive sound of spitting, Ree splooshed back out and into the water, cold hitting her on all sides.

She dropped her lightsaber, flailing to get her feet under her.

Ree kept her mouth closed, but sewer water rushed up her nose. Sputtering and bleeding and aching, Ree found solid ground with her feet, and she pushed herself up, head clearing the water once more.

In the distance, Scale swam-crawled into the distance at ridiculous speed.

And there was Drake, draped over the side, head flat against the sewer ledge, gasping.

"That was . . . bracing."

"I'd call it a fucking scary time, but yeah, 'bracing' fits, too."

The demon birds were also gone, the cloud following the self-declared Lord of the Sewer.

"What a night," Ree said.

"You may repeat that for emphasis," Drake said.

"What a night." Ree kicked around in the sludge until she found her lightsaber again, then went bobbing for disgustingly-coated apples, retrieving her lightsaber once more. There was no point in wiping it off, but she did it anyway. That sword had saved her life once again, and Drake's besides.

"Indeed. I suggest we away presently, lest another

sewer-dwelling monstrosity try to stake its claim. I owe you a milkshake."

"Let's hit the showers first, please. Dear God, please."

They escaped the sewers without further incident. Drenched in muck, Ree refused to do anything until they'd showered and changed. But since their relationship had started all of two hours ago, if it could be called that, neither had a change of clothes at the abode of the other.

This was a time when having already gone public with her friends really paid off. Ree didn't have to sneak into the Shithole, instead kicking her boots off at the door, announcing, "Sorry. Magic crap," and stuffing the shreds of her coat into a garbage bag. She put a towel, shampoo and body wash, and a full change of clothes into a day bag, tossed some PowerBars in as well, and thundered down the stairs to meet Drake. Her backup coat wasn't up to the winter, so Drake sprang for a cab.

Once they were ensconced in his apartment, Drake tossed his ichor-stained coat into a corner.

"After you," he said, gesturing at the bathroom.

"Ditching the coat was almost half the battle. Plus, if I dive into hot water right away now, wouldn't be good for my system. Your home; you should go first."

Drake raised an eyebrow, and Ree shooed him toward the bathroom.

Plus this way, she could join him once he got started.

"Please make yourself at home. The kettle is on, if you care to make tea," Drake said, stepping into the restroom.

Ree waited for several minutes, pacing out the time it would take to make the necessary ablutions. Then she shed her jeans and her top and knocked on the door.

"Can I join you?" she called, loud enough (she hoped) to be heard over the shower.

"Yes," Drake answered, just barely audible over the water.

"Woot," Ree said under her breath, opening the door. Drake's bathroom had a sink on the left, a stack of parts and toiletries on the right, and an opaque brown shower curtain covered in gears and gizmos, a gift from one of his not-actually-magical Steampunk compatriots.

Ree shed the rest of her clothes and pulled back the curtain with a "Hellooo?" in a singsong voice.

Drake's figure told the tale of an active life, and an interesting one. He had a number of scars that she'd never seen before, on his stomach, his thigh, and across his ribs. Nice butt, too, though his pants had made that clear long ago. His hand already covered his junk, but that would be resolved soon enough.

Turning to see Ree, Drake froze. "Ree?!" he shouted in surprise, covering up even more, his cheeks going beet red. "What are you doing?" he stuttered, flustered as she'd ever seen him.

Shitshitshitshit. Ree slid the curtain closed and jumped back, Drake's surprise sending her into a guilt-embarassment panic.

Clearly, he had in fact *not* said, "Yes, you should join me," but "Yes, I can hear you, what?"

"Shit!" she said from beyond the curtain, thankful that it was opaque as she realized she'd sashayed right past several boundaries in her eagerness.

"I'm so sorry. I asked if I could join you, and I thought you said yes, when clearly that's not what you said, because otherwise I wouldn't have freaked you out, and I'm sorry for freaking you out and I'm going to leave now, okay?"

Ree scooped her clothes up with one motion, then practically jumped out of the bathroom.

She dressed at lightning speed, overcompensating for her massive faux pas. Most people she'd dated jumped at the chance for shower sex, but Drake was, as she'd established and should have remembered, not like other people she'd dated.

But she'd imagined that Drake had been having mad aetherial adventurer sex with the Contessa, given the way he went on about her. But even so, why wouldn't he be prudish about sex?

You have led me astray, libido, she told herself, taking long breaths to get her cool back.

Two minutes that felt like two hours later, Drake emerged from the bathroom in a fresh set of clothes, his hair slicked against his head, and one hand over his eyes, a sliver opening between fingers to look at Ree. He dropped the hand, seeing she was fully dressed. He was still red, though part of that was being flushed from the shower.

She hoped.

He opened his mouth to speak. She stopped him, jumping in. "I'm sorry. Can I shower and then apologize some more, or do we need to figure it out now?"

Drake stepped aside and gestured to the bathroom.

"Thanks. Five minutes."

"Take your time, please. I rather need a sit-down."

"Five minutes."

Ree shut the bathroom door behind her and continued to beat herself up while she disrobed. The glory of hot water helped wash away a lot of the embarrassment, but not all of it. It wasn't that she was embarrassed to be seen naked, much more about how Drake freaking meant that she'd been the one to embarrass him, and that wasn't cool. Sex-positivity was all well and good, but it was a whole lot of crap without mutual consent.

She took as quick and utilitarian a shower as she could manage, given that she still had to get sludge off her. Ichor dissolved off streets and crap within a few minutes. But if it got onto clothing or flesh? Then the crap had damage resistance for miles. The third shampooing got the stench out of her hair, so she finished up and dressed.

She knocked on the door. "I'm done, and I'm clothed. Okay to come out?"

"By all means."

Ree stepped back into the room, seeing Drake on his love seat, no longer covered in a heaping pile of gear and equipment.

"I am sorry for startling you," he said.

Ree laughed. Just laughed. Here she was, running rough-shod over his boundaries, and then he goes and apologizes.

"You don't have to apologize for anything, man. This is all me. I tried to jump straight from makeouts to shower sex without being clear. I'm sorry for making you uncomfort-able," she said, emphasizing *I'm* and *you*, with pointing.

Drake was still pink, from the shower or from embarrass-ment or probably a bit of both.

"I . . . was not expecting that, at all. Your courting customs are radically distinct from those of my time."

Drake stopped for a second, just looking at her. "And might I say, now that I'm not panicking, you look quite rav-ishing straight from your ablutions."

"Shall we have tea to help combat awkwardness?" she of-fered, borrowing from *Questionable Content*.

"Quite."

And so, Drake went to make tea. Ree did some mental math to recalculate how she was expecting the evening to go.

A few minutes passed in silence while the water boiled.

ACHIEVEMENT UNLOCKED: 15G

TEA VS. AWKWARDNESS

Drake started up again as he poured the tea, an herbal concoction with hibiscus.

"That was rather not how I imagined the evening would proceed, though given the activity that Eastwood's plight in-terrupted, I might have been better prepared."

"My bad," Ree said, both hands up. "How would you like to see this evening go?" she asked, giving her best flirty eyebrows over the steaming mug, floral scents opening up as leaves and hot water engaged in their magical process of becoming tea.

"I had rather imagined that we would discern how to track down the Strega using that fragment from the device, but I get the sense you might have more sensual pursuits on your agenda."

"Right in one. But it takes two to tango. I've played the bold card twice, and gone offsides once already. This time, I'm playing good. You seem to be on board with the smooches, but what do you think about us? Should there be an us, and what sort? Usually this comes up later, but this isn't exactly a arranged date kind of situation."

Drake took a long, studied sip of his tea, looking like a painting you'd buy at a corner booth at a Steampunk convention.

"Indeed. I am tremendously fond of you, Ree, and were we in Avalon, I would be calling upon your family, asking for permission to court you." Drake set his tea down, and the corner of his lip curled up. "But as we are on Earth, and as you are you, I will say that I would be your boyfriend, and have you as my girlfriend, and seek to make your happiness in all things my highest calling."

Ree took her own sip of wits-gathering, heart pounding at machine-gun pace.

"That's very sweet. And since we already know each other and have been through lots of shit, I get that this isn't going to be like a Match.com relationship or anything. But how about we start with hanging out like we did, plus smooching and making googly eyes at each other? I'll back off the macking, and we both hold off on the 'You are my everything'?"

"I believe I am amenable to these terms. But for clarity's sake, would you be so kind as to unpack what *googly eyes* and *macking* are?"

Ree laughed. It took the edge off of the "Squishy feelings, ack!" tension, so she laughed again.

"Sure thing. Macking is kissing, making out, French kissing, etc."

Drake nodded. "Though I never could understand what made it French. Also the fries."

Ree coughed, bringing Drake back on task. "And googly eyes?" She leveled a lovey-dovey look at the strange and wonderful man who'd been a part of her life for very nearly the entire time it'd been magically bizarre, and thank Jeebus for that.

"These are googly eyes."

Drake met her gaze for a moment, then blushed again and set down his tea.

"I see. In that case, agreed. Shall we take a brief respite for macking, and then get to our heroic endeavors?"

"Now you're talking. But in the interest of heroism, is there something we should be doing first, device- and doodad-wise?"

"Just so," Drake said, standing up and crossing to his laboratory. "We will need to calibrate the tracking device to seek out either material like itself, leading us to other parts of the trap, or to trace semiotic ties, which should lead us back to the trap's creator, our ultimate target."

"Cool. How do I help, aside from refraining from make-outs—which I assure you is, in fact, rather difficult. A heroic effort, really."

Drake chuckled. "So noted. I can set the tracking device to begin calibration, which will then free us for amorous pursuits for some time."

"Very reasonable," Ree said, happy to be back to equilibrium quickly. For all that Drake was old-fashioned, he knew how *not* old-fashioned Ree was. Advantage of dating someone you've known for a year and faced death alongside.

Looking for Group: How to Hook Up with the Partner of Your Dreams by Building an Adventuring Party and Risking Your Life a Bunch—*coming soon from some publisher that publishes weirdly specific gimmicky dating books.*

Though with this one, maybe she could get Quirkmillan interested.

Ree hovered while Drake set up the machine, the piece of lever from the Rube Goldberg trap set on the platform at the top of the device. Interrupting the process wouldn't really do any of them any good except in the fun way, so she kept herself occupied with chatter.

"So, if you didn't have an idea what I was asking you over for tonight, would you have made a move?"

Drake crouched by the machine, adjusting dials and knobs. "Were that the case, I would have been stymied by the social entanglement of wishing to procure a blessing by way of forgiveness from Priya, given the faux pas of courting a member of her inner circle after so famously bungling the previous courtship."

"Taken care of. But how would you have actually asked me out or made a declaration of intent or whatever it is you would want to do? My way was what I imagine you'd call abrupt, and I bet you would have been a lot more Drake-y about it."

Drake looked up at Ree, eyes narrowed. "I'd like to lodge an official complaint as to the use of my name as a diminutive adjective."

"So noted. Your complaint will be taken into advisement by the hilarity bureau."

"And who, pray tell, sits on the hilarity bureau?"

"That would be me, myself, and I."

"Somehow, I imagine that my suit's chances would be rather slim in that case."

"Normally, yes, but the bureau is incredibly biased, and doesn't like making people uncomfortable if it's actually a bother and not just being cute."

A valve started spouting steam, and Drake jumped. "Wells's ghost, what are you doing?" he asked the machine, hands jumping back and forth as he adjusted more knobs and dials.

"Everything okay?"

Note to self: Revise Drake's Devices drinking game to add "Wells's ghost."

"So, what would you have done, if you got Priya's blessing? Flowers? A finely-calligraphed letter?"

"I considered both of those options, but in truth, I was somewhat left at a loss. Televisual programs provide few reasonable examples, as most couples tend to take your approach, as you say, 'going for it.'"

"Yeah, TV and movies aren't the place to go to learn how to date."

"In truth, is there a better resource for modern courtship?"

"Other than trial and error? Not really. Most dating books I've read are crap, save for the ones that are so reasonable and remedial they might as well be stick-figure anatomy lessons."

"In that case, I must express my most sincere gratitude that you spared me the indignity of attempting to synthesize our disparate worldviews for an acceptable declaration of intent, though your 'going for it' very nearly gave me a heart attack."

Ree's heartbeat stirred. *This isn't exactly doing a good job of keeping my eye on the ball*, she admitted in a guilty-not-actually-guilty fashion. "You're healthy. I knew you'd make it. Unless of course I'd been completely misreading signals and what everyone else was saying and you actually weren't interested."

"Of course I am. . . ." Drake looked up again. "Wait. Who would 'everyone else' be, in this case?"

"Pretty much everyone. There's this thing that happens when people who have chemistry don't get together, which mostly involves amusing and annoying everyone that they both know. They share significant glances and gossip behind the would-be lovers' backs. I've been on the outside of that several times, and it's hilarious."

Ree continued, "Sandra and Darren were 'friends' for about two months before they hooked up. We all met him at a party that one of Sandra's friends threw. They talked all night, and then they started circling immediately. He came over to hang out, they'd go see movies together, shop at bookstores, and even did the 'meet on a Saturday morning to go shopping at a farmer's market then hang out all day and cook stuff from farmer's market for dinner' thing, and it wasn't until Anya and I told her to make her move that she even considered it. She thought he was too preppy for her, what with the 'oh no, he's a doctoral student and I'm a washout' angst. I wrote that shit into a rom-com called *Matriculation*. Didn't go anywhere, though."

"I see," Drake said. "I'm very glad that they had an easier time of it. It does seem rather preposterous that so many of us are unable to see what is clearly in front of us." Drake pressed a button and set the device to a consistent buzzing hum, the lever shaking on the platform. "I'm uncertain how long it will take to calibrate, so we will have to come back and check on it."

"What, this one doesn't go *ding* when there's stuff?" Ree asked.

"For unknown reasons, I was not able to get such an alarm to sound at anything less than seventy-three decibels, which is rather too loud given the close proximity of neighbors."

"But just how soundproof is this apartment, then?" Ree asked, eyebrows raised.

"This, like many things, requires experimentation." Drake crossed toward his bedroom, then turned and extended a hand. "Shall we?"

"I love science," Ree said, taking Drake's hand in hers.

CHAPTER SIXTEEN

Private Inquiry

A beautiful forever later, Drake stumbled out of bed to go check on the tracking device. Ree watched him go, letting out a happy sigh.

Another way that Drake proved himself old-fashioned was his stance on running the bases. Ree had assumed she was in position to go straight for a double, but Drake waved her off at first base. Not that first base was anything bad, as Drake brought the same creative, slightly melodramatic gusto to kissing as he did everything else in life. A little much at times, but a little much was way better than not enough.

Every two people had their own specific way of kissing, the middle ground between each person's personal style. Just like each relationship was its own thing. Ree and Drake were still definitely setting those boundaries, figuring out what worked. And it was the best kind of exploration imaginable.

Quite happily disheveled, Ree settled into the bed, looking at Drake's bedroom. Where the living room had been completely converted into a laboratory, his bedroom was relatively spare, appointed with antique-style furniture (maybe it actually was antique, but it seemed really sturdy), including a gorgeous carved and lacquered bed and headboard.

Those would be *very* useful if/when (hopefully when) Drake gave the go-ahead on more.

Drake returned a minute later. Light from the living room framed him in silhouette, shirt untucked, hair mussed. And damned if he didn't look every bit as marvelous as the sunrise on the first day of summer.

"I have good news, and less-good news."

Ree flipped through several lascivious dialogue options before settling on the comparatively mild, "Which one applies to our most recent scientific endeavor?" she said, patting the bed.

"The good, fortunately. The less-good news is that the calibration failed, and I will need to try another method, which will require the device to work all night."

"Oh no, what will we do with a whole night of waiting?" Ree said, planting the back of her hand on her forehead as if swooning.

"I imagined that might be your reaction. Resetting the machine will take several minutes, I'm afraid. But then I promise to continue our experiment. Replication of results is important for rigorous inquiry."

"Rigor, eh?" Ree gave her best Groucho eyebrows, tipping a fake cigar.

"I shall return."

"You better," Ree said, leaning back into the bed.

She took a long, satisfied breath.

About. Goddamned. Time.

Ree fished her phone out of her discarded jacket, and dialed Anya. It was nearly 3 AM for her dad, and even though he'd be elated to hear her good news, she didn't want to wake him. But Anya was on a night schedule already, due to rehearsals, and she was always down for some kiss-and-tell.

"Hey, what's up?" Anya answered.

"You done with showbiz for the moment?"

"I wish. Madame Wesselman just gutted the entire second act. We're on break while she tears the stage manager a new one."

"Shit," Ree said. The opera director was legendarily draconian and was the subject of many of Anya's favorite "Show Business Is Wild" stories.

"I just had to call and request telekinetic high fives."

"And how high were those fives?" Anya asked, giving the countersign. The Rhyming Ladies had a custom of sharing their excitement about dates, hookups, and all things love life.

"High, but not super-high," Ree said. "Not too surprising when high-fiving a temporally-displaced Victorian adventurer."

"Ooooh, I see," Anya said, voice low. The phone was quiet for a moment. "Shit, we're back on. High fives, and good luck!"

"Right back at you. Remember, murdering your director never got anyone ahead in showbiz."

"I'm sure that's not the case, but thanks." Anya hung up, and Ree looked at her phone, seeing the red battery. If they were going straight for adventuring in the morning, she'd need to get her workhorse acharging.

"Now, where are you, little charger?" Ree said, rummaging around in her pile of stuff, a patented mix of purse goods and geeky crime-fighting gear.

When Drake returned, Ree was scrolling through Tumblr, phone charge climbing back out of the red zone.

"Science under way?"

"From one experiment to another. Science waits for no man," Drake said, climbing back into bed.

"Try hard enough, and there may be a Nobel Peace Prize in it for you. Goodness knows the world could stand to hand out more prizes for good sex," Ree said.

Drake froze, like a deer caught in the headlights going "Shit, what am I doing? I should have stayed home and eaten the berries there!"

Fuuck. "Sorry. Overeager again."

Drake's whole body relaxed. He slid forward, running

a hand through Ree's hair, tugging ever so slightly at her roots before letting go. "For now, let us resume the experiment, and see what further inquiries the results invite."

"Deal," Ree said, wrapping her arms around the adventurer and pulling him close.

Despite all efforts to the contrary, morning eventually rolled in with an alarm sounding some weird version of reveille.

"Whaaat?" Ree asked, pawing at the sound.

Drake sat up in bed all at once. "Oh, bother."

"Bother?" Ree mumbled, still holding tightly to sleep, a woman doomed to waking but not ready to give up the label of *asleep*.

As Drake slid off the bed, Ree sprawled out, taking the space he'd warmed in the night. They'd slept with their clothes on (most of them), and while the experimentation had never passed first base, Ree hadn't had a night of make-outs that good since she was in high school.

The floor stretched with Drake's steps, proving just how shoddily the building was put together. Spring floors were great for dancing but made quite a lot more noise when people were padding across the floor silencing alarms.

"Why is it so morning right now?" Ree asked.

"It's already half-nine, Ree."

"I roll to disbelieve. Come back to bed."

Three more squeaking moans of the floor brought Drake back to the bed. He placed a kiss on the back of her head, then said, "I shall prepare breakfast. Do you prefer griddle cakes or omelets?"

"Pancakes," Ree said, then fell one more step toward waking. "Wait. Cook?" she asked. Certainty was indefinitely suspended before coffee, but she'd never heard of him cooking before. He was the king of carryout and delivery.

Drake changed his socks, tucked in his shirt, and pulled down an identical brown duster from his closet. "I am apt enough for these few dishes. But shall I retrieve you a cappuccino first?"

"Marry me," Ree said.

Beat.

"I should not hold you to anything said before caffeine, should I?" Drake asked.

"Nope. Thank you."

"I shall return presently. You needn't leave the bed."

"Mm hmm," Ree said, burrowing further into bed.

Some indeterminate amount of time later, Drake returned, announcing his return. "I come bearing caffeine, my slumbering companion."

"Not slumbering anymore. I'm merely draped coquettishly in repose. Or something."

"Truly? This is a wonder to which I must bear witness." He stepped back into the bedroom, a takeout cup from Stardust Coffee in hand. Stardust was barely half as good as Zombie Café when it came to bean quality, but for her first drink of the day, the caffeine content was more important than the taste. Plus, it was coffee in bed. This was very rare in her world, and was to be savored.

She took a long sniff, the first vapors of caffeine hitting her system like the chill of a polar-bear swim upon first plunge. She popped the top off and took a sip, then a gulp of the cappuccino. The foam was better than she remembered. Someone had leveled up.

"This is really well made," Ree said.

"I told the proprietor that I was bringing the drink to the most beautiful woman in the land, who happened to also be a veteran barista. I rather think the barista took it as a challenge. She sent me off with a 'Go get her, tiger.' Are tigers associated with virility here? I rather thought they were more directly associated with Asia and Europe."

"If the barista was a redhead, then it was a comic book

reference."

"She was blond. Or, the blond of bottles."

Ree took another sip. "Probably still a comic book reference. But she did a damned good job, regardless."

A memory struck her as fog fell from her mind. "How's the doohickey?"

Drake's head quirked to the side, almost birdlike. "I did not check. One moment."

"Curses!" Ree said. "I mean, forget that terrible thing and come keep me warm. It's too cold in here!"

"I shall turn on the heat," Drake said, voice carrying through the apartment.

"That's too expensive!"

"I do believe you are trying to have one over on me again."

"Guilty. So, what's the word?"

"We are ready to proceed."

Ree climbed out of bed and slid on her pants, which had been strategically dumped by the heater. She walked out into the living room.

"Not quite. I was promised griddle cakes."

"I am not one to break my promises."

Ree made her way to the kitchen, padding along the cold floor, wishing she'd stopped for her socks.

"Good man. I can help, too. This isn't a bed-and-breakfast; I can pull my weight around here."

"Foul woman," Drake said, following her. "You put me in an untenable position. I cannot deny a guest, but neither can I allow a guest to do their own cooking."

Ree pulled Drake's one spatula out of the mason jar of cooking implements and leveled it at Drake. "Then how about I cook your breakfast, and you cook mine?"

"Brilliant."

⋅✕⋅⬡⋅✕⋅

If it weren't for the imminent chase and fight scenes she expected to follow shortly, Ree would have declared it a perfect day at 10:15 AM. Every bit of the fun, energetic banter was still there, but now with added makeouts and proximal comfort. Instead of trying to dance around each other in the tiny kitchen, they happily glided past each other, moving like dancers in and out of the embrace.

Fucking heavenly, it was.

But when the pancakes were done, the dishes washed and put away, there was nothing left to distract them from the tracking machine, lights blue and expectant, ready to guide them on a wild-goose chase.

"I guess we should get going, then?" Ree asked, pointing at the machine, the broken-off lever sitting atop the machine's dish.

"Indeed. It seems likely that Madame Lachesis will want to make another attempt on Eastwood before the season passes its zenith tonight."

"Shit, that is tonight, isn't it? Guess I'll skip the shower, then."

"Knowing our luck, we will be bound once more for the sewers," Drake said, collecting his weapons.

Ree put all of her Geekomantic tools back in order, but that still left her without a good winter coat.

"You got another coat in that bag of holding? Or at least a sweater, maybe?" The buff jacket could pass in a pinch, as long as they went inside every half hour and the Hoth levels for the day were low.

They weren't. Her phone showed a high of 17, a low of 5, -12 with windchill.

"It is not fitting for your beauty, but this should be of assistance," Drake said, handing her a PU hoodie.

"Where did you get this?"

"It was left in the apartment when I moved in. Will it fit?"

Ree slipped the hoodie on. It smelled vaguely of motor oil. "Did you use this as a work rag?"

"Oh. Just the once."

"It's all good. Just wanted to make sure it wasn't leftover from the original owners."

"That would be rather more unsettling, wouldn't it?"

"Yep. You good to go with the trackamagigger?" Ree asked, gesturing at the machine.

Drake pulled off a piece that looked like the controller for an RC car, then turned with it in hand, pulling out an antenna. "Ready to go."

Off on another wild-goose chase. Drake walked out the door. *Good company, though.*

Now just make sure he doesn't die or you don't fuck it up, her brain told her.

Fuck you, brain. Let's go fight things.

Word.

CHAPTER SEVENTEEN

Defender's Creed

Drake's RC tracker led them west, past the U-District and toward the water.

The adventurer stopped on a street corner, staring intently at the tracker's readout.

"How we doing?" Ree asked, stamping her feet. Her second-string boots were for going out and dancing, not for turning aside winter.

Note to self: Inquire about all-season muck-proof boots. No price too high.

Amended: Many prices are too high. Still a priority.

"The source appears to be leading farther still to the west, into the industrial district."

"Great, straight into gangland territory," Ree chattered, teeth rattling.

"So it would seem. It is likely, however, that most of their number will just be waking up now, and less likely to go chasing after strange adventurers."

"Yeah, but what about me?" Ree asked, winking.

Drake resumed, crossing the street. This time, he managed to wait for the light. "Your protestations of normalcy have been noted and will be attended to with all appropriate consideration, filed under 'Owner of three complete sets of the *Star Wars* films.'"

"That's totally reasonable. The VHS set, a Laserdisc of the remastered but not special edition trilogy, and the second edition of not-quite-as-terrible special edition DVDs. Also, magic."

"None of the above is lending any credit to your case for normalcy."

"Okay, I give up. Plus, the weird adventurers have more fun."

"I would think this rather more fun were we not forging through weather more frigid than the outposts on Europa."

"No disagreement on that here."

✕✕⬡✕✕

Forty bone-chilling minutes later (including a ten-minute thawing break in a coffee shop), they reached a warehouse building two blocks in from the wharf.

"The signal originates somewhere in that building, give or take twenty yards."

"Okay, how do you want to enter?"

Ree walked down the street, taking the building in through her peripheral vision, in case Lachesis had surveillance running. The building was three stories tall, with double doors on the ground floor, and probably a back entrance on the wharf side. Some Spider-Mojo could get them up onto the second or third floor, but a lot depended on who else was there. Bad thing about being a hero (aka a moral human being) was worrying about collateral damage.

"Breaking and entering is rather more your area of expertise."

"Are you saying that because I'm Latina, or because I'm the one with the lock-picking skills?" Ree joked.

"I was thinking more of your bold, aggressive combat style."

"I'll allow it. Looks like there may be another way in around back, probably less guarded. If we pop inside for a minute, I can run a reverse yellow pages search on this address, see what businesses pop up. Maybe we'll get lucky and she'll have left a paper trail."

"Well thought. I saw a delicatessen around the corner, and I would happily provide a cup of soup, should you be interested in some warm broth to fortify the constitution."

"I'll take every constitution bonus I can get in this Winter of Ree's Discontent module."

By the time the soup was done, several things were different:

1) Ree could feel her nose again.

2) Her hands had stopped burning.

3) She knew that there were three businesses associated with the address: an import/export business on the first floor, an upholstery show on the second floor, and something called Lachesis Logistics on the third floor. Bingo.

4) This place's soup was awesome.

Ree went back to tip the guys at Otrowski's an extra dollar, earning a nod of approval from the balding proprietor.

Rather than coming back at the building the same way, they went around the block, approaching the building from the wharf side.

"Okay, we're looking for the third floor. Lachesis Logistics is a dummy company name if ever I've heard one. Strega number one was Connie Clothos-Line, and this one is Lachesis."

"The Greek Fates. Fitting for women styling themselves as Strega."

"Natch. Though that means the next one is Atropos, who is supposed to be the nastiest of them all. Death-bringer, life-ender, so on and so forth. That'll be fun."

"Again, I find your definitions of things such as 'fun' and 'normal' to be rather disassociated with what I've come to know as reality."

Ree held her hood close as the wind howled, blowing snowflakes into her eyes despite her glasses. "I learned to embrace the ridiculous. It's safer inside the clown house than next door."

"That is one way of coping, I suppose. Now, how do you propose we gain entry to the third floor?"

"I'm sure as hell not going to just go up and knock. With as trap-happy as Lachesis seems to be, we need to think laterally. I see a skylight up there, so step one is getting up to the roof."

Drake brightened. "For that, I have a solution." He opened his coat and reached almost cartoonishly deep into a jacket pocket, pulling out a stumpy gun with a grapple in the barrel. "It is a far cry from an ornithopter, but I wagered that we might need to move vertically in the near future."

"Will that support two?" Ree asked.

"The winch is only rated to two hundred pounds, so we will need to go one at a time, I'm afraid. I have inquiries out for a superior spring crank, but as it involves what Wickham calls 'cheating Steampunk,' my resources are rather more limited."

"That corner looks promising," Ree said, pointing at the near edge of the building, with thicker crenellations around the lip of the roof.

"That should suffice, yes." Drake stopped next to a fire hydrant, squared his stance, and raised the grapple gun. He aimed and waited for a moment, the winter wind whipping his coat around and nearly pulling Ree off her feet as it filled her coat. She turned in profile to the wind, no longer feeling like an umbrella about to be whisked off to see Mary Poppins.

Drake fired, and the hook arced right over the lip of the building. He pulled the grapple gun tight, then wrapped the bottom around the hydrant.

Their totally conspicuous adventures went unnoticed, since again, fucking blizzard cold out. Anyone and everyone who *could* stay inside *was* staying inside.

"When I am safely atop the building, untie the rope and press this button, and the winch will retract. You should then be able to climb up the side of the building."

" 'Should'? Have you tested this thing?"

"You said that you liked adventure, yes?"

Ree's face fell.

"I jest. Yes, I have tested this function. It has performed marvelously."

"Why don't you just winch your way up and toss the gun back down to me?"

"The device is too fragile. And this is not my first time brachiating up to break and enter an enemy's lair."

Ree said, "You really are my kind of weirdo." She pecked Drake on the cheek, then squeezed his forearm. "Be careful."

"I will take as much care as I can, though a certain bravado is necessary for such ventures." Drake rubbed his hands together, pulled his gloves tight, then jogged over and leaped up, grabbing the rope with both hands. The cable stayed taut, sparing Drake from a slacklining climb.

The adventurer scaled his way up toward the building as quickly as a five-year-old on a jungle gym.

"Impressive," she said, just as the reality of what she was about to do pinged her fear of heights.

You know, like climbing up a three-story building, Adam West Batman–style.

"Gulp," she said.

Some panic-stolen amount of time later, a whistle cut above the wind. Ree looked up to see Drake gesticulating at the grapple gun.

"Time to face the music," Ree said. She could power-up with something to fly, to climb, or some other way of making it up the wall, but a street-level hero with a fear of heights was a recipe for trouble, and situations like this were the best possible way to fight through that fear.

"I can do this," Ree told herself, untying the grapple gun from the fire hydrant, cable already slicked by melting snow.

Taking the grapple gun in hand, she walked over to the warehouse, as nonchalantly as it was possible to approach a building you have no business approaching while holding a grappling gun in your hands and trying not to retch.

Easy-peasey, Ree thought, trying to hype herself up. *You've seen this a thousand times. You've climbed up buildings with just your hands and toes; you've survived dogfights through downtown and crashing into a labyrinth.*

It was like a ropes course on rails. Easier than the big climb in leadership camp. Ree's dad had responded to her shyness and fear of heights in the way that only an overly supportive marine could—he'd enrolled her in a "leadership" course that mostly involved team puzzle athletics (The floor is lava! You have a small supply of lava-proof two-by-fours! Go!) and indoor wall-climbing. Ree had made it up the fifty-foot-high course only once and had puked her guts right out afterward. That was the end of the leadership course.

Ree put a foot up on the concrete wall of the warehouse, exhaled, and pressed the button. The grapple gun's winch started spinning, pulling the cable in from the slack she'd generated. She watched the cable move like a venomous serpent, snaking across the ground, coming toward her.

"Here goes nothing," Ree said, responding to the cable's tug by pulling up, starting her ascent.

The first few steps went easily, just tracking with the motion of the grapple gun. It was doing all of the work; she just had to support her weight.

"Next time, can we bring a harness? Or a kiddie seat?" Ree yelled up the wall, not expecting to be heard. But snarking let her take her attention off the situation.

She pretended that forward was down, and that like

the old Batman show, it was the camera that was sideways, not her body. That illusion lasted until the second floor, when a wind gust knocked her off her feet. Her right side bounced off the concrete wall, sending a double-shot of terror down her spine. She wrapped a hand around the cable and tried to get her feet back under her, in that "under" that was actually on the side and . . .

Ack.

Her climbing instructor's voice came to her. *Stop. Breathe. Check your rope.*

She squeezed the cable, still retracting. "Check."

Check your footing.

"In progress," she said, continuing to bounce off the wall, the wind doing its inanimate best to twist her up in the cable and shear her arm off or some shit. She got one foot on the wall, then the other, and shuffled up to resume her ninety-degrees-from-upright stance.

"You're almost there, Ree," Drake called from the roof. She looked up, and what did you know, he was right. Drake leaned over the lip of the roof, lips tight.

"Keep talking. Anything, just keep talking, please," Ree asked, shaking from hand to toes, and trying very, very hard to ignore the category-four storm rumbling in her stomach.

"This was rather brave of you; we could have done this. . . ."

"Not. That. Anything else," Ree almost hissed through gritted teeth.

"Ah, my apologies. The gravel coating the roof here reminds me of the volcanic rock in the terrain of the Incarnate duel." Ree zoomed in on his words, wrapped the familiarity of his patter and cadence around her as armor against fear, the sounds crafted into parapets, each word another brick to hold back the panic. *Fifteen feet, come on.*

"I went back and watched the video, did I tell you? You were magnificent." She slowed her breath as best as she could. *Ten feet more. Almost there.* "Not that there was any doubt that you would be magnificent, but I agree with Grognard that based on my understanding of the rules, Lucretia could not have Incarnated that quickly all three times."

Five feet. She wanted to reach out for Drake's waiting hand, but she didn't dare let go of her death grip on the grapple gun. Drake helped haul up the cable, and grabbed her forearm, giving her enough to pull back on and get a foot over the lip of the roof.

She rolled onto the roof, going flat onto her back, hyperventilating.

I made it.

I made it.

That's your cue to resume normal service, lungs.

A minute later, she could breathe again.

Ree opened her eyes and saw Drake waiting, lips still thin. "I'm fine," she said. "That was more of a thing than I wanted it to be. Should have used mojo to get up. The grapple gun does work, but next time I would like a harness, please."

"Understood. That will be rather easier to arrange, as opposed to the cushions on the ornithopter."

"Any plans to make another one?"

"The materials necessary would require a journey into Deep Spirit, as replicating such a working without those materials entails alchemical talents beyond my ken."

"Road trip?"

"So to speak. First we would need a vessel capable . . ." Drake stopped himself. "Another time. Shall we attend to the matter at hand?"

Ree stood, shaking out the jitters. "I'm good. Did you get a look into the skylight?"

"I did not." Drake smiled. "I was rather more focused on the well-being of the beautiful woman with the fear of heights."

"Okay, let's get to it, then. You have something to break the glass with that won't lead to us jumping through jagged shards? Something quiet, maybe?"

"You don't just want to try to pick that lock?" Drake asked, pointing at a roof access door.

"I'm going to blame that on the fear. Yep, the fear," Ree said, walking over to the door, giving the skylight a wide berth. Again, cameras. Or Mark-1 eyeballs.

Ree took one glove off and rummaged through her bag for her lock picks. They were low-end since, of all the things in her bag of tricks, these were the most likely to get her on someone's police watch list, even with her friends in SWAT. She could get set up as a bonded locksmith, but that was way too much hassle for a skill that was only occasionally more useful than just getting superpowers.

"Stand watch, okay?" Ree asked, kneeling into the compacted snow that had frozen into the rough rocks. Her knee would be numb in a minute, at this temperature.

Fuck winter.

Between the cold killing her sensitivity and numbing her hands and possibly sticking the lock, she got a whole lot of nowhere.

"I could tap into Parker from *Leverage* and probably get it, but with normal skills, this is a no go."

"How long would it take to activate that power?"

"Ten minutes maybe? That's a while to stand around in the cold. And it's not exactly easy to focus with this weather." As if to illustrate her point, the wind picked up, howling as it blew crystalline needles in her face.

"Shall we try the more direct version, then?"

"Didn't we just talk about this?" Ree grinned.

She pulled out her lightsaber, her best choice for a quiet breaking-and-entering method. Plus, it would confuse the hell out of the cops if they came and investigated. Unless they called in SWAT, who would probably guess the method of ingress right off. They might come knocking, but Ree was pretty sure she had enough cachet with Officer Washington and Captain Chu to get away with it.

"We've got to be ready to go as soon as I cut the glass, okay? It might be as much as a fifteen-foot fall, so tuck and roll is the name of the game."

"Indeed. After you," Drake said, holding his rifle leaned against one shoulder.

Ree activated the lightsaber, took two quick steps over to the triangular skylight, and made a quick circular cut, controlled at the wrist, cutting open a yard-wide hole in the skylight.

She leaned down to look into the warehouse space, which was stacked high with parts and bits and bobs straight out of the set of *Metropolis*.

Jackpot.

Ree dropped through the hole, and tucked and rolled as she hit the concrete floor, coming up to her knees, lightsaber blazing.

"As I suspected," said a voice from behind her. Ree pivoted on the balls of her feet and saw a woman with a pale Scandinavian complexion wearing a gauzy black bodysuit-dress combo, flowing in some places, tight around the waist, legs, and arms. Her hair was held up in a bun by a gold pin that was as art deco as the rest of her outfit.

Drake thudded to the ground next to Ree, dropping into his own roll.

"Enter the aberration's lackeys. Come to avenge your master and defy the prophecy?" she asked in a vague European-ish accent that floated up and down the North Sea.

"I don't put much stock in prophecies that boil down to 'Just you wait, my siblings will get you!' The Billy Goats Gruff played that game out a few centuries ago. Get a new schtick."

"And we are no one's lackeys, Lachesis," Drake added.

In the split second that Ree's attention drifted to her side to listen to Drake, the Strega was off in a sprint, headed for the window at the far end of the warehouse space.

"Oh, no you don't," Ree said, pushing up into a run to pursue.

And now, a chase scene.

Lachesis made a quick gesture with one finely-manicured hand and said something Ree couldn't make out, geometric lines in gold and silver unfolding from her gesture. The window in front of the Strega shattered, falling to the floor and making room as she leaped through the open pane, legs tucked up like a le parkour traceur.

Ree ran to the window, and saw Lachesis land softly on something covered by a huge blue tarp that had been swept clean of all but a small dusting of snow.

"Git," Ree declared, then backed up to make the jump herself. "She's on the run. Hit the tarp!" she said, diving out the window.

Ree flipped in midair, remembering summers with her Taekwondo classes learning how to do flips and dives off the diving board at the local pool. She'd always found the practice martially suspect, but it had been amazing fun.

And now, she reaped the benefits. She landed on her back, sinking onto what felt like foam. Ree scrambled out of the pile, locking onto Lachesis, nearly sixty feet away already, running like a top-end marathoner, headed straight for a trio of people on a street corner looking at a laminated map.

Ree pulled out her phaser, set to stun by default, and shaved right, resetting her angle to avoid putting the lost tourists in the line of fire. The zap went wide. She could stop and take aim, but she was already far enough way that she didn't count on her markswomanship skills.

Instead, she stuffed the phaser back in her jacket and pulled out the lightsaber, leaving it off until she got closer.

Drake's voice came from behind, accompanied by the pounding of boots. "Following!"

"We've got to close the gap so someone can get a shot off," Ree shouted.

"Understood," Drake said.

Ree poured it on as much as she could, admitting that she was a bit out of shape what with the bizzaro weather.

It's not like she had access to a gym or anything. Her exercise regimen was fighting monsters and running around in sewers or on rooftops, and it wasn't exactly regular. Cross-training, sure, but maybe not the best for this kind of flat-out run.

And Lachesis wasn't staying on the sidewalks. She angled into an alley and bounced off a Dumpster and a wall, then grabbed hold of a fire escape, pulling herself up.

Parkour indeed. Just great. Between the architecture yen and the parkour, Ree started to piece together a profile of an eccentric mastermind, a match to Lucretia's grand design and certainty of purpose. Whoever these Strega were at home, when they were at work, they all had cases of gods-given authority.

Ree just had morality, and a sideboard of CCGs.

She reached back into her jacket, thumbing through the sideboard, wildly moving cards aside, counting down to the card she'd need. Doing so at a flat run was just about impossible, but any lead she could get on pulling the card before she needed it would close the gap.

But she needed more than just a one-person jump if Drake was going to be able to make it. She kept thumbing down, then pulled out a card.

Fireball. Not the one.

Sacrificing precious time as she came up to the fire escape, ten feet up, Ree drew the card she'd actually been going for: a Green Lantern card. She tore it and tossed the pieces to the floor, gathering the energy into a one-shot energy construct: a green trampoline that she crammed into the edge of the alleyway. She jumped up, tucked her feet, then bounced on the trampoline for all it was worth, reaching up and taking hold of the bottom of the fire escape.

Ree scrambled up and onto the wrought-iron grate, swinging herself around to the first set of stairs.

She caught a glimpse of Drake fifteen feet back. "Hurry! That thing won't last long!"

Drake leaped and bounded off the trampoline as well, catching the fire escape with one hand, his rifle slung over his back once more. Trusting that the interdimensional adventurer could handle it from there, she focused on the stairs, scaling two at a time, hoping that her boots would be enough to avoid slipping.

Lachesis disappeared over the lip of the roof, and Ree pushed on. Drake stomped behind her, two flights down.

Ree hopped over the lip, pushing off with one hand and kicking her feet over, landing with a double-crunch on the snow. Lachesis was already at the far end of the black-tar roof lined with solar panels.

The Strega waved her hands, sang a quick lick in Norwegian or something, and bounded across a ten-foot gap with ease, leaving contrails of magic in connecting geometric art deco shapes.

"Hexomancers," Ree cursed, reaching for her sideboard once more. She pulled out a Giant Strength card from the pile, tore it up, and then headed for a solar panel. She ripped the whole thing up from the roof, and swung it like a two-by-four over to the gap. It barely bridged the gap, and might not be that stable.

Drake hurdled over the side of the building, landing in a crunch behind her.

"Up and over!" she called, jumping up to the panel. If it broke while she was on it, she had the sideboard. And Drake had his grapple gun. It'd have to do, or they'd have to give up the chase and try again later, when Lachesis knew they were on her trail.

Ree held out both hands for balance, hustling over the gap as fast as she could in the still-howling winds, glasses smudged by fat snowflakes.

A rifle burst zipped past her foot. A field of gold and silver geometric patterns flashed into sight and sparked as something bounced off.

Great, Hex shield, Ree thought.

The witch turned and smiled, waving with Steve Ditko-esque finger gestures. Then she looked over the side, jumped up to the lip, and dropped out of sight once more.

But the delay had closed ten feet's worth of lead as Ree booked across the second roof. She reached the edge of the building, looking over. Lachesis was already on the ground again, heading north. Ree tried to reconstruct the woman's method of descent. Storm drain to second-floor veranda to open Dumpster.

Again, not something Ree could do on her own. She pored through her sideboard, looking for a way down. She settled on another Swiss Army–Green Lantern card. This time she fashioned a slide that led down off the roof and into Lachesis's trail.

"Chutes and Ladders this time!" Ree called. She kept her eyes locked on Lachesis, who looked over her shoulder at Ree. Ree waved hello as she slid down the construct, the wetness on her coat slowing her descent.

Ree would gladly have kept a Green Lantern ring on hand to do stuff like this all the time, but it took incredible mental effort to make constructs straight from the ring, as Eastwood had shown several times. These one-shots were way less taxing, but she was already running short. She had one more GL card, then she'd have to come up with other tricks.

Drake hit the slide as she hopped off. Lungs already heaving, she continued after Lachesis, considering pulling out a fatigue token to get her wind back.

"Ah!" Drake called, and Ree skidded to a stop. Turning, she saw Drake collapse to the ground, the slide disappearing faster than it should have.

I hate Hexomancy, Ree thought.

"I'm fine! Keep going!" he called, picking himself up.

She did.

When I catch this witch, there is going to be a face-punching the likes of which the world has not seen since the third age.

CHAPTER EIGHTEEN

Geekomancy vs. Le Parkour

Ree and Drake chased Lachesis across three more city blocks, the woman gaining on them, bit by bit. Between Hexomancy giving her a boost and dropping black ice and inconvenient crowds in their way, she was building herself the buffer she'd need to escape entirely, resetting their efforts to following with Drake's tracking machine.

And that would just not fucking do.

Ree bit into another fatigue token, shredding the cardboard and feeling a rush of energy fill her up, washing away the tearing pain in her legs and the burning in her lungs. She pushed forward.

Ahead, Lachesis hopped over a switchback without losing any steam, reversing direction down to an outdoor mall.

And what's worse, they were starting to get witnesses. More than a few.

"Urban tag!" she shouted to a cluster of tutting elderly women, who very well might be clutching their pearls under their massive powder-blue and salmon coats.

Drake continued to lag behind, his arsenal of tricks and gadgets good for getting up, but not nearly as versatile as Ree's for speed, strength, and weird situations.

"Don't mind me! I have the tracker!" he shouted as she slowed to keep him in sight, then gave her best overexaggerated stage wink and set off again.

She tore up a Flash card from the *Vs.* card game and watched the world go slow-mo as she kept booking at the same speed, moving faster than a time-lapse video. The Doubt was going to be working overtime today, but so be it. Two blocks later, Ree slipped on a patch of black ice, scrambling for footing in super-speed. It wasn't coming, so she dove into a roll, trying to bleed off some speed before she collided with the very-solid wall beside a café with a sickening crunch that could only have been her.

Groaning, Ree fumbled for a healing potion token. She ripped the cardboard between her teeth and the overwhelming pain washed away with a full-body tingle.

There was no way that was a real chunk of ice. *Hexomancy strikes again.* As long as Lachesis had the lead to burn in bits and pieces to drop hexes, she'd be able to escape the pair indefinitely. And if she was an experienced traceur, she probably had the lungs to outrun both her and Drake.

Getting to her feet, Ree pulled out her deck to look for another way to catch up with the Strega.

The entire deck flew out of her hands with a gust of gold and silver magic.

"Witch!" Ree shouted, wanting to use a different word but not around the cluster of kids playing in the snow nearby. She managed to grab one card before it could flutter away. It was a Hulk, probably good for one super-bound.

Ahead, Lachesis jumped, pushed off a wall, then turned and jumped again, grabbing on to the bottom of a second-floor balcony of some ritzy apartment building. Ree did the math based on the size of Hulk's super-jumps in films and comics, aimed so that even with Hexomantic interference she'd still end up on the building's roof, and then ripped the card mid-run.

As the energy seeped into her legs, Ree took one mighty leap. She arced high over the street, keeping her eyes on Lachesis, who looked over to see Ree heading for the roof above. She wove another Hex, gold and silver energy arcing up to send her careening off-course even farther than the woman's curses had sent her before.

Ree did the math and realized she was going to miss the roof. But barely. Hyping herself up and hoping for residual magic, she shouted, "Puny Strega!" and flipped around, grabbing the lip of the roof, her hands crushing the marble in their grip, her feet cracking the brick of the outer wall.

The landing knocked the power straight out of Ree, but she'd made the landing. She pulled herself up and onto the roof with not-even-Banner-level strength.

"Head her off, Drake!" Ree shouted as she ran across the roof, hoping to catch the Strega between them.

Lachesis popped up to the roof of the building as Ree crossed the halfway point. Ree drew her phaser and fired, but the Strega tossed it off with a gesture, another gold-silver field protecting her. Ree kept firing as she closed, also drawing and tossing one of her knives. The Strega slowed, focusing more on the shield, then took off after the dagger hit. Ree drew her lightsaber, no longer willing to play nice, especially if she could wear the Strega down to take her out with an old-fashioned right cross.

Ree was on track to head the Strega off, as long as she could keep Lachesis's focus on defense, not Hexy offense. She feather-touched the phaser's trigger, borrowing out of her experience gaming Quick Time Events by spamming a button, and reached for another throwing dagger.

A green glob of zap crossed through her vision, signaling that Drake had made it up to the roof. The Strega stopped, turning to face both of them.

"The abomination has chosen his minions well."

"Is that Strega for 'I give up'?" Ree asked, closing in. "If so,

I accept your surrender. Now get on your knees and keep your hands still."

Lachesis's smile was a bloody knife drawn across a goat's neck. The zealotry burned bright in her eyes, and Ree lost a step. The woman was far from giving up. Which meant that the fight was on.

Ree slipped the lightsaber back into her coat, not liking what would come of a Hexomantically-misdirected laser sword, especially as she and Drake moved into their combined melee approach, the man out of time jogging forward as he fired on his rifle's best impression of full auto.

Lachesis struck Jean Grey psychic poses as Drake fired, and angled the shield so that it deflected the shots straight at Ree. She dodged and dove, still closing on the Strega. This woman didn't have Connie's mass, and if her major physical chops were in evasion, maybe she wouldn't be as good in hand-to-hand.

Ree decided to skip striking and move directly in for the grapple, taking small steps to minimize her exposure to Hex whammies.

As Drake's rifle slipped from his hands, still firing, the adventurer dove to the side, taking Lachesis's focus with him. Ree shuffle-stepped through where the shield would have been, happy to discover that it wasn't a full dome or plane, more like the Dune shields—all about the individual attacks, slow blade pierces the shield and all.

Ree locked a hand around the Strega's wrist with a "Gotcha!"

But where Lucretia would have struggled ineffectually, Lachesis threw her arm down and around in a circle, breaking Ree's grip.

Okay, sticky hands it is. She'd played it only a few times with her dojang-mates that cross-trained in Daiji, but the idea was simple enough. Keep pushing and pulling and grabbing until something stuck and you could knock your opponent off their balance. If she could get her to the ground long enough for Drake to dog-pile, they'd have her.

Ree lashed out with grabs, strikes, and pushes, trying to get the Strega off her balance, and especially to occupy her hands. The Teutonic Strega met her move for move, showing herself to be no melee slouch.

But still, it was two to one. Drake joined the fight, kukri taking cautious swipes at the Strega's flank while Ree and Lachesis parried and riposted with punches and grapples.

"Keep it at the ninety to one hundred and fifty," Ree said. At that angle, they'd have less chance of missing what the other was doing and opening themselves up to a Hexomantic disaster.

Lachesis knocked the kukri out of Drake's hand, then spun and caught Ree across the chin with a hook kick. Reeling back, she came up to see a quick flash of gold and silver. Drake tripped directly on his knife, cutting his arm.

"Oh, now you've fucking done it," Ree said, rolling back up to her feet. Another Hex and she flopped straight to the ground, tucking her chin to avoid biting her tongue.

Hex by Hex, step by step, she slipped, rolled, and tripped her way back to Lachesis, a growing mound of bruises, but still going.

Lachesis picked up Drake's bloodied kukri, holding it up to catch the winter sun as Ree wobbled to her feet once more.

"Your blood will ensure the other's doom and the completion of the prophecy," she said, voice thick with hate.

Ree fell forward, her feet still confounded by hexes, but this time she was close enough to topple into the Strega, sending them both to the ground and the kukri off to the side.

The woman struggled, elbowing Ree in the collarbone as they rolled on the snowy roof. Ree bit down on her lip and snaked an arm around the woman's neck, moving to the side and putting pressure on the Strega's larynx. Lachesis's nails bit into Ree's arm, but she held fast. Ree snaked her other arm around Lachesis, starting what would be a fight-ending half nelson.

Drake kicked out at Lachesis, catching her in the wrist. The woman grunted, breath strained, and Ree took the opportunity to apply the other half of the half nelson (the other quarter nelson?).

"Now would be the time to give up," Ree said, putting pressure on the back of the Strega's neck, keeping her hips above the small of the woman's back. Lachesis didn't have the mass or strength to break this hold without magic, and with no hands free, no magic.

"You going to come quietly?"

Lachesis screamed, frustration and rage bypassing words.

Ree let one arm slip, leaning her shoulder into the biceps of the woman's freed arm, and grabbed the manacles that Eastwood had given to her when they left Dr. Wells's.

She snapped the Mana Sink manacles on one hand, then the other, then relaxed her hold. Lachesis wasn't going to be able to escape her again now. Her phaser still had a good two stun shots left in its charge.

Three paces away, Drake had a bandage out, wrapping his bloodied arm.

"You okay?"

Drake's face was pale, drained. He'd caught up without any magical speed boosts, but the effort had winded him.

"May I trouble you for one of those healing potions of Eastwood's?" he asked.

At Eastwood's name, the woman screamed again.

"You got it," Ree said. "Can you help me with Lachie here?"

Drake offered his unwounded arm, looping it around the Strega's.

A quick survey of the not-quite alley beside the building didn't provide anything handy, which meant this would go the hard way.

She reclaimed the phaser from where she'd dropped it, now wet in the snow beside the grill.

Ree hauled the Strega forward. "We're going to get down,

and then you're going to come with us, okay?"

"Bufoon. Nearsighted, uncivilized, primitive bufoon," Lachesis said, a nearly Elvis-level 'tude on her snarl.

"Then why are you the one in chains, and I'm the one with the gun?" Ree prodded the Strega in the shoulder with the business end of the phaser. "Now, over the side."

Lachesis swung one leg over the balcony ledge, then the other, hopping down and landing with ease. Ree jumped right after, landing in a crouch. On a good day, she'd look nearly as good as Lachesis.

This wasn't a good day. She toppled to the side, remembering to keep the phaser trained on the Strega.

"Shortsighted, too. The cowboy must die, lest others be emboldened by his continued existence. He has stained the pattern, disrupted the flow of the river. I should have set those ball bearings to detonate, made them jagged, something. Atropos will not be so easily stopped."

"Atropos. That your third sister, along with you and Connie Clothos-Line?" Ree asked as they walked out of the alley.

"Stop, police!" came a call from the street level.

"Fucksicles." The officer had his gun out and ready but not trained on them.

She sorted through possible responses, taking inventory of what tools she had on hand.

"I'm a federal marshal," she said after a moment. "This woman is a bail jumper, indicted on three counts of attempted murder. Cover me as I come down and I will be happy to show my badge."

Ree climbed down the fire escape and dropped into the slush by the officer, leaving Lachesis with Drake, still on the fire escape.

"Going for my badge," she said, fishing around in her jacket, pulling out the psychic paper she had on loan from Eastwood since he didn't exactly need it while he was in traction. She showed it to the cop, hoping that the zillions of hexes Lachesis had been throwing around wouldn't cancel out the artifact's magic.

"And if you're still not satisfied, you can call Captain Chu with SWAT. He knows me."

The cop's whole stance changed when she mentioned Chu. "You worked with SWAT?"

"Yep. The fugitive here is one of those," she said.

The Pearson PD were clued in on the supernatural. Or at least some of them were.

The cop gave her ID a look, then nodded, holstering his gun.

"Can we bum a ride?" Ree added. "My partner here took a nasty cut, and this one gave us a hell of a run."

The cop looked at Drake's coat and his bloody arm. "Your partner, eh?"

"Independent consultant."

The cop nodded, returning to his squad car. "Yeah, I hear SWAT has a lot of those. Come on, and see if your partner can keep from bleeding on the backseat."

Ree rode in the back, keeping an eye on Lachesis, watching the manacles. She went ahead and gagged the Strega after two minutes of incoherent, nearly evangelistic raving about the prophecy and her sister's revenge.

The patrolman dropped them off a block from the Dork-cave, leaving them to walk the Strega the rest of the way. Ree consciously locked Lachesis up by a different set of stacks than where Eastwood had bound Connie, leaving the gag in place for a minute while she reactivated all of the wards and traps.

They cleaned and dressed Drake's injury, then he downed another healing potion and took a seat to recover, leaving Ree with the Strega, still struggling against her restraints.

Ree squatted down in front of the Hexomancer and pulled out the woman's gag, taking care to stay out of biting range.

"Okay, start talking. Why are you after Eastwood, and what's this Atropos like?"

Lachesis laughed. But it wasn't arrogant laughter, defensive laughter, or anything like it. This was full-on Mark Hamill's Joker.

Ree asked the questions again, but Lachesis just kept laughing.

She didn't want to veer into the abuse-and-torture side of captive-holding, but it was getting a shade more tempting, the woman's laughs cutting at the top edge of her hearing like bamboo shoots under the fingernails.

"When I break free of these simple chains, I will delight in reading the bloody details of your death in the entrails of the pretty one here. I smell him on you. That will make my vision all that much clearer. And you'll be there, of course you will. When it comes to foretelling death, there's nothing quite like viscera. The ancient Chinese preferred the tortoise shells, the Yorubans knucklebones, but viscera. Yes, viscera give the truest insight."

Ree turned to Drake and whispered, "She's a lot."

"It does seem. Though it may be a ploy for dealing with interrogation."

"Could be."

Lachesis jumped forward, biting at Drake while the two were distracted. Ree reacted on instinct, throwing a jab at Lachesis's nose. The woman's head thunked against the steel shelves, and Ree's hand came back bloody.

Ree shook her head, wiping her hand off. "I don't believe in torture, but you go after me, I will protect myself. Then we'll see whose death we can see."

"You haven't the talent. Child of the die, the controller, not the Hex. Fate and Fortune trump mere muddling enthusiasm. He has shown this."

"One, I'm pretty sure we just proved the opposite. And two, who is 'he'?

"*He*," Lachesis said, murder replaced by longing on her face. "Him. He grants us grace and shows us the path, that we might set things right. Visions of wrongs to be righted, transgressions by the Cowboy and his apprentice."

"I'm not. His. Apprentice," Ree said, her own gorge rising.

"Ree . . ." Drake put a hand on her shoulder, the touch light, tentative.

She shrugged off his hand, more forcefully than she'd meant. She turned and squeezed his hand. "I got this."

Turning back to Lachesis. "I didn't come after you because he's my master, because of anything but the fact that you pose a danger to this city. My city. You hear me, or are you back in Homicide City counting bloody sheep?"

"You're the sheep. Following your blond shepherd and your bearded false prophet."

The woman continued to struggle against her bonds, practically foaming at the mouth.

"Yeah, enough of that." Ree hit Lachesis with the phaser, point-blank on stun.

The woman collapsed.

"Okay, let's dig up those oracles. They were in the 'O' section, should all be in a plastic tub."

While Lachesis was out, Ree tied the duct-tape bindings double-thick, even with the manacles in place.

Lucretia was intolerable and carried a boulder-size chip on her shoulder, but until Grognard's, she'd played relatively nice, contributed to the magical underground community in Pearson, such as it was. Connie had been strong and determined, but ultimately rational, a woman with a job to do, an enemy to defeat. Stripping her power eliminated the threat, but in a squicky overkill manner.

But Lachesis? She was just scary.

Keep justifying it to yourself, a voice in her mind said, chiding.

Did PPD have facilities to hold her? Was that a thing they could do?

"Found them!" Drake declared. Ree stayed put, keeping Lachesis dead in her sights, even though she was zonked out, not even snoring, thanks to the stunning.

"Hold that for a minute. I'm going to exhaust our options first."

Ree scanned her directory for the number she'd gotten for SWAT, the police team that had pitched in during the production of *Awakenings* when Alex Walters was unleashing all hell, from killer apes to orcs to a freaking dragon. His team had been top-notch, and if they could handle Lachesis, they'd be welcome to have her.

The desk sergeant passed the call up to Captain Chu.

"This is Captain Chu. Ms. Reyes?"

"Yeah, thanks for picking up. I've got a homicidal Hexomancer in custody. She tried to kill Eastwood, and then when Drake and I tracked her down, caused no small amount of mayhem before we caught her."

"That was you, then. Since when are you a marshal?"

"I needed to get out of that situation as quickly and discreetly as possible. I hope you understand. This Strega nearly took us both out. Trick is, she's totally beyond reason. I can't in good faith just kick her out of town and expect she'll grab a bus and leave the area with her tail between her legs. Can you help me out?"

"If I bring her in, we need to charge her regular-style. Do you have enough evidence to indict her in front of a mundane judge?"

Ree removed her glasses and pinched the bridge of her nose. "I don't know. Magical signatures are all over, and we have two eyewitnesses she tried to kill, but mostly with magic. Are you telling me I'm on my own?"

"Eastwood said the magical community has its own ways of solving these problems."

"About that. This woman is part of a sisterhood, and this whole thing kicked off when her sister cheated during a trial.

So I'm not inclined to trust in Magical Underground justice right now. She's totally off her rocker, but my way of dealing with her is pretty harsh."

Captain Chu paused for a second. "To be perfectly honest, Ms. Reyes, I really don't need to hear about your plans for vigilante justice."

"Got it. Then I'll leave you with plausible deniability. Thanks for taking the call, and give my best to the squad. Especially Washington. The invitation to Grognard's stands, by the way."

"Thank you. Best of luck."

And with that, Captain Chu hung up, having squarely kicked the ball back into Ree's court.

Drake stood by with a cardboard box filled with dusty card decks and assorted oracular paraphernalia.

"I take it the call did not produce a workable solution?"

"Yep. It's on us. What do you think we should do?"

Drake set the box down, looked at the Strega, still unconscious, and bit his lip. "Frankly, this woman scares me. The pair of us were barely able to best her, and we did only because she accepted a confrontation thinking she could Hex her way to victory. She's clearly dangerous to more than just Eastwood, and is unlikely to be reached with reason. I would offer her a way out if our safety can be guaranteed."

"And Eastwood's?"

"He is his own man. My loyalty is not to him," Drake said, looking at Ree as if to make it very clear where his loyalty did lie. Which was flattering, but it once again put the ball in her court.

Her collar, her decision. She consulted her personal oracle/ conscience.

Try for the high road and offer her a chance to walk away.

Ree rummaged through Eastwood's stacks until she found some smelling salts, because of course he had smelling salts.

The fact that they were in a section labeled NEEDFUL THINGS was creepy, though.

And after all, this was to protect Eastwood. She was going out of her way, risking her and Drake's necks for a guy who was still very firmly in the gray area, even with his hero-ing.

But this woman hadn't just threatened Eastwood. She had to be countered, checked, or removed from the equation somehow, but without leaving the ashy taste of fail in her mouth.

Lachesis snarled to consciousness, fixing dagger eyes on Ree and Drake.

"What? Didn't have the courage to take the smart path?"

"I don't want to kill you. In fact, I'd rather not hurt you at all. But you've made it pretty clear you're not going to negotiate or play nice. So what I need to know is whether I can get your word, your binding word, that you'll give up on the prophecy and this vengeance schtick. You leave Pearson, never come back, and never use your power against me, Drake, or Eastwood. Swear that, and do it again under giese, and you'll be free to go."

Lachesis laughed. Cackled, really. She contorted her head back and away, shaking her restraints, just laughing. The laughter cut through Ree's confidence and left her feeling naked and weaponless. If the Joker were real, this was what his laugh would sound like.

And Ree wanted nothing to do with it.

She fumbled for the phaser, dropping it as she drew it from her coat, snatching it out of the air with a quick save. She made sure it was still set to stun and zapped Lachesis back into unconsciousness.

"Fuck," she said, stepping back and grabbing Drake's hand. "I don't think there's a good way out of this."

Drake nodded. "I'm afraid not. Do you recall how Eastwood conducted the severing of Connie from her power?"

"No, but we have cell phones for situations like this." She hadn't had the time to use any genre emulation during the chase, so her phone was still sitting on plenty of power. She just hoped that Dr. Wells had thought to ensure there was a cell signal in her new lab.

Ring.

Ring.

Ring.

"Yes?" answered a female voice, faint, as if from the bottom of a well built into a movie theater. Seriously, those things must be actively paying to mute cell signal.

"Doc, this is Ree. Can you put Eastwood on?"

"Ah. He's just coming up. I'll take you to him."

A minute later, Eastwood was cogent enough to relay the steps of the ritual to her, and grumpy enough to do so with all of his patented condescension and a side order of "I told you so."

"What happened to 'How dare you take her power, you monster?'"

"Yeah, yeah. Laugh it up, Captain Traction. This one makes Connie look like pre-jail-time Martha Stewart. I offered her a way to walk away, and she went banshee laughter on me. This is the kind of time when you disarm someone. Is there anything else I need to know about the ritual?"

"Just make sure she inhales the ash as soon as the ritual is complete and the oracle has burned."

He waited a second.

"Thank you, Ree. You bought me another three months."

"Both of us, this time. You work on not dying. I plan on being angry at you for years to come."

Eastwood laughed, then devolved into moans of pain.

A moment later, he croaked out, "I'm looking forward to it."

"That will be all. He needs to rest," Dr. Wells said, cutting in.

"Thanks, Doc. And good on you for making sure there's cell signal. Saved me a trip through the muck."

"It comes in handy. Now be thorough, and report when you're done."

"You're not the boss of me, but I like having a cleric on call, so sure." She hung up and slipped her phone back into the jacket. "Okay, so here's what we need. . . ."

⨯×⬡×⨯

Ree wasn't much for rituals. She usually left that crap to Eastwood, or figured out some genre emulation work-around when the Grumpy Cowboy wasn't available or when they were on talking-but-not-really-talking terms. But with Eastwood's instructions, she managed to only burn off all the hair on the back of her hand before getting the ritual to take, the blood sizzling on the correct oracle, the smoke bursting into colors.

She held the mini-brazier up to Lachesis, and the woman's eyes went wide as she breathed in the magicked ash, awake again in a flash.

The woman's eyes went white, and she convulsed, rattling the shelf in violation of most sensible versions of physics. Small woman, heavy shelf, and yet there they were.

Ree reached a hand out to cover Drake and guided them both back two steps.

"Did the previous Strega do this?"

"Nope," Ree said. "And I don't know if this is a good thing or a bad thing."

"I tend to leap directly to bad when I see convulsions such as that. It reminds me of the exstasis of the Listeners of Da'roun, receiving testament from the Four-mouthed godhead."

"Awesome."

"It was that, quite literally. Do you think we should summon Dr. Wells?" he asked.

But then, Lachesis stopped, slumping forward in her bindings. She looked up and locked her eyes on Ree. "My sister told me you tried to stop the cowboy from doing this to her. It seems that you've given up even that shred of good."

"I have this strange personality quirk where I react poorly to people threatening to eviscerate my friends and use them for divination on how best to kill me. I know that might be weird in Strega country, but here in Pearson, that makes me humane."

Lachesis's voice dropped, the venom gone for a moment. "Humane would be to just kill me. Set me free. He will not tolerate this failure."

"Who is 'he'?" Drake asked.

"You will find out, soon enough. He will reveal himself. And when our sister comes, her shears will cut off the overlong threads of your lives, all of you, the cowboy first. I have seen his corruption, witnessed his arrogance with my own eyes, heard the dissonance he brings to the world with my ears—"

"Got it," Ree said, tuning the woman out. "Next step is getting her out of town. You up for a road trip? My best guess is it'll take most of an hour to get to the city limits, more if the snow doesn't let up."

"That will make for a rather expensive taxi service," Drake said.

"Yep. That's why we're borrowing a car. You watch Parkour Strega here while I call Anya. Her roommate has a car."

As predicted, it took them three hours round-trip to drive Lachesis to the edge of town and leave her on the highway, handcuffed. Ree was tempted to take the woman's boots, but she was already going to be out in the cold without a coat, and without whatever magic was keeping her warm. She'd suffer just fine.

Drake called Eastwood and Dr. Wells on the way back to let them know it was done. The clock showed 4:15 as they finally made it back into the U-District, having successfully dodged black ice, northwest drivers who had never dealt with snow and ice accumulation, and several streets filled with cars dumped over the side of the road.

"I think this calls for a milkshake," Ree said.

"Seconded. Would it be audacious to declare this celebratory milkshake the actual first date for our nascent relationship?"

"It's only a date if we don't run into any monsters," Ree said.

"Understood. I will make a request with the universe to spare us this one afternoon."

"While you're at it, can you ask for the evening, too? I was thinking we could wander down and catch *The Hobbit*."

"Didn't you say that the reviews called it 'bloated and undisciplined'?" Drake asked.

Ree threw on her turn signal, pulling into an abandoned parking space, snow and ice heaped around it in a rim. The wheels and chassis crunched over the lip, then slid nicely into place. "Yeah, but that doesn't mean I don't want to see it for myself. Plus, if it's terrible, we can just move to the back and make out like teenagers."

"That sounds rather expensive, given the free alternatives."

"Well, then we'll just have to try extra hard to enjoy the movie, won't we?" she said, pouring all of the rakishness she could muster into a smile. "But first, milkshakes." Ree shut the car off.

The passenger-side door cut into a mound of ice, and it took Drake another two tries to push through and step out. "Perhaps this time I will ask for the fine proprietors to add whipped cream. This was a particularly trying day."

"So almost dying justifies an upgrade from vanilla to vanilla with whipped cream?" Ree asked, looping an arm around Drake's as they walked.

"Vanilla is a perfectly acceptable flavor choice. Especially with beans as fine as those used by the Burger Bin. I have not found their equal. Vanilla may be bland in some establishments, it is true, but why condemn the flavor for its weakest pretenders to the name?"

Ree leaned into Drake's shoulders, thinking *I could listen to this man rattle on about vanilla for hours.*

And so she did.

Walking out of the movie theater, Ree knew she was ranting, but she didn't care.

"I don't recall seeing anything in Tolkien's notes that terminal velocity on Middle-earth was low enough that a pile of dwarves could have a couple tons of wood and metal fall on them without anyone ending up in traction. I must have skimmed that part of *The Silmarillion*."

"But did you enjoy it?" Drake asked, the pair walking hand-in-hand.

"Yeah, but it is my gods-given right as a geek to complain about the things I love, and I'll not have that taken away by anyone, let alone myself. I've got another good ten minutes of complaining in me, and then I will download the Misty Mountains song and listen to it on repeat for the whole weekend."

"That was quite excellently done. Did I see that it gave you chills, or was that merely an intimation that you wished me to hold your hand again?"

They turned the corner from the art-house-and-geeky-stuff theater in the U-District, heading back to the Shithole, where Anya would swing by and pick up the keys to get groceries and return the car. The wind had died down, the air crisp but still. Her weather app showed tomorrow's highs in the 50s. "Little bit of column A, little bit of column B. Tolkien's all about the songs, and the *Lord of the Rings* movies really cut out a lot of that, so it was cool to get that song, at least. Not that I really missed 'Where There's a Whip, There's a Way' from the Bakshi version."

"Again, you leave me far behind, my dear."

"That I can fix. Wait. Have you read *The Hobbit*?"

"I have not. It is on the list you gave me, which if represented in physical volumes would tower over Mt. Rainier."

"Yeah, but *The Hobbit*'s a kid's book. You could finish it in an afternoon. What do you say to a reading date? I could tackle my own TBR mountain."

"Only if you allow me to ply you with my tea collection as we go. There is an oolong that I believe may be the perfect companion to a snowy day of reading."

"As long as I can still start my day out with espresso to hit my caffeine baseline."

"I would think that goes without saying."

They turned the corner as a male voice cried out from down the street, a scream of pure panic. Not just mugging panic. Twenty bucks said this was monster action.

"I think this might have to become retroactively not a date."

"Well, we could always abandon our self-appointed sacred duty and leave him to his fate," Drake said, checking his rifle.

"Yeah, because that's going to happen," Ree said, pulling out her lightsaber.

"After you."

Ree dashed down the street, and Drake followed.

CHAPTER NINETEEN

Welcome Back, Cowboy

SPRING

Ree leaned back in her bed, a bulletproof smile on her face. "So then, he says, 'Your moods are more mercurial than tropical storms, more beautiful than the triple sunset over the Ajerian horizon.'"

"What's an Ajerian?" Ree's dad asked.

"Hell if I know, but I'm pretty sure he meant it as a compliment, so that's how I'm taking it. He still doesn't get half of the things I say, so it's only fair that he get to drop references I have no fucking clue about."

"And it's not like he's wrong about your moods," her dad said. His voice dropped, and she could hear the shadow pass over his face. "That's your mom coming through."

For the hundredth time, Ree's heart broke for her dad, who still didn't know what had happened to his wife, Sionnan Reyes, aka Branwen nic Catrin—the late Jedi of Pearson. As far as he knew, she'd just run off, leaving him alone with Ree.

But she'd gone off to resume her Geekomantic career, eventually dying years ago under mysterious circumstances that threw her straight into the clutches of the Thrice-Ret-conned Duke of Pwn, Dork Lord of Hell. And in between running away from home and getting killed, she had shacked up with Eastwood for several years. You know, just your standard midlife crisis.

And while she'd come clean to her dad about basically everything else about her magical life, Ree had kept this part a secret. Her dad was dating again, had a good thing going with an economics lecturer at IUPUI. He didn't need the gaping wound of his wife ripped back open with phosphorous and brimstone thrown into the gap for bad measure.

"Yeah, go Mom," Ree said, matching her dad's tone. "But he takes me as I am, and I take him as he is. We're a walking romantic comedy, but it works, largely by actually communicating about shit that bugs us instead of flouncing off and requiring a song-and-dance to be won back."

"Have you learned nothing from John Hughes movies?" her dad asked, the sarcasm as thick in his voice as red sauce on his enchiladas. Her dad positively drowned his enchiladas. So much that Ree was always a bit disappointed whenever she had them out in the world and she could sometimes actually see the tortilla through the sauce.

"I learned plenty. If I were a Cinemancer, I could make my life a romantic comedy, but unless I want to channel *My Super Ex-Girlfriend* all the time or try to base my relationship on the hate, bicker, love arc of *The Empire Strikes Back*, I'm strangely stuck being a grown-up about the whole thing."

Her dad laughed, a deep belly laugh. She could imagine him crossing his arms as he did it, the way he'd done a zillion times before. "Who are you, and what have you done with my daughter? Are you a changeling? I can call Grognard and put together a search party."

Note to self: Need to visit home soon. Maybe bring Drake?

A shiv of worry hit her in the gut. *Shit. What about his parents?*

He doesn't mention them. Never mentions them. Will he ever be able to see them again?

"What can I say? I've matured. When you're dating a temporally- and dimensionally-displaced Steampunk Technomancer, you have to work a bit harder to be grounded. Plus, he gets on really well with the Ladies, even Priya. I mean, as well as you can get along with your current girlfriend's best friend, who is also your ex."

"Again, you're not really living a romantic comedy." Her dad waited a beat. "It's nine here. Didn't you need to head off and pick up Eastwood?"

Ree pulled her phone away from her head to check the time. "Shit, yes. I promised Grognard I'd help him clean up and come down to the bar for a welcome-back party. Thanks for chatting, Daddy-o."

"Love you, Ree-bee."

"Love you, too," Ree said, sighed a smiling sigh, and hung up. She launched herself off the bed and grabbed her already-prepped bag, heading out the door.

⋅✕ˣ⬡ˣ✕⋅

Eastwood was in strangely good spirits when she arrived at the Dorkcave.

He'd shaved, even, his beard as well groomed as she'd seen since the trial.

"I spent two months in traction. You get to missing things—like feeling human. And plus, an old friend is in town. She's coming by Grognard's tonight."

That was news to her. "Oh, yeah? What kind of old friend?"

Eastwood's blush told her exactly what kind.

"Oh, yeah? Who is it? Dish." Ree's gossip-mongering overpowered her anger at Eastwood, which, to be fair, had mellowed over the months since Lachesis's hit had nearly left him six feet under. The third Strega was due soon, and the law of threes plus the Billy Goats Gruff vibe had her looking over her shoulder in a big way.

Lachesis, over-the-top as she was, had been very clear about how much bad news Atropos was. And considering how rough Connie and Lachesis had been, whoever took up their Atropos spot was likely to earn the label of The Heavy.

Hence the party, a full week before the equinox.

Even so, Eastwood was loaded for bear. His Han Solo vest was packed with several sideboards, his psychic paper, and Gygax only knew what else. His trench coat was crisp, and practically glowed with magical protections. The cowboy look was strong with him; no doubt he'd cleaned up for his old friend.

The trip through the unseasonably warm spring and down into the humid sewers passed without incident, and before she knew it, they were knocking on Grognard's still new-seeming door.

The zillion-times-warded steel door swung open. The bar was as crowded as it had been during the grand reopening, if not more. The regulars had come back right away, but it took a few months after that for the casual patrons to drift back in, for new folks to join the circle after making connections at the Midnight Market.

"Eastwood!" they shouted in unison, channeling *Cheers*.

Ree took the stein that Uncle Joe had been holding, waiting by the door as Grognard's plan demanded. She handed Eastwood his stein, and he raised it to toast the assembled.

At the bar, Grognard was also in his best, an unbuttoned vest lying open over his Deathmøle T-shirt.

Sheesh, everyone shaved, Ree noted. Uncle Joe was put together, and Chandra was wearing makeup (aside from eyeliner). Talon was the same as ever, thank goodness.

The crowd shifted, and Drake emerged without moving. Thanks to the neurochemical joys of limerence, the room brightened. Ree felt three inches taller, walking on platform shoes made out of giddy.

She had it bad. And it felt awesome. A permanent +2 morale bonus on basically every roll, ever.

Drop salsa on her shirt? Meh. Miss the bus? Whatever. Monster popping out of the sewer? That's what lightsabers were for. She didn't know if the neurochemical hack would be permanent, and suspected that at some point, it might fade to a more comfortable, worn-in-pair-of-jeans affection, but damned if she was going to let it go if she could avoid it.

Ree wrapped her arms around Drake and planted a big smacker right on his lips. "Hey, babe."

Drake chuckled. "How is it that I ended up saddled with that as your pet name for me?"

"You vetoed Drake-y, and rightly so."

"I suppose I could retaliate by declaring you my Ree-splendent One, or something equally nauseating."

"Yes, but that takes much longer to say. Wouldn't stick."

"So are you saying that the name will not stick because it takes too long, she who quotes *The Middleman* perfectly, including always saying the entire phrase of The Booty Chest, the pirate-themed sports bar with the scantily-clad waitresses?"

"Touché. Cider?" she asked, releasing her hold. She was on the clock tonight, after all. Grognard was fairly lenient when it came to canoodling and making googly eyes on the clock, but judging by the crowd, tonight was going to be slammed.

"Always. Thank you," Drake said, pulling Ree's left hand up to kiss on the knuckles. It was a totally chaste move, but Drake managed to make it positively roguish. Needles of self-fiving thrills washed over her like a tidal wave. She squeezed his hand, then headed to the bar to activate Super-Server Mode.

"You weren't kidding about a crowd, man," Ree said as she stepped behind the bar with Grognard, who Monkey Gripped three bottles of booze at once, pouring an AMF.

"Nothing less for the return of my best customer. Plus, we hadn't thrown a big blowout in a while."

"And what does New Year's count as, if not a blowout?" Ree asked, chuckling.

"That was just a fucking mess. This will be much better."

Ree grabbed the apron from the shelf under the register and strapped it on like a Bat-belt. She stuffed her phone and lightsaber into the apron, then checked her notepad, the small bills, and the credit card envelopes. Everything was in order. "Uh-huh, sure. Where you want I should start?"

"Pitchers for Eastwood. Take them to his friend in the corner, there."

Grognard nodded to the corner booth, where a stunning Japanese woman in a trench coat sat, arms spread around the booth like she owned the place. She was maybe forty, attitude for miles. That'd be Eastwood's old friend, then.

Her spiky hair would fit right into an anime but wasn't quite so outrageous that people would stop her and ask where the Comic-Con was if she walked down the street. It'd take the rest of her outfit to do that. She wore a black-and-red bodysuit, glowing red trim sending off *Tron* signals in Ree's mind. Over that, a coat that could have been a twin to Eastwood's. *Ah, so that's a thing.*

"Critical Hit, then?" Ree asked, checking that they'd be drinking Eastwood's favorite of Grognard's brews.

Grognard nodded without looking at her, operating two martini shakers at once, deftly popping the tops off and pouring four drinks' worth of shots in a single go.

Ree slotted a pitcher under the tap, and said to herself, "Time to go meet Cowboy-Ko, then."

Once the pitcher was full, she grabbed a tray, stacked some pint glasses, and headed out into the crowd. She took a wide path around a pitched card game with a crowd.

The woman embraced Eastwood with a hug, their touch lingering long enough to lend more weight to Ree's suspicions. Shade joined them, rounding out the trio with his OC (Original Cyberpunk) look.

"Pitcher of Critical Hit for you folks."

Shade brightened, giving his best salesman-not-trying-to-sell-you-something smile. "Thanks, Ree. How's tricks?"

"Good. Those shades of yours saved me a lot of hassle a couple of months back, don't remember if I told you."

Shade put a hand over his heart, everything exaggerated. "It warms my Amiga heart."

Pouring a pint, Ree said, "I'm Ree, and I'll be taking care of you all tonight. Eastwood, are you going to introduce me to your friend?"

"Eriko, this is Ree, my former apprentice. She's still angry at me for some reason or another." Ree gave him a mild glare. He knew damned well why, just didn't want to mention it to his ex. "Ree, this is Eriko Miguchi, one of the finest hackers I've ever had the privilege of working with. She's the one who helped me try to backtrack Lachesis."

Ree nodded, and Eriko returned the motion with a slight incline of her head. "Good work," Ree said. "That woman was ten pounds of scary in a five-pound bag. It's good we got her out of town when we did."

"I'm glad to be of assistance." Hints of a Northern California accent peeked through at the edges of Eriko's vowels.

"Anything to eat for you folks? Cheese sticks are going to be good today; we just got in fresh basil."

"An order of those, and the queso fundido, please," Shade said.

Ree waited a beat for the others. "Anything else?"

Nope.

"I'll put that right in. Let me know if you need anything. *Apples to Apples* starts at eight, and shots will be half off during the game."

"Even for Uncle Joe?" Eastwood asked. Uncle Joe had the alcohol tolerance of a three-year-old. And when he was drunk, nonstandard cards had a tendency to appear in his hands for games.

"Only way to see is to buy in."

"You have *Apples to Apples* tournaments?" Eriko asked, leaning forward, a crack of enthusiasm piercing her cool demeanor.

Eastwood beamed like a kid showing his friend around FAO Schwarz for the first time. "That's just half of it. You should see the *Warmachine* armies folks have here."

"You really have retired, haven't you?" Eriko asked as Ree stepped away from the table.

Ree made the rounds, picking up enough orders to back-log the kitchen for an hour. She dialed in to the job, laughing and joking with the regulars, greeting the newbies, and playing up the evening as much as possible, feeling a bit disingenuous as she did. Was it wrong to help other people celebrate someone you've got major problems with? When harshing that joy is all about prioritizing your own feelings over others'? Add the compromised position of working for tips and the whole thing became a headache.

Chop wood, carry water, she told herself. *Or in this case, chop limes, carry beer.*

⋅✕˟⬡˟✕⋅

After the *Apples to Apples* game finished, Eriko waved Ree over to the corner booth.

"Sit down! You've been going nonstop since you got here."

"Well, my boyfriend is over there," Ree started, pointing over her shoulder.

"Screw your boyfriend; he can wait."

"Those are kind of mutually exclusive, aren't they?" Ree asked.

Shade slapped the table. "Point, Reyes."

They were into their cups. Several cups. All three were flushed at the cheeks, Eriko's buttoned-up facade dropping off to reveal a hard-drinking, shoulder-punching counter to Eastwood's tipsy taciturnity.

"So, Eastwood tells me that you're Branwen's kid. D'you grow up in all of this, then?" Eriko gestured vaguely in an everywhere direction.

"I grew up in geekdom, but not in the weird-ass magical subculture version."

Eastwood cut in, lurching forward, forearms rattling the table. "Branwen was in retirement for a while. But why don't you tell her about the thing with Joe from the EFF . . ." he said, clearly trying to lead the conversation away from the topic of her mom and his ex. *Thanks for that*, she thought.

"She was a good mom, until she was gone. And it's a super-pleasant memory, so thanks for bringing it up. I'll bring you all some water."

"Hold on." Eriko reached across the table and grabbed Ree's wrist. Ree tensed, nearly ready to wrench the woman's arm over and pull her into Shade. But he hadn't done anything to deserve getting someone tossed on him, and the woman was drunk. Treat her like a drunk.

"I'll just bring that water. . . ." she said, sliding out of Eriko's grip. The older woman tightened her grip, clamping around Ree's wrist.

"Wait a minute, spring chicken. You oughta know that Eastwood here has devoted his whole life to saving people. He and I are the reason regular people can even use the Internet anymore. We kept the digital frontier safe, kept the Neo-Luddites from using Trojans to send the country back to the 1850s.

"The EFF wasn't just about keeping the Internet free from corporatist control. The shit we saw, the blood we shed, all for you kids to scream at each other on Tumblr and post cat videos. . . ." Eriko let Ree's wrist go and slumped back, shrugging deep into her coat.

Shade jumped on the silence. "The Internet has always been a weird, wonderful place, it's true. I wasn't the same kind of active as these folks, but I've got some stories of my own. Did I ever tell you who Max Headroom is really based off of?"

"You haven't," Ree said, happy to spare a smile for Shade, who switched from slightly-sleazy-but-not-creepy salesman to lovable uncle very easily. "But I've got to make rounds again, or take a real break. And if I'm taking a real break, it's going to be to snog that handsome Steampunk over there." Ree pointed a gun-finger at Drake. He held court at the bar, speaking with expansive gestures.

"I'll be back to hear the stories later. I do want to hear them, really. I've been using the Internet since BBS days, but Eastwood's never been that forthcoming with his Wild Wild Web stories."

That seemed to calm the suddenly-sullen Eriko, and Ree managed to escape back to the bar to pour a pitcher of ice water. Some H_2O to dim the edge on Eriko's drunk, then she could make rounds later for the war stories.

"Mind if I sit with Drake for a fifteen?" she asked Grognard, who had his own crowd gathered to hear about the Assault on Grognard's, or the Tale of Grognard's Heroes, whatever he was calling it now.

He gave her a vague nod of approval, which was more than enough to help her feel justified in de-aproning and sneaking over to plant a big one on Drake, inserting herself into the discussion.

"Hello, my dear! I was just regaling some new friends with the tale of the time that we conducted a dogfight across the skies of Pearson with the fiendish Aberrant Muse."

Ree leaned against the bar and grabbed Drake's stein, taking a drag on his Angry Orchard cider. Grognard didn't brew cider, but he kept a good stock on hand (mostly for Drake). This varietal was a bit sweet for her taste, but it suited him.

Drake continued his story, and after a couple of minutes, Ree pulled him away into the office for some discreet snogging before heading back to work. She was a big PDA fan, but he was . . . not. So if she wanted to get her mack on when they were out in the world, they had to head off to the bathroom or office or whatever it was.

It had made for some hilarious memories, like being the first of two couples making time in the restroom, the second couple being *far* louder. It was just another part of their normally-abnormal relationship.

"Have you had the chance to speak with Eastwood's companion? They appear to be quite old companions. I'd be fascinated—"

Ree placed a friendly hand on Drake's shoulder. "I don't really want to talk about Eriko and Eastwood right now, if that's okay."

"Perfectly fine. Shall I return to singing the praises of your versatility and creativity in all things, especially your kinesthetic intelligence?"

"I gotta admit, you're better at grandiloquent dirty talk than all of the grad students I've known. But they were MFAs, so they were mostly worrying about impressing one another with how much they loved Jonathan Franzen."

"I doubt that is truly all they spoke about." Drake held her close, heads resting together as they sat on Grognard's desk.

"Yeah, they also complained about whiny comp students. Understandably so."

"Let us not speak of them, then. What would you like to do tomorrow? I imagine that things will start exploding any day now, so I was thinking we could have a dedicated day for pantsless reading."

"I see my efforts to pull you into my habits of calculated laziness are having an effect."

"There is great wisdom in measured, deliberate periods of repose."

"Deal. We'll be like firefighters in the firehouse. Though we'd need to install a pole in your apartment. Think the super will allow it?"

"I might need to fix the water heaters a few times before she would permit such a substantial change, but I will make the proper inquiries."

Ree grinned. "Liar."

"Touché. Should you get back to your rounds?" he asked.

Ree craned her head around to check the clock. "Yeah. Walk me home tonight?"

"As always. I think I will go to join Eastwood, Shade, and their fellow technophile, perhaps trade some tall tales, as you call them."

Ree pulled Drake into one more kiss for good measure. Then she put her server face back on, heading out to the crowd.

CHAPTER TWENTY

Tall Tales

The hours whirred by with drinks, food, and chatter about games and films and more. By 1 AM, most of the crowd had cleared out, leaving Eastwood, Drake, and Eriko in the corner, Uncle Joe sorting and re-sorting his cards, and a trio of regulars around a table playing *Netrunner*.

Eriko waved Ree over to their corner booth. "Take a seat. Hanging out with us, you're serving half of the patrons here. I'm sure Grognard won't mind."

And +2 points for using social pressure via my job to make me hang. Well played, cowgirl.

Years of working retail had prepared her for interacting pleasantly with people she'd rather bite her nails off for her dinner than deal with, and this would at least give her a chance to find out more about Eriko and Eastwood's Console Cowboy past.

Ree poured herself some Adamantine Ale and took a seat next to Drake, settling in, squared up to talk to Eriko, ignoring Eastwood as much as she could manage.

Which didn't turn out to be much, as Eriko and Eastwood spent the next hour trading stories of their adventuring days together, fighting domain rustlers, tech bubble robber barons, demon bandits, and more.

Eriko had pulled back from her drunkest state, her words coming out smooth. "So there we are, backed up against the cliff, squared off against a half-dozen hired guns from Boo. com, slick city boys with top-of-the-line astral rides but not a lick of sense among them."

Then Eastwood chimed in, spirits raised by his companion. "And then their leader, this prim British-Indian woman, says, 'You've got nowhere to go. This part of the web is ours. You Console Cowboys have had your time. You can't stand in the way of progress.'"

They laughed. Drake jumped in, his tie metaphorically loosened after several hours of ciders. "When a person's dialogue sounds stilted to me, it is at that time that one knows that one has truly entered the land of the cartoonish."

Eriko clapped, lapping it all up. "Too true. She was at most twenty-three, some hotshot marketing exec straight out of an MBA program and plugged straight into the secret IP address wars that mirrored the dot-com bubble, and what does she do? She goes full-on black hat, reading lines straight out of spaghetti Westerns with aetheric winds blowing digital tumbleweeds in front of her."

"We got used to it," Eastwood said. "But that whole era was more than a little ridiculous, looking back on it now."

Eriko shrugged. "That's the nineties for you. Y2K just around the bend, seemed like the world was either going to implode or crank on toward infinite profits. It's a damned good thing I had some money in Apple, or the bust would have cleaned me out."

"Nice! Enough that you're rolling in it, or what?" Ree asked, tromping right over the 'Oh, we don't talk about money' norm that dominated in the U.S., more because she was genuinely curious than out of any sense of being anarchic or jealous.

"I wish. Had to liquidate all but three shares when the rest of my portfolio evaporated. But I kept a hand in, and even though the landscape's a complete one eighty from what it was like in Eastwood's and my time, the net is still full of plenty of adventure. It's just way more William Gibson than Louis L'Amour these days. The spirits adapted right quick, though. Our conception of the world changes, they change right along with it."

"Their world is a shadow of ours; they can't help but change," Eastwood said. "Especially after we colonized the space so intensely. There's too much human emotion caught up in the net. It's nothing but communication, people reaching out to one another."

"Sometimes to throttle one another," Ree added.

"Well, yes," Eastwood said.

"He gets all nostalgic and utopian talking about the net," Eriko said, lending him a wistful look.

There was a whole lot of there there, after all, Ree thought.

"But what happened with the Boo.com chick and her thugs?" Ree asked.

"Yes, go on," Drake said.

Eriko and Eastwood traded looks, jockeying to see who should continue the story.

"You do it," Eastwood said. "You do her voice better than I do."

"So the suit's all, 'You can't stand in the way of progress,' while Eastwood and I are signaling each other with shifts in weight. We took the range of nervous movements and flexing, all of that stuff you see when people are getting ready to draw down in shootouts, turned it into shorthand. So when she finished up her monologue, I'd started a DDoS attack on Boo's server, which ripped half of her goons right out of Spirit, their tethers too weak to hold on to. The others were good enough to reroute on the fly, but all of a sudden, six on one becomes three on one. . . ." Eriko said, shrugging with practiced ease.

Eastwood brought the story home. "And we sent them running. The suit was all bark, no bite. Her gun didn't even clear the holster before Eriko put one between her eyes, de-rezzed her avatar, sending her screaming back into her cushy leather chair back in start-up country."

"I'm still a little rough on the details. This is in Spirit, but you're using tech to hack one another's connections and crap?"

Eriko nodded. "Technomancy. Cowboy here did all of his through his geeky bits, consoles and game books and all; I came at it from the techie side. Drake was saying he gets to Spirit with a . . . What did you call it?"

"Breakthrough Actuator. It works based on Braga's theory of space folding, with a sympathetic alignment system that equates its surroundings with that of an equivalent space in Spirit."

Eriko waved him off. "Yeah, that. There're a million ways to get to Spirit. When folks started buying up space on the World Wide Web, a few of us got together to make sure there was enough space for the everyone else, for regular folks to make a living, set up their own space, get their packets across the wilderness. A lot of money started pouring in all at once, a digital gold rush. We were almost always outgunned, but our crew? Some of the best techies you've ever seen behind a keyboard."

"We were at the keyboard and in Spirit at the same time, our spirits moving around while our bodies stay grounded in the physical plane. It meant that if we got smoked in Spirit, we popped back home with a migraine but got to live to fight another day," Eastwood said.

"Sweet. Why don't you do that now?" Ree asked.

"My tech's outdated. Plus, I can't do Geekomancy as a projection. Props and the like don't work; I just have to use spiritual armaments."

"So you shot people with spiritual pistols?"

"You envision your reality there and make it so. When the dominant meme was the frontier, it was all cowboys and six-shooters. Now it's chrome and glass and monoblades."

"I've got to check this place out sometime," Ree said.

"Anytime, kid. There's not much left of the frontier. A friend of ours maintains a saloon called The Gulch. It used to be the Last Homely House of the Wild Wild Web. Now it's a curiosity, a throwback, surrounded by high-rises, Google and Apple and Facebook, so on and so forth."

"So all of these countries are set up in Spirit?" Ree asked.

"Some more than others. But everyone's got a presence, if only to be able to protect it. Otherwise folks like us," Eastwood said, gesturing to Eriko and himself, "could pop in and waltz out with all of their data. Spirit hacking's big business these days. Identity theft, big data harvesting, all that jazz."

"Why is the world so weird?" Ree asked.

"There are more possibilities and permutations of imagination and wonder than a single mind, even a group, could imagine. The multiverse is as expansive as the factorial sum of all human imagination," Drake said.

Ree cocked her head to the side, struck with surprise.

"Oh, homeboy's getting philosophical. You better take him home," Eriko said, all toothy grin. It was very hard to dislike this woman. She treated everyone like an old friend and was confident in her badassery without stepping on anyone's back to get there. She could see what Eastwood had been into. And she was in damned good shape—yoga or martial arts or whatever she did to stay fit. It was certainly more than Ree's urban fantasista cross-training regimen. Where Ree kept in decent shape, Eriko was toned as all hell.

Ree checked the clock. They weren't due to close up for another half hour. "Not quite yet. I've got to help Grognard close up shop. Will you folks take care of him in the meantime?"

"If by 'take care of' you mean 'extract gossip from,' then you got it, kid."

Ree didn't know if Eastwood had picked up the *kid* appellation from Eriko, or vice versa, but it still rankled. Where it always sounded dismissive coming from Eastwood, from Eriko, it came off more sisterly. Some serious Charisma score on that one.

She grabbed a round of empty glasses and headed back to the bar. Dishes, cleanup, and a drawer countdown later and it was 2:30. Uncle Joe had been ushered off on his merry way, and the few, the proud, the tipsy joined Ree and Grognard as they scaled back up into the city.

Grognard shook Eriko's hand, then grabbed Eastwood to give him a bear hug. "Glad to have you back. Don't make a habit of doing that, okay?"

Eastwood grunted assent, slightly blue in the face with Grognard's grip.

Ree and Grognard bid farewell with their three-stage handshake, ending in a fist bump, then Grognard wandered off to wherever it was he lived. She'd asked three times and had never gotten an answer. After that, she'd stopped asking.

Eriko and Eastwood yelled and rambled like college kids as they made their way home, the weather crisp but not cutting. The freak winter had disappeared as soon as Lachesis did. Weather control was apparently not outside the control of Hexomancy, either.

Looking at the older pair, Ree told herself in Yoda voice, *When forty-five years old I am, rock that much I will not.*

By the time they got to the Dorkcave, Eastwood was draped over Eriko's shoulders, the woman keeping him upright with impressive drunk-management skills.

"We need to get into the door, Tony," Eriko said in a soft voice, the quartet waiting at the door.

"Tony," Ree whispered to Drake, noting her use of his given name.

Eastwood got the door open, and Eriko turned, the door open into the cavernous warehouse/den/man cave.

"A pleasure meeting both of you. Thanks for humoring an old cowgirl."

"The pleasure was ours," Drake responded.

"Good night," Ree said. "I don't know what he liked when you were together, but he's partial to Cap'n Crunch and bacon last I checked."

Eriko nodded. "It used to be Froot Loops, but it's always been bacon."

"You staying in town long?" Ree asked.

"Just a few days, I think. He asked for some backup this week."

"Good call. Give me a ring if any shit goes down," Ree said.

Eriko nodded. She hauled Eastwood up, and said, "Come on, hero. Let's get you to bed."

As the heavy door swung closed, Ree turned to Drake. "So, your place or mine?"

"Given that your abode is better appointed for breakfast and received our last allotment of groceries, it would seem the wise choice, if acceptable."

"Yep," Ree said, and so they went. Ree's inquiries about rounding second base had all been waved off, but waking up gracelessly and unself-consciously intertwined was good enough, for now.

⊗

A leisurely waking at ten, breakfast until noon, and then by two, Ree and Drake were out and about, on "patrol" that was 80 percent walking date, 20 percent actual vigilance. They ran into trouble one time in ten but never stopped gearing up. Ree went for a media power-up only about half of the time, rocking some Buffy mojo that afternoon, having just finished watching "Faith, Hope, and Trick."

Which is why when the lights went out a block away on Stephenson, she was ready.

"That block just lost power," Ree said, turning on like a light switch.

Drake looked around. "It stops on this side of the street. Perhaps just an outage."

"Let's go take a look, just in case," Ree said, power-walking down the street toward the Dorkcave.

Past the divide of Stephenson, everything was out. Drake held his not-a-cane rifle over his shoulder, ready to sling down and fire from the hip in a single motion she'd seen him use a dozen times.

A woman walked down onto the street, holding her phone up for signal. Lights were off across the whole block.

Cars were still in the street, the drivers getting out of their cars. Behind them, drivers in functioning cars honked at the stopped traffic.

"What's going on?"

"My car's dead."

"Is anyone else's phone working?"

The street, empty of the buzz of machinery or automobiles, grew loud again with voices, slivers of worry working their way in at the edges.

"It appears that all machinery has been affected," Drake said.

Ree checked her phone, which was still working, charge holding steady at 82%. She picked up her pace. "There's not a whole lot that would take out lights, power, and cars. And it's not ongoing. It was a one-time thing."

"An electromagnetic pulse, or similar effect."

"If I was going to come after Eastwood, an EMP would be a pretty fantastic opening play," Ree said.

"And you've considered this before?"

"I take my lessons from Batman. I even made plans on how I'd fight you if you went evil."

"Really?" Drake asked.

"Don't be surprised. I have plans of how I'd fight Anya if she went evil. By-product of a lifetime of devotion to the Dark Knight and watching mind-controlled-hero plots on TV."

They reached the block with Eastwood's Dorkcave, which was as dead as the ones around it. People had abandoned their cars and stood and sat in clusters, most staring at their phones.

With the power out, Ree and Drake had to force the door but didn't have to deal with any of the countermeasures. Ree held her phone out on flashlight mode, other hand resting on the hilt of her lightsaber.

"Eastwood? You there?"

No answer. Drake flipped on his shoulder-mounted light, more than doubling the available light.

The room was silent, save for their footfalls.

Two chairs stood facing the screens, each holding a body.

"Shit, shit, shit," Ree said, running.

She stopped a step past the chairs, turning to see Eastwood and Eriko, keyboards on their laps, heads lolled back.

"Wake up!" she shouted, loud enough to wake the dead.

No response.

She checked Eriko's pulse, which was low, but steady.

Eastwood's was the same.

She tapped Eriko on the shoulders, light, then harder. She punched Eastwood in the shoulder, the walls of the room growing closer as her own heartbeat started racing.

"Are they . . . ?" Drake asked.

"They still have pulses; they're breathing, but they're totally unresponsive. If they were jacked in when the EMP went off, what would that do to them?"

Drake stood still, his eyes moving from the pair to the screens, then back. "I . . . I don't know. We should contact Shade, and Grognard. Get Dr. Wells here to tend to them."

"You call Dr. Wells?" she asked, her phone out and dialing Shade before she was done speaking.

The hacker-maker picked up on the first ring. He answered in an affected Max Headroom glitch cadence. "H-h-h-howdy."

"Shade, it's Ree. I'm at Eastwood's, and someone's set off an EMP. He and Eriko . . . I think they were jacked in. They're alive, but totally zoned out. I don't know what to do for them."

Shade said, the cheer dropping straight out of his voice, "Oh, hells. Make sure they keep breathing. Eastwood should have an oxygen kit. I've got a life-support kit for cut-cord victims. I'll be right over. You called Dr. Wells?"

Ree looked to Drake, who was on the phone, other hand plugging his opposite ear. "Yeah, think so. I'm going to call Grognard next."

"Good. I'll be there in twenty-five minutes, traffic permitting. Someone's going to have to go in after them. Their bodies won't last very long without their spirits unless we get them into full-body life support."

"How long is long?"

"A few hours, at most."

"Shit," Ree said. "If this is the third Strega, what would she do next?"

"Try to destroy their bodies, or trap them in Spirit long enough that they fade away. With the connection to their bodies severed, their spirits will have nowhere to return to, and they'll be easy prey. My bet is you've got company coming, maybe before I can get there."

"Got it," Ree said, pulling her lightsaber out of her jacket.

"Keep cool," Shade answered, then hung up.

Ree dialed Grognard, explained the situation. The brewmaster announced he'd be over in twenty minutes, and he'd have Talon show up as well. That was a lot of firepower all of a sudden, though Shade wasn't much for up-close and personal.

"Dr. Wells impressed upon me the fact that she does not make house calls, but that given the situation, she would make an exception. She expects to arrive within the hour."

"An hour?"

Drake shrugged. "She noted that negotiating the sewers with the sort of equipment she'd need takes, and I quote, 'More than a little doing, so hold your horses.'"

"Got it. We need to get eyes on outside. I don't want someone to just blow the building."

"Do you think the Strega would go to those lengths? That

would be a rather conspicuous amount of collateral damage."

Ree found that she was pacing. "I don't even know what to expect. I mean, how much firepower do you need to set off an EMP that kills eight square blocks?"

Drake's trigger finger tapped along the stock of his rifle. "It would be quite an undertaking. Especially to do so without an accompanying burst of sound. I am imagining it was an elaborate working of Hexomancy, specifically directed."

"Bet you're right. But that's some big fucking Hexing. To kill everything, not just shut it off but keep it off? That's a whole order of magnitude above and beyond what Lucretia did with Grognard's."

"Right you are."

Ree and Drake did their best to get ready for a siege, pulling down artifacts and props, arraying an arsenal divided into categories such as "Stuff only Geekomancers can use," "Anyone can use this," and "For sanity's sake, don't touch."

All that remained was the waiting.

It didn't last long. The door creaked and then swung open, revealing a wide silhouette.

Grognard stomped down the stairs into the Dorkcave, his leather coat on fire.

CHAPTER TWENTY-ONE

16-bit Soul

"What happened?!" Ree shouted as Grognard stripped off his jacket and stamped out the flames.

"Fireball trap, I think. Frakking thing hit me dead-on."

"Shit!" Ree said. "Warded?"

Grognard picked the smoking jacket up from the floor and shook it out as she approached. "Damned right. This thing's been with me nearly as long as you've been alive."

Ree whipped out her phone, setting up a mass text to Talon, Shade, and Dr. Wells.

The area around the Dorkcave is trapped. Keep on your toes.

Shade's response came almost instantly, thanks to his smart-shades, no doubt. *Way ahead of you. Also, I'm glad Dr. Wells is coming.*

Talon was followed by a trio of bat-demons and Shade walked in with a bloodied arm. Later, Dr. Wells rang, prompting Ree to open the freight door Drake had installed to handle large deliveries. She rolled in a cart loaded down with gear, a caduceus wand held in her teeth, glowing white and green.

"You okay?"

"Eastwood's not going to like this invoice, I can tell you that much."

As Ree pulled the chain to lower the freight door, it started hailing.

It hadn't been raining or snowing before, nor did Ree remember any clouds in the sky.

"This is bad," Talon said, looping her gladius in slow arcs, a nervous tic that made folks keep their distance. Talon was loaded down in complete Hoplite kit, shield, spear, and all.

Dr. Wells took control, shooing Drake from Eriko and Eastwood's side.

"How long since the EMP?"

Ree double-checked her phone. "Forty-five minutes."

Dr. Wells pulled out a generator and started connecting cables to ports, turning her mobile kit from pile of stuff to Aesclepiomancer's best friend. "Okay. Help me get this set up."

They had Eastwood and Eriko on life support within minutes. In the meantime, the hail got even louder, pounding the freight door and the windows.

"We should get someone outside to make sure Mega-Strega doesn't just drive a bomb into the building or whatever else."

"You volunteering to go out in that?" Grognard pointed to a side window, where golf-ball-size hail stacked up against the glass.

"What you need to do is get someone into Spirit and retrieve these two's souls. Then we can all get out of here," Shade said.

"We could use my Breakthrough Actuator, but it is at my apartment, and I would not be excited to try our luck passing through that gauntlet twice, once with delicate equipment."

"No need. I've got a deck right here." Shade pulled a two-foot-square piece of tech out of his coat. Shade's gear was all over-sized and clunky, but its '80s sheen belied its power. "I can get you jacked in, but it only works for two."

Ree looked to Drake. He nodded. They'd been working together long enough to be on the same page about these things, even before the smooching. "Drake and me. We've handled Spirit before, and we can track Eastwood."

"They will be in the web rather than the regular Spirit realm. My device will take you straight to the web, but I don't have a way of tracking these two's spiritual IP addresses. Once you're in, you're on your own to find them."

"If they're together, I bet I know where they went," Ree said, thinking of the saloon Eriko had mentioned the night before.

"Indeed. The Gulch is our best waypoint," Drake said. "We mustn't tarry."

Grognard tapped his holster. "And when the bad things come knocking, Talon and I will keep them out."

The swordswoman nodded. "I haven't had a good fight in kit in a while. It'll be good to put the new blade through its paces."

"Sounds like a plan," Ree said. "Will you need to pull us out if we have to bug out of the Dorkcave?" she asked Shade.

"Too many bodies to move. We'd need you back here."

"Any way of communicating with us while we're there?"

"Of course. I'll be your shoulder angel the whole way through. Just where I like to be."

Ree dragged over two fold-out metal chairs that Eastwood used for his movie nights. "Sweet. Let's make it happen."

Five minutes later, Shade threw the switch, and Ree's world folded in on itself. The Dorkcave was replaced by a shining green-and-gray landscape, pixelated moons overhead. Everything was rendered in 16 bits, accompanied by a rustling midi wind. Drake included. It was both cool and incredibly disconcerting, a pair of feelings that had become all too common in her weird-ass urban fantasy life. Ree stood up and saw herself in the same 16-bit graphics.

Now, that's weird. She turned her hands back and forth, taking it all in.

They were sitting in an outdoor café, hacker types of every race and denomination sitting and chatting, from '80s neon-clad Cyberpunks like Shade through Matrix-esque folks in PVC to mustachioed hipsters with half of their heads shaved, revealing what she imagined might be "ironic" data ports.

"Shade?" she asked, checking the connection.

"Right here," Shade answered, patented newscaster cheer back in place.

"Why are we in a Mode Seven universe?"

"This is my home port. Renraku Café. Ask for Molly; she'll get you oriented. If you had the time, I'd say you should try out the CPU hot chocolate. It's in-vi-vi-vigorating," he said, sounding like he was about to launch into an infomercial.

"Molly?" Ree asked, thinking of the Sprawl trilogy's heroine.

"The manager and I go way back."

"Got it. You let me know the second we need to move, okay?" Ree said, standing and making her way to the door, trying to keep from freaking out that she had a limited range of motion and a total lack of head control; it bobbed up and down as she walked.

She spotted the server with the mirror shades and tried to hail her. Her coloration meant she was probably a fellow Latina. The woman skated around on rubber wheels whose axles were her feet. She braked to say, "You're new." The woman's accent was odd. She'd need to hear more to place it.

"Yeah, we're friends of Shade. He said you could point us to The Gulch?"

"The Gulch? That's clear on the other side of the city," the woman said, the accent pinging Ree's ears as South African. "You'll need to go through Neo Tokyo and Xian Cubed. Best bet would be to contract a cab. Mel's just finishing up his lunch; I'll see if he can take you."

Ree flashed her best "I love helpful waitstaff!" smile and stood by while the woman skated off, snatching empties from tables in mid-stride.

"How helpful," Drake said.

"I know, right? I wonder how long it'll take us to get across the city, if we've got hounds at the gates."

Ree turned and looked out from the foyer of the café into the city outside. The street had glowing circuitry in the streets and throughout the buildings like veins, all in older green-scale like the computers of her youth. Her dad had sat Ree on his lap with their Commodore Amiga and his older TRS-80, both hand-me-downs from marine buddies.

"This is all rather disconcerting. I have spent time in strange realms, even places where one's form was expressed in a different visual schema, but never have I been whatever this is."

"It's 16-bit graphics; '90s-era video game look."

"That gives me information, but not understanding."

"It means that if we go out to a world map, we may get a bit queasy as things move around."

"Oh, lovely," Drake said.

The server came rolling back, leading a short man with bright green skin, his color intense in contrast to the muted palette around them.

"I'm Mel. Molly says you need to get to The Gulch?"

"That's us. I'm Ree; this is Drake. Can you take us?"

"Yeah, but it'll cost you. Contrast is throttling packets, and traffic's especially bad this time of day."

"As fast as you can get us there is great. And you can bill Shade; we're here on his rig."

The man nodded, moving to the street. They approached a silver car with bright blue accents and no visible wheels. He waved his hand and the doors opened vertically, Delorean-style. "Get in, and buckle up, okay?"

Drake slid into the backseat, leaving Ree to ride shotgun.

Mel slapped on a cabbie hat and started revving up the

cab. The car's startup checklist was extensive, and looked all the more complicated for the limited resolution of their world. But the car did start, and then took off. Straight up. Mel pulled into a lane of flying traffic, the car weaving between flying shipping containers being dragged forward by flying tugs and spirits themselves, in every color, their tails condensing to wispy points in classic Casper fashion.

"So what brings you to the neighborhood? Don't think Shade's mentioned you folks before."

"We're here to check in on some friends," Ree said, not eager to spill the beans about the whole situation to a cabbie they'd only just met. Not that she knew the guy from Adam, but in the TV Tropes universe, cabbies were notorious gossips, and she didn't need word getting out any more than it already would.

Gods only knew how much influence Cosmic Pictures had in the Spirit realms, and they were doubtless still sore about the black eye Ree and the gang had given them in the last days of *Awakenings's* production, Jane's throw down with Rachel McKenzie, and acing their apparently-a-monster-the-whole-time knee-breaker Alex Walters.

Mel didn't push after that, seeming to pick up Ree's desire to play things close to the chest. Between watching the wondrously weird landscape and worrying about the rogues' gallery worth of entities that might be after her at any given moment, she didn't really have the time or temperament for small talk, though there were a hundred questions she wanted to ask about this area.

Fortunately, Drake had her covered.

"How large is this city, in all?"

"We're just one of the clusters, there're another five around the globe. We feed in from the Pacific Northwest and Nor-Cal, so you've got Google, Apple, and Facebook all set up across town." Mel pointed out the window to a mini-skyline with a half-dozen spires shooting up into the clouds.

They passed out of 16-bit land into a higher-res area, and everything changed. Ree looked down to see herself in mid-2000s graphics, as well as the car and the world around them. She felt fuller, less flattened out. And sadly, a bit nauseated.

"That's a hell of a thing," she said.

"Yeah, sorry. It's a bit disorienting the first few times, I hear."

"You hear?" Drake asked. "As to indicate it was never disconcerting to you?"

Mel shrugged. "I'm a Spirit original, coded and patched. Woke up in the late '80s as the first outposts started staking their claim in the area. As parts of the city got upgraded, I adapted."

"Fascinating." Drake was lapping it all up. "What percentage of the city's occupants are mortals, as compared to spirits such as yourself?"

"We're about seventy–thirty, even with the shift workers coming in for the big corps. Everyone's been all about automation and crap. The Amazon Pyramid is more like ninety-ten, the spiders and bots keeping everything going while the bigwigs just pull the big levers at the top."

Mel zigged and zagged the car through traffic, but ahead, the sky grew crowded, a three-dimensional traffic jam. Ree was reminded of the *Doctor Who* episode "Gridlock."

"Nope. Like I said. Contrast is throttling traffic." Far above, a layer of traffic moved smoothly. "Folks who can pay for the fast lane are doing fine."

"How much does that cost?" Ree asked.

"More than you or I could afford, unless you're secretly an employee of a Fortune 500 company."

"Not so much," Ree said. She turned to Drake. "You haven't been holding out on me, have you? You're not secretly a deep-cover Amazon market research agent?"

"I do not even know of what you speak," Drake said, looking a mix of confounded and amused.

"Yeah, that doesn't really exist. Or does it? No, it doesn't." She turned back to Mel. "Any other ways of getting across town?"

"Well, if you want to go back to the street and hoof it, you might make it across town in four hours. Or I could try something really ludicrous."

Shade's voice crackled in, filling Ree's ear. "We've got company, Ree. You better hurry. Talon and Grognard went out to meet it. I think it's a giant robot."

"Got it," Ree said, slightly sad she was missing the giant-robot fight. But when she saw a different giant robot flipping off someone that cut it off in the flying traffic lane, she felt less left out.

Ree sighed, returning to the conversation in the cab. "Tell me about the ludicrous plan."

The ludicrous plan involved flying around back alleys through Neo Tokyo. Which, given the fact that street-level grief-ers had spiritual rocket launchers, turned out to be worse than expected.

"Shit!" Mel said, hauling hard on the wheel and sending the car sideways, driver's side down, passenger side up, and Ree's lunch about to make a reappearance.

A rocket streaked past them, flying through where Ree's seat had been.

"Like I said, this is the ludicrous plan," Mel said.

Drake asked, "Why, pray tell, did you suggest it, then?"

"I get blown up, I just pop up in my garage. And you kids are on tethers, so you'll just head home. I get that you need to see your friends, so I decide to throw out the wild idea. And now, here we are."

The car turned back to right-side up, Ree's stomach dropping like an anvil hitting a Jell-O cake. "Get us to The Gulch in good health, and I'll make sure that Shade pays you handsomely."

"Of course he'll pay me handsomely. He's a slick guy if there ever was one. He don't do nothing he don't do handsomely."

"Great. You go on being complimentary, and I'm going to try to not hurl, 'kay?" Ree said, clutching the dash and the door handle for anything resembling a stable hold.

They raced past and over two- and three-story buildings, under spiritual overpasses, through localized rainstorms, and past a hundred different neon signs in Chinese. If they had been going slower and Ree had been feeling less like she needed to vomit, she was sure she'd have been impressed by how beautiful everything was.

"I believe those youths on the bikes are intending something rather untoward," Drake said. Ree checked the side mirror and saw a trio of red-skinned spirits straight out of *Akira* aiming machine guns and a 50-caliber cannon at Mel's cab.

"Punks," Mel said, hauling on the parking brake as the car burst out of the alley and into a busy street.

The car screamed, metal-on-metal-on-aether, smuggler's turn, the car spinning 270 degrees. As the cab straightened out, he gunned the gas, and Ree lurched back in the seat.

"Sweet Muppety Jesus, please protect me in my time of ridiculous." A hand wrapped around her white-knuckled grip on the seat beside her. She looked back to Drake with a strained smile. It was a terrible and terribly sweet attempt to distract her. She wanted to release her hand and squeeze back, but at just that moment, she wasn't certain that she wouldn't start bouncing around the cab like a Super Ball if she let go of her death-grip on the car.

A minute later, Mel eased up on the throttle and resumed following what Ree took to be the traffic laws, flying in formation with the spirits just fifteen feet above the street.

"See? That wasn't too bad."

"Next time you have a wild idea, please keep it to yourself," Ree said, hyperventilating.

"Indubitably," Drake added. Ree let go of her seat to squeeze Drake's hand.

"Whatever, you know that was fun. A little something to prime the engines, eh, brother?" Mel winked back to Drake.

"Of a sort," Drake said.

"How much longer, taking this way?" Ree asked, her eyes locked on the horizon in a feeble attempt to settle her stomach. The mega-corp towers pierced the cloud layer ahead, shining with neon night light, or maybe just glowing of their own accord.

"Not ten minutes. You kids should loosen up, enjoy the sights. The Google campus has the best adult playground you ever saw, guaranteed. And their jungle gym isn't half bad, either," he said, winking companionably. She leaned against the passenger's-side door, uninterested.

Sexytimes were the furthest thing from her mind, as her stomach was ready to ex-plode, im-plode, and ab-plode at the same time.

But, true to his word, ten minutes later, Mel brought the car down into a parking spot. They'd crossed another dimensional threshold, and were now rendered in photo-realistic CG.

"Shade on the line there?" he asked.

"Hey, Shade?" Ree asked.

"Present," Shade said, his voice thin.

"Everything okay there?"

"Don't know. I haven't heard from Grognard or Talon, but it's quiet outside. How are you doing?"

"Mel wants to rake you over the coals for a bunch of money," Ree said. Mel grinned, his teeth becoming like a shark's.

"Of course. Tell him I've sent an extra little something to be dropped in his box."

"That's not dirty, is it?"

"Cross my heart and hope to die," Shade answered, his bravado forced.

Ree unbuckled her seat belt. "You're all taken care of. Thanks for not getting us killed."

Triumphantly not vomiting, Ree wobbled to her feet and took in the neighborhood. It looked like a cross between the

Seattle of *Shadowrun Returns* and the shadow realm out of the *Lord of the Rings* movies, super-windy shapes attached to everything.

"Is this supposed to be like that?" Ree asked, leaning down to the window level to ask Mel.

The car zoomed off, pulling a half-Immelman to reverse and jet its way out of the neighborhood.

"I suppose he would want to get off to his next fare," Drake said.

"Yeah, not sure it's that," Ree said, eyeing the streets. The empty streets.

"Where'd everybody go?" she asked.

Looking around, the streets and surrounding buildings were strangely quiet. The streets' circuit board lights were flickering, and the buildings around them were all locked up tight, steel grates and gates and bars over windows and doors.

"Either this is a bad part of town, or a normal part of town freaking the fuck out," Ree said.

Looking the opposite direction, Drake said, "I believe it to be the latter. We have company."

Ree turned and saw two almost-cartoonish dust devils, each around five feet tall. Except that as they passed over the street, the circuit boards cracked, sparked, and shattered.

And they were headed right for the pair.

"How are we supposed to fight those?" Ree asked.

"I suggest we run," Drake answered, turning and setting off.

Ree followed suit, and the two raced down the street, looking for any open door or source of higher ground. The shattering and sparks followed them, getting closer.

"Anyone home?" Ree shouted. "A little help here!"

No answer.

A block later Ree played a game of "One of These Things (Is Not Like the Others)." In the middle of the block, between five-story-tall chrome apartment buildings and office buildings, was an all-wood (in appearance at least) saloon, complete with a horse post, a wooden sign, and swinging double doors, though they were full height. Above the door, spelled out in vacuum tubes, was THE GULCH.

"There!" Ree said, gesticulating at the saloon.

Ree poured on the speed, and the two of them practically dove through the door, which proved to be made of not-actually-solid wood.

The pair fell into a tumbling, bruised mass of bodies, and as Ree got her bearings, trying to make the world stop spinning, a voice greeted her.

"Oh, you made it."

"Hi, Eastwood," Ree said. "We're in trouble."

CHAPTER TWENTY-TWO

The Old-School Brigade

The inside of The Gulch was all saloon, all the time, with strong touches of '80s Cyberpunk. Every booth had a screen built into the wall, and instead of the piano, there was a Virtual Reality rig, oversized gloves, and a helmet that looked like the halfway point between the blast shield helmet Luke used to train with and a rejected Daft Punk design.

A pole-thin woman stood behind the bar, one hand on a shotgun. Eriko stood beside Eastwood, and three more Console Cowboys sat at the bar, hands on their sidearms.

"We come in peace!" Ree said, hands up as she stood.

"She's fine." Eastwood put a staying hand out, and the other cowgirls and cowboys stood down, returning to their drinks.

"There're some nasty customers coming along. Good money says they're black-hat Stregas, come to settle the score."

"You don't need to use the cowboy lingo just because we're here."

"Thank gods. You'll catch me dead before you catch me in a poncho or a sombrero."

"Catching us dead may be not outside the realm of possibility," Drake said, one eye on the door.

"So, there's nasty coming," Ree said. "We're here to help people not get dead. What can we do?"

Eastwood looked over to the bartender.

"Marianne, this is Ree and Drake. They're okay. Geekomancer and a Steampunk Tech. Where do you want them?"

The bartender looked Ree up and down. Marianne stood just under six foot tall, plus or minus boots. Ree pegged her as no small part Native American, braided onyx-black hair, with cheekbones that could sharpen a bowie knife. She wore a denim shirt, sleeves rolled back.

"The wards here will hold for a while," Marianne said. "But I won't have us be trapped in here while she just throws crap at us. I want a party to ride out and bloody their noses before they can get to the saloon. You take Eriko and the twins."

A black woman and man stood. Their complexions were smooth and dark. The man had locs; the woman's head was shaved clean. The man had a scar along his neck and the woman hefted a big-ass shotgun over her shoulder.

"Abraham, Luisa, this is Ree and Drake."

The scarred man extended a gloved hand. His voice had the smooth cadence she associated with West Africa, Sierra Leone or the surrounding area. "Abraham. Pleased to meet you."

Handshakes all around, and Ree cranked a thumb at the door. "So how do y'all want to handle the posse out there?"

"We kick their asses, and they leave," said Luisa.

"An admirable plan, but it may be desirable to coordinate more closely," Eriko said.

Marianne gestured to the Cyberpunks. "It's our turf, so we'll take point. You two can watch our back and play swing support."

Eastwood picked up the thread. "Ree, your tricks won't work nearly so well here; it's all mental might-makes-right. Fight like you would normally, but you have to visualize your actions, otherwise the magic won't work. Lightsaber won't ignite, blaster won't fire. Better to make mental constructs and keep them throughout the fight than to switch up. It was the biggest change I had to make, getting all versatile with props. But here, it's Green Lantern–style, got it?"

"You better try it out before we get going," Eriko said.

Ree pulled out her lightsaber and thumbed it on. The blade did nothing. She switched it off, then on again, visualizing her blade springing to life.

And so it did. Delighted, she held her focus, and waved it around in a slow pattern, making sure the blade maintained its integrity.

"Draw," Marianne said, tossing an empty bottle at Ree. She spun and cleaved the bottle in two, pieces clattering to the floor.

"And now you," Eriko said to Drake.

"Where do I fire?" Drake asked.

A pair of the regulars stepped away from a portion of the wall. A third had short hair an androgynous figure—flipped a panel to reveal a shooting gallery, cans and pins twenty yards back.

"Nice trick," Ree said.

"Comes in handy," Marianne answered. "Spirit isn't nearly as restrictive when it comes to the laws of physics controlling things like buildings being bigger on the inside. Give it a shot, Hornblower."

Drake squared off, took aim, and then knocked three pins down in a row, the bursts from his rifle coming out pure white, glowing.

"That'll do," Eastwood said. "Everyone else, you better be ready to lend a hand, or I'm cutting you all off from my screener copies, got it?"

Grunts and murmurs of assent seemed to be good enough for Eastwood. He drew his blaster and looked to Eriko. "After you."

She laughed. "Screw that. You take point!"

Once they got outside, the Console Cowfolk out in front,

the crowd waiting for them included a half-dozen dust dev-ils and several humanoid shadow-figures with glowing red eyes, riding half-transparent spirit-horses.

"You here for me?" Eastwood asked.

Whinnies and growls came in response.

"Where's the Strega? Or is she like the last one, too cow-ardly to face me in person?"

A voice spoke from all around them. It was a woman's voice, gravelly, a five-packs-a-day kind of strained. "You al-ways thought you were so special. And so good at getting other people to die for you. My sisters and I have seen your crimes, and now I am here to cut your overstretched thread and restore balance."

"You gonna do that by voice-over-ing at me, then?" East-wood asked.

Instead of another response, the creatures charged.

Ree focused on her lightsaber prop, and a blue-white blade of focus popped on. The blade felt different in her hand, less weighty but more substantial, somehow. She spun the blade as the creatures approached, then dropped into stance.

The fight turned into a messy melee faster than servers dropping on an MMO's launch day. The Console Cowboys and Cowgirls mowed down the spirits, fanning the hammer and lashing out with knives. But the creatures just came back for more punishment.

All the while, guns jammed, blades broke, and Eastwood's friends slipped and tripped, Hexomancy running wild. This Strega's hexes had a red-and-black hue and smelled of sulfur.

Ree fought around the edges, keeping anyone from get-ting flanked. Drake took a high position and played sniper, downing horses and stopping two-on-ones before they could happen.

Spiritual lightsaber blazing, she chopped through the dust devils, speared demon horses, and took the heads off shadowy figures.

But when one dissolved, another sprung up.

"They just keep coming!" Ree hissed through gritted teeth, chopping and weaving as quickly as she could. But it was like ghostly whack-a-mole, and nowhere near as satisfying as walloping things with a mallet.

"The summoning spell has to give out sometime," Eastwood said. Beside him, Abraham dropped to a knee. Above him, a demon horse reared up to kick. A shot from Drake took the creature's head off at the neck, dropping the spirit to the ground.

But they kept coming. Luisa lost her shotgun in the gullet of a horse, and the weapon vanished when the spirit vaporized. She returned to the fight with a pair of spiritual pistols.

Drake's bursts came more sporadically. Ree checked over her shoulder to see him sweating like he'd been in a sauna. Her slicked hair told her she wasn't doing much better, her mental exhaustion expressing in her spiritual form.

But the damned things just kept coming.

"Back inside!" Ree yelled, seeing the writing on the wall. They needed reinforcements in a big way. Ree cut apart two dust devils, making her way to give Abraham a hand up. Eriko buried a bowie knife in a shadow-man, then joined the group.

But Eastwood kept fighting.

"We need a tactical retreat!" she yelled. Eastwood snarled, cut the leg off a spirit-horse, then broke off and joined the group. Ree stood aside and covered their retreat with a construct phaser, ushering Drake inside before she dived through the double doors.

The saloon doors sealed as she hit the door, becoming a flat wall. The rest of the windows had done the same, the building going into lockdown.

"Well, that was an exercise in frakking frustration," Eastwood said, tromping to the bar.

"That bad?" Marianne asked. The others had gathered around one table, weapons out and ready.

"It's bad. The spirits re-form or are replaced as soon as we ace them. The Strega's got a ton of power here."

Shade's voice came back through to Ree. "You there? Ree? The door is breached, but Grognard and Talon are still keeping the things out. Grognard keeps yelling things about how he wishes he had his beer with him this time. I don't think we have long before we'll need to move, which means you need to come back, pronto."

"No can do, Shade," Ree said out loud, for the cowfolk to hear. "We're under siege here, and I don't think this barkeep is going to abandon her post, either."

"Then do whatever you can to siphon off some power or whatever. The waves slowed in the last two minutes, but now they're surging again."

Lightbulb.

"The more we fight here, the easier it is for the folks guarding our bodies," Ree said. That got people moving, the remaining gunslinger-hackers on their feet.

"This time, we all go out to face them," Eastwood said.

The barkeep pulled a hatchet and a peacemaker out from behind the bar. "Tony, when this is all over, you and I are going to have some words about your crap-ass timing, you hear me?"

"Yes, ma'am," Eastwood said, taking some gauze out from his coat and awkwardly wrapping it around a bite on his left hand. Eriko rolled her eyes at Eastwood with a smile and took over the binding.

"We have to stay together, keep them from overwhelming us," Ree said.

Marianne chuckled. "Girl, I know your momma was somebody, but we've been fighting rogue spirits since you were running around in Wonder Woman Underoos."

"That's basically my whole life," Ree countered. "I wore Wonder Woman underwear yesterday. They're great."

"Good for you. Now listen to your elders." Marianne stopped by the door. "Teams of three or four. Keep by the door so we can retreat into here and take up cover. Things go sour, I'll call the retreat, then we all go out the back to the rides. But I ain't gonna retreat. We've held this place through two centuries in Internet time, and damned if some mono-loguing witch is going to kick me out. You hear me?"

"Yeah!" shouted the gunslingers.

"Now let's kick their spectral asses all the way back to Hades!" Marianne said, shouldering her way through the once-again-door.

The group poured out, the Cyberpunks moving smoothly, psyching themselves up. Ree and Drake flanked Eastwood and Eriko. Outside, the monstrous crowd had shrunk. But at the center stood one important addition: a black-cloaked figure, face shrouded.

"Finally," said the figure, in the same smoke-stained voice as had taunted them before. "This is long overdue. His Grace will be overjoyed when I present your head and your blade."

The woman held out a hilt, and flicked on a ghostly red light-saber. Eastwood flicked on his own blade, and the battle resumed.

"I've got a bad feeling about this," Ree said as she followed Eastwood into battle, Eriko on her right, Drake on her left.

Willing her own spirit-sword into being, she waded into the mooks, pushing them back so that Eastwood could en-gage the Strega straight-on.

The dust devils were easy to deal with; she just had to keep her grip strong on the lightsaber, which meant not los-ing focus. She did her best impression of a Jedi Battle Mind, flowing from strike to strike, weaving back and forth, watch-ing as Eriko fired point-blank, mowing down sprits and Hex creatures of all types. All of a sudden, the badassery of the Witch Hunter in *Diablo III* seemed far more feasible, seeing this woman stand within melee range with creatures of all sorts and keep her cool, keeping up her fire.

But keeping creatures off of Eastwood was a harder task than Eriko was making it look. Ree was practically jumping around the street, pushing spirits back, cutting down those that broke from the pack to attack Eastwood, who was in full-on Duel of the Fates mode with the Strega.

The pair cut and thrust and jumped and spun, the Strega's strikes aggressive, risky, which Eastwood met with careful, defensive blocks and cuts. Eastwood liked to figure out an opponent's weakness and then go for the kill, a fighting style oddly more measured than his frequent devil-may-care attitude toward the weird and wonderful world of magic.

Ree wanted to clear out the spirits so she could dive in to help Eastwood, end the duel before one of the Strega's strong-arm strikes could push past Eastwood's defenses.

But the spirits kept coming.

Drake sniped dust devils out from around Ree, keeping the creatures from overwhelming her. Drake was scarily good at firing where she had just been, providing covering fire despite the chaos of the melee. It was an utter delight and ass-saver to see the Precise Shot feat at work.

Ree speared one spirit through the gut and tripped another, spinning her blade to finish it off. She saw Darth Atropos blow right through Eastwood's defenses and slash him across the left shoulder. The arm went limp like someone had shut it off, and he retreated, fighting one-handed.

Do or do not; there is no try, she told herself, and jumped into the fray, raising her blade to catch Darth Atropos's downward slash, which would have taken Eastwood's head. The blades met, clashed, and the blade cast the inside of the Strega's hood red, the face still shadowed.

"Foolish girl. His fate is inevitable; it has been foretold. You broke my sisters, but I cannot be stopped. He has decreed it. If you give him up, I may let you live."

Ree pushed the Strega's blade away and backed up, giving herself space. "Somehow, I doubt that."

Drake fired into the duel, but the Strega swatted his shots away with ease, disdain clear in her movements. She was a quicksilver juggernaut, confident and inexorable.

Why the Strega didn't just send Atropos first, Ree couldn't say. But that's how it went. Everything with them worked in threes, a progression. Might have something to do with elemental association. Hex storms associated with spring, spring Strega, spring equinox. The magical world was full of often-imperceptible rules and traditions that bounded magicians and monsters into habits, nervous tics turned into ontological boundaries.

Less thinking, more fighting, she told herself. She kept her movements as small as possible to give herself the time to counter Darth Atropos's incredible speed.

Eastwood reentered the fight, pressing the Strega from the flank, making her parry around her back and over her head while she assaulted Ree. But it barely slowed her down.

The Strega pushed Ree's parry over to her right side, then chopped at her neck. Her buff jacket turned most of the blow, but she lost feeling at her shoulder, like someone had toggled that part of her body off. Reeling, Ree watched through watering eyes as the Strega turned toward Eastwood, raising dust as she spun, raining blows down on him like lightning strikes.

Ree took a quick survey of the field. Several of the gunslingers were injured, clustered back by the saloon. Luisa and Abraham fought back-to-back, bloodied but holding on. Eriko was slowing, but still rocking, always two steps ahead of the creatures.

Until one materialized right behind her. The action was too far away for Ree to reach her, so instead she reached forward and imagined a bolt of energy lancing out at the dust devil. A phaser appeared in her hand, and she fired, disintegrating the creature, a cloud of dissolving pixels breaking on the woman's shoulders.

Eriko turned and saluted Ree, then resumed her dance.

But saving one gunslinger's back had put the other in jeopardy.

Eastwood was on the ground, his lightsaber gone.

"Hey, you!" Ree yelled, too pressed for time to come up with a quip. She dashed forward and swung at the woman's shoulder level. The Strega turned and parried the blow, quick-stepping in a circle to turn and push Ree's blow through, sending her off balance and toppling to the ground beside Eastwood.

Ree brought up her lightsaber, guarding both of them. Drake shot again, and the Strega parried the shot, sending it lancing into the hip of Abraham. Luisa leaped up to cover him.

"You all need to get out of here," Eastwood said. "I'm the one she wants. I won't let anyone else die for me."

"Git!" Marianne said, recalling the wounded gunslingers. Drake covered their retreat, the spirit posse diminished, but big enough to keep tying up the cowboys.

The pair got to their feet, glowing spirit blades up and active once more, blue and green matched against red.

"That means you two, too," Eastwood said, blades whirring, the Strega a match for both of them at once, her blade moving exactly where it needed to be to cover her from every angle. Darth Atropos had obviously spent a lot of time with a blade, and the Force or Hexomancy or something kept her one step ahead of the game. She didn't even look like she was pushing herself all that hard, though if she was maintaining the Hex storm and the assault on the Dorkcave, that'd explain where the rest of her focus was going.

"How we doing, Shade?" she asked, hoping for better news in the real world.

"They just keep coming, Ree. Not as many, but Grognard's getting real ornery. He wants to leave."

"No can do. Keep it up. Maybe throw some of Eastwood's weird, dangerous crap at them."

"I heard that," Eastwood said, dodging back and leaping forward with a thrust. Darth Atropos parried down into the lunge and then lashed out with a roundhouse kick to the face, dropping the cowboy in a heap, spiritual dust rising around him.

Ree cut at the woman's head, trying to flow through to where the woman's blade wasn't. She didn't get the headshot, but she cut into the cloak. The woman's hair flipped free, draped down over her eyes in classic heavy-metal-baddie fashion.

Recognition hit Ree like the fist of an angry god.

The haunted features, the curly hair. The upturn at the edge of her mouth.

Ree's voice cracked as she said, "Mom?"

CHAPTER TWENTY-THREE

Darth Atropos

Branwen didn't respond. There was no recognition on the woman's face.

She raised her blade, pointing it at Eastwood. "The Duke has ordered your death. His will be done."

Just a whole lot of hate.

The Strega lunged, and Ree parried on instinct, back-pedaling as fast as she could, late to every parry, the blows sending shock up her arm. Ree jumped to the side, covering herself with her blade, and saw the Strega cut through the pillar at the corner of the saloon, spinning with a snarl.

Ree came up, ready to face the spirits that had doubtlessly been flanking her.

But they were all gone, the street empty. Ree heard the sounds of engines from behind the saloon, then the howling of winds.

Must have let them go to focus on us. It was nice to be worth someone's full attention, especially when that person is your brainwashed undead-or-something mother, returned to exact revenge on behalf of the Dork Lord of Hell that controlled her soul.

Or something. Ree was waaaay off book here, making it all up as she went.

Dear Dad,

Not that I've told you any of this, but Mom's back, and she's gone all Dark Side. I'm really afraid that the only way I'll be able to keep her from killing Drake, me, or Eastwood, is to kill her. And that's way easier said than done, though saying it would make me barf up my stomach and lower intestine.

If you could arrange for the universe to give me a break, maybe some cosmic paternal counterforce or something, that'd be awesome.

I'm sorry I didn't tell you. I hope I get the chance to say so in person,

Your Loving but Harried Daughter,

Ree

Branwen chopped and slashed and stabbed at Ree, who could barely keep up with her parries as she tried to circle back around to let Eastwood back her up.

"Mom, it's me. It's Ree. Your daughter!" Ree kicked at her mother's leg. The woman took the blow and stepped back to gain her balance. Ree took the opportunity to jump back and talk. "You sat me on your knee and we watched *Star Wars* a hundred times. You'd crawl in bed with me when I was sick and we'd listen to the BBC *Lord of the Rings* tapes."

Branwen charged again.

Ree's voice grew strained as her focus wavered. "You made me a Princess Leia outfit when I was four and the wig was so itchy that I broke out in hives.

"Don't you remember any of that?"

Eastwood swung at Branwen's back, and the woman ducked to roll beneath the blow, cutting at Ree's knee.

The blade passed just over her kneecap, cutting through the buff jacket and slicing through her thigh. The blade wasn't really a lightsaber, but her leg wasn't really her leg. The pain was sure as hell real, though. Ree put all of her weight on her other leg, holding her guard down to keep her mother at bay.

Eastwood took point, slicing and stabbing with his good hand.

"Listen, damnit! It's me, Eastwood! You got me out of more scrapes than I could count, pulled me literally out of a gutter and out of the bottle, and now you're what, a puppet for the Duke? Do you know what he's made me do, what he's put me through to get you back?"

"That woman is dead. The Duke has shown me what must be done." Branwen stepped back and leveled her lightsaber at Eastwood. "You must die." A blast from behind took Branwen across the shoulder, her blade too far away to block.

"But first, the adventurer." Branwen turned and shot spirit force lightning at Drake. The electricity came out red, and the smell of sulfur filled Ree's nose once more. Somehow, the Duke had taken her mother's specialized Geekomancy and super-charged it with his power, Hexomancy layered on top of her existing power. Or maybe she had always been that powerful.

Drake half jumped, half fell off his perch, missing part of the blast. But not nearly all. The errant hero writhed on the ground, red energy arcing off him and onto the circuit-board streets.

"No!" Ree plodded forward, putting weight onto her in-jured leg. Pain stabbed out like a grenade exploding inside her muscles, but she pushed onward. She cut at Branwen, Eastwood on her left, pulling the Strega off of Drake.

"You deal with me first! Don't you dare ignore me, ignore him. Do you know what you did to to my dad? Your hus-band? It nearly broke him. He worked seventy-hour weeks for years when you left, trying to make ends meet."

Ree cut and slashed, parried and pushed, her anger giving her strength. "We moved a half-dozen times, chasing opportunity after opportunity. He was lost without you, and so was I. All so you could go off and get yourself killed and brought back as a monster? No fucking way. You wake the fuck up so I can yell at you properly."

Working together, Ree and Drake found a rhythm. And slowly, they turned the tide of the fight. Eastwood stayed mobile, pressing Branwen when she tried to isolate Ree. Ree kept her weight on her good leg, refusing to give ground.

Branwen knocked Ree's blade aside with a double-handed slash, powering through Ree's guard. Branwen followed it up with a spinning back kick that knocked Ree off her feet. Ree landed hard, biting her lip.

Pain spilled over as she lay crumpled on the ground, bruised, cut, and tired.

With Ree out of the way for a moment, Branwen tore into Eastwood. Eastwood swung his dead arm out to take the cut. This time, the blade didn't just pass through and kill the nerves, it sliced the geek's hand off at the wrist. Eastwood cried out, dropping to his knees.

Branwen brought her blade up, ready to take his head off. And with the rig he used to get into Spirit fried, there'd be no tether, no golden parachute. It'd be game over.

Yelling louder than she knew she could, Ree reached out with her free hand, and a wave of energy knocked both Branwen and Eastwood off of their feet. Ree stood and plodded forward, feeling like a busted-ass Terminator, but a Terminator nonetheless.

"Stop now, Mom. This is the man you love. If you won't wake up for me, won't wake up for Julio, do it for him. Someone in your life has to be important enough to you for you to push through the Duke's bullshit. The mom I knew was a loving woman, who taught me compassion, to love humanity for all of the wonderful things we've done, to focus on joy, and to look for the best in people. That's why I'm not going to give up on you, even if it kills me."

Ree lowered her blade, leaving herself defenseless. This was a Jedi fight, so she'd take the high road. Because she couldn't do the other thing, couldn't strike down her own mother.

"You're giving up?" Branwen asked, raising her blade for the killing blow.

"No. I'm believing."

Something passed over Branwen.

Her voice came out thin, uncertain. "Ree?"

"Yes, it's fucking Ree! Are you still in there?"

Branwen stepped back and shut her blade off. She raised a shaking hand to Ree.

"My little girl," she said, and every bit of tension dropped out of Ree like rain out of a cloud. Her mother wrapped her in her arms for the first time in more than fifteen years.

Ree dropped her own spirit-blade and returned the hug, her face hot with tears. "Thank gods, Mom. I thought you were all the way gone; it wasn't you anymore."

"It wasn't. Wasn't all of me, at least," Branwen sobbed. She squeezed Ree tighter, injuries flaring. But Ree did not give one flying fuck about those, because her mom was back. The woman who had left a lifetime ago, who had first introduced her to *Star Wars*, who had taught her to be a storyteller. It was like the return of a phantom limb, all pins and needles, but with such a sense of familiarity and comfort she could just fall asleep right there.

Except.

"Drake!" Ree said, pulling back from her mom. She rushed over to the adventurer, forgetting her injuries. She took the fall well, rolling through the accumulated dust from the spirits and checking Drake's pulse.

"He's still breathing."

"Shade, get him out, if you can. He's hurt here; he needs some of that soul goop he makes. I'm working on getting everyone out of here."

"I can't leave," Branwen said. "He'll know. Hells, he's probably already on his way. You two need to go, now.

He'll wipe my memory again, and keep sending me after you. I'm sorry." She looked to Eastwood. "You've crossed him too many times, Tony. This isn't like with the Frats, or the *Clone Wars* fights. He's calling in all of his cards to get this done. The Dork Lords are turning on him, think he's weak, can't keep his house in order."

Branwen's eyes darkened, her lip curling in a snarl. She took a breath and the darkness passed. "The Strega are all souls he's claimed and put to work. He's got another dozen where we came from. He enhances their power and warps their minds with prophecies and this sense of purpose, blows smoke up their asses about preserving the balance. It's a de-monic Room 101, wrapped in chains and force-fed hate. You can't resist, not for long. You can't help but take in his poison. It gets in your blood, in your head. He'll keep sending the Strega, as many as it takes. You have to run, now."

"I'm not letting you go again," Eastwood said. "Not after all of the lines I've crossed to bring you back. Let the Duke come."

"You rang?" spoke a deep, resonant voice.

Hairs on the back of Ree's neck shot out like she'd been electrocuted. Ree turned on her good leg to see the Thrice-Retconned Duke of Pwn, Chief of the Dork Lords of Hell, standing in the street, his midnight-black suit in perfect con-dition, red-gray skin and a too-wide smile under his fedora.

"I didn't expect that you'd be able to shake her free of the memory curse I laid. That was quite impressive. But I see every-thing my Strega see, so it doesn't matter what you remember. In fact, this whole prophecy, this year of skirmishes, has done me a great deal of good, as now I get to settle two accounts at once."

"Go choke on a VHS of *Highlander 2*, asshole," Ree spat.

"Charming," the Duke said. "Come now, Branwen. We have bills to collect." He stepped forward, a hand held out, palm up.

Branwen grabbed Ree around the wrist, squeezing tight. "No. I'm not turning on them. Punish away, do whatever you want. But you're not going to make me hurt them again."

"Oh, but I am."

"Not likely," Eastwood said, pulling out a sphere in chrome and silver, the size of a softball. "This is an aether bomb. Are you familiar with them?"

The Duke said nothing, just took a step back.

"I thought so. This goes off, it will crater ten city blocks of Spirit. And when the Censors come along to figure out what happened, they'll get a whiff of your influence, and then all of Spirit will come to you looking for reparations, including those tech bigwigs," Eastwood said, pointing up to the towers of Apple, Google, and more, well within the range of the bomb.

"Where did you get an aether bomb?" the Duke asked.

"It's impressive what you can find when you tell people that you're aiming to kill one of the Dork Lords of Hell. Seems like you've racked up an even bigger list of enemies than I have. And that's impressive; just ask Ree."

Ree laughed, half in agreement, half nerves. Okay, mostly nerves.

"Here's how this goes," Eastwood said. "You make a move, I set off the bomb and a statistically significant portion of Spirit gets wiped off the map, all signs pointing back to you. The Dork Lords offer you up on a plate to assuage the Censors, and your empire goes poof."

Eastwood took a step forward. "Or, you release Branwen from her bondage, return her to Earth alive and well. Along with Drake, Ree, Eriko, and all of the Console Cowboys."

The Duke laughed, but it sounded hollow, forced. "Your perception of how black-and-white this situation is would be charming if I didn't know you so well. If you set off the bomb, you die permanently and will be remembered as the worst villain Spirit has seen since the inquisition."

"I'm all out of fucks to give, Dukey. The only people I care about are right beside me. I do right by them, or I'm nothing."

Eastwood grinned. "Plus, if you let them go, you get something even better. You get me."

Fuuuck, Ree thought, seeing Eastwood's gambit for what it really was. This was his Hail Mary of redemption, his Iron Man in the portal, his *Matrix* Crucifixion.

The Duke's eyes lit up. "Interesting. You would come, without contest, and do my bidding for all time?"

"You sign, I'm all yours. But you leave them out of it, and renounce all claim on their souls," he said, pointing to Branwen, Ree, and Drake in turn. "Those are the terms. Otherwise we all go up in a big puff of nothing."

"Don't do this, Tony," Branwen said. "You don't know what he'll do to you."

"Nothing I don't deserve," Eastwood said. "This is the best way, for everyone. The world needs you in it. Ree needs you. It doesn't need me anymore. That's what this year taught me."

"Like hell!" Ree said. "You're an asshole, but you've saved countless lives."

"Not countless. Three hundred and seven," Eastwood said. "And it's not enough. I've gotten people killed, stood by while they died. It doesn't matter how many lives I save, if I can't save you all."

Eastwood took another step forward, still ten feet away from the Duke.

"You make the oath on your power, and then it's all over."

The Duke's smile grew even wilder, his face making a decidedly Cheshire cat–like shape. "Oh, but I'm so enjoying the tension. The noble self-sacrifice, the grand gesture." The Duke stepped forward. "How you must have stayed up nights thinking about what you would do if it came to this." Another step.

Eastwood matched him, backing off, keeping his distance, hand still on the aether bomb.

The Duke continued. "How you must have swelled at the thought of getting to burn out and not fade away."

"Talk all you want. The offer is the offer. You swear on your power, or this all goes up in screams."

"There's got to be another way, Tony," Branwen said. "To lose you after you've spent all this time trying to save me . . ."

Eriko's voice cut out of the darkness. "Do it, Tony. It's the right call." She limped out of an alley, spirit-revolver in one hand, the other wrapped tight around her middle, like she was holding something in, stanching a wound.

Eastwood looked to Eriko, then to Branwen, like he was pulled in seven directions at once. The conflict played out on his face, but only for a second. He'd made his choice, and he'd stick with it. The dude was nothing if not stubborn.

"If only one of us gets to live out our lives, it should be you," Eastwood said to Branwen. "Be a mother again. I was a shitty father figure, anyway."

Ree's heart was pounding so fast, so loud, that she let the moment to snark pass right by.

Eriko limped over to join the group. Ree wrapped an arm around the wounded cyberpunk, bracing her up.

"So, Dukey, what do you say? The catch of the day, or years of blame, trials, cold wars, and infighting down in Hell, the Dork Lords carving up your kingdom into a hundred conventions and fiefdoms?"

The Duke laughed, the sound like an avalanche at the bottom of the Grand Canyon. "You'll have your deal, Eastwood. I just wanted to wait for you all to fall over one another being noble and repressed."

Ree was still on a hair trigger, ready to run, fight, or both at the same time. Her emotional landscape was a fucking disaster zone, love and fear and gratitude and anger and compassion adding up to a near-suffocating pool of feeling. . . .

The Duke flicked his hand, and a worn vellum parchment appeared, text blazing into existence, ornate red lettering filling the page. The Duke put thumb to the contract in the bottom left corner, then rolled it back up and lobbed the parchment to Eastwood. The geek tossed the bomb sideways to Branwen, who snatched it out of the air without blinking.

Eastwood caught the contract and unfurled, reading, one eye still on the Duke.

Ree kept a hand on the spiritual blaster, though she had every reason to believe that these weapons would likely do jack-all to the Duke.

"Ree?" Eastwood asked, indicating the contract. She stepped over and held the parchment in the air, unmoving thanks to the not-quite-physics of the Spirit realm.

Eastwood signed the contract, which burst into black light, then flew back over to the Duke, rolling up into his hand. The Duke opened his mouth wide and stuffed the contract down his throat like a sword-swallower.

He smiled, then snapped his fingers. "Now, boy. We should away. You have one minute for goodbyes, as per the contract."

Eastwood handed the bomb to Branwen, then hugged her like he'd never let go.

Ree stepped back to let them have their moment, lovers reconnected after years. She imagined what she'd have to say to Drake if she were in the same position. *I'd never put myself in such a crappy situation.* Though really, she had no way of knowing.

A few moments later, they disentangled. Branwen stepped back, and Eriko limped up, grabbing on to Eastwood like he was a life raft. But not for balance. She dug her nails into the man's coat, whispering something in his ear. Her eyes were wet, puffy. Not that Ree's were any better, with the emotional roller coaster they'd all been through, one last drop just around the corner.

Eriko squeezed Eastwood tight one last time, then let go. Branwen offered a hand to help, but Eriko shrugged away, standing on her own two feet.

Finally, Eastwood extended a hand to Ree. "You've done more and better than I could have asked for, even if you were a pain in the ass."

Ree took his hand, and shook. "Right back at you. The pain-in-the-ass part."

Eastwood stepped back, turning to the Duke.

"You come back at us, I won't hesitate to put you down," Ree said.

"Please don't," Eastwood said, walking forward to the Duke, hands shaking, clearly trying to put on a strong face, to see his heroic gesture through to the end.

The Duke spoke again. "Know that The Gulch is not safe, never will be safe. Branwen, Ree. I'll be seeing you later." He gave them the same wave that Vir gave Mr. Morden, making it as creepy as a cute gesture has ever been, menace and delight mixed like a cocktail. He wrapped his red hands around Eastwood, pulled the man into his form, and the pair imploded, collapsing into a puff of sulfur.

And then, nothing.

Branwen dropped to her knees and screamed. It was a scream of defeat, of triumph, of freedom, of loneliness. It was a hundred different things all at once. It was open season in her heart, every doubt and joy and frustration all exploding and rampaging at once.

Ree went to her mother, hugging and crying, overjoyed and deflated.

An indeterminate minute later, she let go and went back to Drake, burned but still breathing.

She touched her earpiece, calling up the line out of Spirit. "Shade, we need a way out. But there's a wrinkle. There's four of us coming back—me, Drake, Eriko, and Branwen."

"Is Eastwood okay?"

"He's gone, Shade. It'll be Branwen coming back with us. We need a way to get her out without a tether or whatever."

"Ah," Shade said.

"I can get myself out," Branwen said. "I've done it before."

Damn, Mom. Ree nodded, impressed.

"Just the three, then."

"Understood," Shade said. "Just a minute.

A silent moment passed, spectral winds passing through the street.

Ree and Branwen pulled Drake up and held him between them, still out for the count. His burns looked nasty, though the jacket had taken much of it. Spiritual armor or something. He had spent years and years adventuring through Spirit realms, after all.

"Portal opening now," Shade said.

A two-yard-tall circle opened up in front of them, the portal showing the Dorkcave, Shade and Dr. Wells standing by.

"You good, Mom?" Ree asked.

Branwen put her hands together, took a long breath, and blinked out of existence.

A moment later, she blinked into sight in the Dorkcave.

The two women stepped through with their unconscious companion, and the world went white.

⚅

Ree woke up in her seat, Drake beside her. He was distinctly not burned to a crisp.

She leaned over and planted a kiss on his cheek, waking him up at a lurch. Ree squeezed his shoulder. "It's fine, we're safe. I'm here."

Drake relaxed into her touch, looking around.

"Where's Eastwood?"

"He's gone," Branwen said. She stood with Shade and Dr. Wells. Eriko reclined in her chair, asleep, but Eastwood's chair was empty.

Ree pointed at the chair. "Where's his body?"

Shade said, "Disappeared shortly before you checked in. From what Branwen tells me, the contract was sufficiently binding to bind his body to his spirit, the both of them transported to hell at once."

Ree hmmphed. She didn't really have energy left for anything else.

She wobbled to her feet and offered a hand to Drake

as he did the same.

Turning, she saw Grognard and Talon, each leaning against a row of the stacks, bloodied and looking three miles past exhausted.

"Thanks for having our backs," Ree said, sufficiently battered and wrung dry that she actively had to focus to put any real emotion into her words.

Grognard raised the head of his halberd an inch in recognition. Talon nodded.

"I think this calls for milkshakes. Lots of milkshakes. Mostly so that we don't collapse from lack of blood sugar," Ree said, looking at the crowd.

Dr. Wells said, "I'll stay here with Eriko. That long spent with a cut tether has weakened her."

"You good to hold the fort, then?" Ree asked, realizing that the Keeper of the Dorkcave wasn't due back anytime soon. Or, really, at all.

At that thought, her phone buzzed a notification.

When she pulled it out, the screen was white, with black text. Eastwood's voice spoke the message.

"If you're hearing this, it means that my eventuality for the Thrice-Retconned Duke of Pwn's return has gone off, and I'm being fitted for torture cuffs or something unimaginably nasty in hell, like watching *Manos: Hands of Fate* for all time alongside a devoted, ecstatic audience that just won't shut up about how awesome it is.

"Ree, if you'll have it, the Dorkcave is yours. If my gambit brings Branwen back, I need the two of you to move on with your lives, keep fighting the good fight, and not try to get me out. That move never works out well, I should know. And even if it did, the Duke's backlash would be even worse.

"I've made my choice, and please let it stand. If I frakked that all up, and neither of them are around, I want Grognard to look after the place. Sorry I couldn't stick it out, brother.

"Whoever else hears this, keep following your passions,

turn them into something positive, some way to help. I got wrapped up in guilt and revenge and arrogance, and I lost sight of what got me into this whole thing: I wanted to be a hero; I wanted to help people. I lost perspective, and now I'm paying the price.

"Eastwood out."

Branwen coughed back a sob, and Ree leaned into Drake, cacophony of emotion still deafening.

"And after milkshakes, I'm going to need a lot to drink," she said.

"I've got that covered," Grognard said, pulling himself up, chain mail rustling. He extended a hand to Talon, who stood as well.

"That was a hell of a thing. Kit worked out fine, though." Her shield was dinged in a hundred places, and the spear was stained red a foot past the blade. But even bone-tired as Talon looked, she was proud and pleased in equal degrees. This was a woman born to fight, and she loved what she did. It was scary but infinitely useful.

"I know the Burger Bin is accepting, but this might push even their limits," Ree said, making her way to the door, shedding weapons and armor as she went to slightly mitigate how badly they'd stick out of the crowd.

Once they'd had food, she could start the daunting task of processing all the crap she'd just gone through.

But first, shakes.

Breath of Life

They got more than a few stares at the Burger Bin, even de-armored and with the big, obvious weapons left at the Dorkcave with Dr. Wells. But money talked, and the group racked up a $120 bill and pushed two tables together to have their version of post-battle shwarma in the form of burgers, fries, and milkshakes.

Oh, the *milkshakes*. Choirs of angels should accompany the Burger Bin's milkshakes. Even their straight-up vanilla was inspired—homemade ice cream, sumptuous texture, and with none of the chalky aftertaste that was endemic among crappy corner-store and chain milkshakes. This was the real shit. And for Ree's favorite, every flavor combined to make a taste symphony, a seventeen-hundred-calorie yumpocalypse.

The world went from 360 to 1080p as caffeine and blood hit Ree's system, and by the time the monstrous concoction was half-gone, she felt like she could rejoin the conversation.

Branwen caught up with Grognard and Shade, going back over several years' worth of milestones. Drake sat beside Ree, a comforting arm around her shoulder, leaving him to eat with his left, which he did quite adeptly. *Clever boy*, she thought.

"I'm going to have a lot of catching up to do, aren't I?" Branwen asked.

Grognard started rattling off titles. "You gotta start with MCU Phase One. It's the most impressive work of cinematic franchising since the James Bond movies."

"The X-Men movies were fine and all, but don't tell me that the Iron Man movie was actually good. RDJ is an inspired bit of casting, but the character is second tier, at best."

"No, seriously, Mom," Ree said, energized by the three major forces in the universe: sugar, caffeine, and squee. "We can go watch it right now. And that's not even the best one of the bunch. They managed to make Captain America not just a retro jingoistic mess, and Branagh directed *Thor*. It's Kirby-tastic."

"*Thor* is quite impressive. Ree says that's because it's as melodramatic as I am, and while the critique may be on point, my praise remains," Drake added.

So, that's one meet-the-parent conversation down, Ree thought, noting the oddity of hanging out and talking magic shop and geekdom with her mom, her mom, who had helped make her the geek she was today, and was, after all, the reason she was in this magical world in the first place. The circularity of it all was kind of overwhelming, so she went back to her milkshake, leaning into Drake's embrace.

This, this made sense. Odd couple though they were, it was one of the best things to come out of her urban fantasy life. The adventure and excitement were definitely up there, but they came with a crap-ton of peril.

And these folks. Her magical family of choice, weirdoes all, just as weird as her, but every single one weird in a different way.

"And more important," Ree said, "George Lucas sold *Star Wars* to Disney. Which means new movies. Lots of them."

At that, Branwen's eyes lit up.

Grognard cleared his throat. "I'm going to order some of

their soda to go, and then you're all going to come down to my place to drink to Eastwood's passing." It wasn't an invitation.

Ree went back up to the servers and slipped them a $20, figuring that a bit of scratch never hurt in keeping up a good relationship with one of her favorite all-hours purveyors of life-giving drugs.

At Grognard's, it took approximately 3.7 seconds for the booze to come out. Grognard wheeled out a barrel of his Critical Hit, in honor of Eastwood. The place was still closed, and would be for the rest of the day, if she knew her boss.

The brewmaster had called Chandra and Uncle Joe on the way, but other than that, it was going to stay a closed wake. There would be a memorial during the next Midnight Market, and even thinking ahead to that meant that Ree opened herself up to a flood of actuarial anxiety, the burden of the Dorkcave and the emotional baggage that came with it coming at her like whitewater.

Glasses full, Grognard started the toasts. "Eastwood wasn't just another guy, just another friend. He was as noble a fuckup as I've ever known, and as a fuckup, I admired him. We didn't always see eye to eye, but that's what friends are good for. They call you on your bullshit, tell you when you're going off the rails. He kept me in check, and I did my best to return the favor."

Raising his stein, he continued. "Here's to Eastwood. He died so others could live."

"To Eastwood," they chorused, and then drank. Ree took a sip, then a longer chug.

Her emotional HP was totally tapped out. She was all out of go, but it was important to be there for everyone. There were too many things to resolve, too many words to say, and all she wanted to do was curl up into a ball and spend a weekend processing everything that had happened over the last year, the highs and lows, the things said that couldn't be taken back, lines crossed, friendships made, strained, and broken.

Twenty minutes later, Grognard came along with a flask. "You look beat. Pearson's going to need you to be strong. With Eastwood gone, they're going to look to you now."

"The hell they will," Ree said. "There're a dozen people more senior than me."

"But they're not the ones pounding the pavement. You've stepped up, and people have noticed. Every community has its champion, and you've built yourself a fine reputation the last year and a half."

Ree accepted the flask and took a shot. It was more Critical Hit, but the fortified version, Grognard's Geekomancy expressing itself through brewing. One sip, and she felt fatigue drain out of her body, the gray cloud in her mind breaking up. "If I'm the champion, then we're in trouble." But this time, she said it with a wink.

"Thanks, boss," she added.

"If you're taking over the Dorkcave, you think you'll still have time for little old Grognard's?"

"Only always. I might ask for a change of job description, get out of the server business."

"You'll miss the tips," he said.

Ree took another sip of the Critical Hit and handed the flask back. "But I won't miss the food stains, so it evens out. Plus, if I'm going to be all Pearson Protector, I may not have time for a night and day job anymore."

"I bet you can handle the cave by day, take the time you need at night," Grognard said. "I'll take whatever help you want to give. Before this all went down, I was going to ask if you wanted to go full partner, stake into the business. The offer still stands."

"No shit?" Ree leaned sideways into the bar. "That's a hell of a thing. Get back to you after I've slept this all off?"

"Of course." Grognard clapped her on the shoulder, and she returned the gesture.

Reenergized, she hopped off her stool and went over to Shade and Branwen, who were chatting up a storm in one of the booths.

"They fought the whole night, kept going out again and again. I was out most of the time, thank goodness. I don't have the stomach for all of the meatspace hand-to-hand," Shade said. "Not like your girl, here. Ree, your mother was telling me that you enrolled in martial arts when you were six?"

"Yep, that's me. Bullies: terrible for a kid's self-confidence, great motivation to take up Taekwondo."

Ree slid into the booth, taking a space by her mother. She blinked and reassured herself that her mother was still, in fact, there. She hadn't ever known her mother as an adult, and see-ing her in the rags of her Darth Atropos outfit, hair stained and ragged, made her as strange as what the years had done to her face, her hair. But spend a few years being tortured and brainwashed by a demon, see how good you look. On second thought, don't. That's what imagination was for.

"She wasn't really serious about it for a few years. And then you started sparring at twelve, right?"

Ree took a long sip from her stein. "Yep. Twelve-year-old girls are terrible. Sparring let me hit things. It was good therapy."

Branwen ran a hand through Ree's hair, the motion familiar and strange all at once. Halfway through, Ree flinched away.

"Sorry."

"No, it's my fault. I shouldn't have assumed."

"We're a regular soap opera here, aren't we?" Ree asked Shade.

The cyberpunk raised his hands. "Far be it from me to tell someone they're strange. My heart and cyber-soul belong in 1986."

"Can we chat for a minute?" Ree asked Branwen.

"Excuse me, my drink appears to be broken," Shade said, catching the hint.

The booth empty, Ree spun through her mental Rolodex, trying to figure out what to say, what she should say.

What came tumbling out was what she'd wanted to say for years.

"You fucked up."

Branwen took the words like a body blow. She righted herself, looked at her drink, took a long sip, and sat for a moment.

"I know. I'm sorry. You got the message I left with Eastwood?" she asked.

"Yep. Still doesn't help. You broke Dad's heart, and my heart. It took us a long, long time to get better. You could have told Dad about the magic stuff, about what the movies and shows were doing to you."

"Just going cold turkey wouldn't have helped. I needed to be free again, to be the most important person in my own life. It's selfish, and I wish I'd figured out a way to be my own person and be a mother and a wife. But I couldn't hack it."

"Are you going to call him?" Ree asked.

Branwen froze, like a deer in the headlights of a demon car.

"I don't even know what I'd say."

"You could say you were sorry. He needs to hear it. But he also needs to keep moving on with his life. So I don't know what to do. Should I forbid you from calling him so you don't open up old wounds and send him right back to where he was when you left? Or keep this secret from him for the rest of his or my life? I don't know, and I figured you'd want to weigh in."

"I loved your father very much. He was the kindest person I'd ever met, and he gave me years of peace. But I can't be that woman."

Branwen pointed to Ree's lightsaber, peeking out of her apron. "That is who I am. I've bound up my whole life in it, can't not be it. The prequels were crap about a lot of things, but for me, a stable family and my calling don't go together."

"What about Eastwood?"

"Eastwood wasn't the type to settle down. Never was,

never would have been. He was good and bad for me, I was good and bad for him. It worked more than it didn't."

"So what are you going to do, then? Stay in Pearson? Go itinerant? Return to Dagobah?"

"My master is dead, years ago now. The only place I know people is here. But this is your city now, not mine."

Ree reached out a hand, rested it on her mother's palm. "It's a big city, Mom. I'd rather not lose you again, if I can avoid it."

Branwen smiled, and Ree saw her mother again, the woman she'd known as a girl, underneath the wrinkles and burns and years of pain.

"Good. Because someone needs to take over the Dorkcave, and that thing is just too Gen X for my taste. Though I would love to keep a key to raid it as an armory, if you don't mind."

Branwen grabbed Ree's hand and turned the touch into a handshake. "On the condition that you come by at least once a week to talk."

"Deal."

That's one thing down. Ree slid out of the booth.

"Awesome. I'm going to go sleep for a week or so, and then I'll come by."

"Can't wait," Branwen said, her familiar glow still going strong.

She found Drake at the bar, recounting the most recent adventure with Talon and Grognard.

"It was a fight for the ages, something out of a saga, every bit as dramatic as any of the films whose props they bore."

Ree grabbed a stool and let him talk, embellishing and digressing from a story only hours old, applying the experience of a man who'd traveled across worlds, who had learned to fit in anywhere, if oddly. But no matter where he went, he stayed himself.

"Pardon me, folks," Ree told her friends. "Can I steal you away for a minute?" she asked Drake.

"No," he said. "You needn't steal that which is freely given."

And he says stuff like that. She held out a hand and led him over to another booth.

"Are you okay?" Ree asked.

"Dr. Wells gave me a restorative, and that in addition to the joyous shake has put me in fine enough condition for one who has been through the wringer."

"Really okay, or not-dead okay?"

Drake leaned in and kissed her. Gently, attentively, like his whole focus was on kissing just right, a sharpshooter's attention to the precise deployment of two lips. "A portion of both, I suppose."

"You wanna get out of here, then?"

"Are you making intimations of an amorous nature?"

Ree waggled her eyebrows in her best impression of Groucho Marx. It was pretty terrible impression, as she'd never gotten remotely close to his control.

But the mere attempt got Drake to chuckle, so it was always worth it.

The pair made their farewells. Hugs from Shade and Talon and Uncle Joe, kisses from her mom, a bear hug capped off with healthy claps on the back from Grognard, and they were off.

×✕⬡✕×

Back at Ree's, they kissed and laughed and tossed off sweaty clothes, making their way as quietly as possible to the bedroom. Ree left a sock on the door, and turned to Drake, already tucked under the covers, his shirt gone.

Drake sat up in the bed. "I've been thinking that it was high time that we celebrate another milestone. Seeing Eastwood's sacrifice, I realized that there is nothing I would hold back from you, nothing I don't want to do together.

"I am yours," he said. "Heart and soul."

Ree slipped into bed and kissed him on the forehead, then the lips. "I love you."

Drake smiled a rakish grin to end all rakish grins. "I know."

Ree waited a moment, then laughed with all the energy she had left. She kissed Drake again, then gave him a high five. They settled into a comfortable embrace, laughing contagiously.

+10 points for Harrison Ford's improv win.

"Also, when you mean you are mine, do you mean . . . ?" Ree asked, trying not to probe right after hitting one milestone and blunder her way toward another.

Drake took a breath, and nodded. "I presume you have supplies?"

"Boy, do I," Ree said, reaching over to her bedside table drawer.

Behind those doors, Ree and Drake laughed and kissed and talked and celebrated making it through another adventure.

That day, Ree had lost a mentor and a sometimes friend, regained her mother, and taken several steps forward with her partner, her partner in every single way.

Falling asleep with Drake's arms around her, pleasantly entangled and disheveled, Ree found more peace than she'd had in years, with two big question marks in her life replaced by exclamation points of joy.

The next afternoon, after more amorous distractions, and a long, long shower to wash off the week's pains, she picked up her phone and called Grognard.

He picked up on the first ring. *Almost like he was waiting for the call, or something,* she thought.

"Yep?" Grognard asked.

Ree smiled. "I'm in. Let's rock this joint."

Acknowledgments

Three novels and a novella later, here we are at the end of the first major arc of the Ree Reyes series. There's more to Ree's story yet to come, somewhere down the road. *Hexomancy* is an ending, but not The Ending.

It's strange to think that as of writing this, it's been only four and a half years since I started working on *Distraction: The Novel*, over Thanksgiving while Meg was studying. *Distraction: The Novel* soon came to be known as *Geekomancy*, and would launch my career as a novelist. Ree has grown as a character as I've grown as a writer, and I think that *Hexomancy* is our best story yet.

And that's all because of the help I've had along the way, from readers, fellow writers, my editor and agent, and many more.

Here are a few specific shout-outs to people who made a substantial difference for this latest novel:

A Muppet-flail of appreciation to Mary Robinette Kowal and my fellow classmates in the "Writing on the Fast Track" class I took in fall of 2013. That class unlocked nothing less than a revolution in process for me. Most of the time, it takes me between three and six months to write a first draft of a novel. I wrote the rough for *Hexomancy* in a month and a day, thanks to having a stronger, richer outline and applying the focus techniques from the class. Mary has also done me the great honor of serving as the voice of the Ree Reyes series for two novels and a novella in audio form, bringing her chops to the series.

And while I'm giving out productivity props, big thanks to Rachel Aaron for her productivity-hacking essay/book *2K to 10K: Writing Faster, Writing Better, and Writing More of What You Love*, which helped round out ideas from Mary's class. Metrics, man, metrics.

A massive woot of gratitude to Beth Cato for detailed notes and insights.

Muchas gracias to Enrique Bertran for his assistance in helping me with Puerto Rican Spanish, all the better to represent Ree's cultural and linguistic heritage.

Geeky cheers for a job well done to Sara Megibow, the Agent of Awesomeness, for helping me shape my career as it grows over the years.

A hearty Wookiee yowl of appreciation to my editor, Adam Wilson, for going with the flow when I called an audible to change gears, and for always challenging me to dig deeper, to enrich the world and its wacky magicks.

Meg, my partner in life and love. The best possible first reader, expert analyzer of character, she of the mighty laser eyes. If Meg weren't such a hard worker, this whole series might not exist.

And to you, dear reader. I was able to go this far with Ree's story because you read and enjoyed the books and told your friends. You have my deepest gratitude.

Baltimore, Maryland

April 2015

2ND EDITION ACKNOWLEDGMENTS

And with *Hexomancy*, the Ree Reyes series comes to a close. At the time, I hoped *Hexomancy* would be the end of the first trilogy for Ree, but the tides of publishing have carried me in different directions. The Ree Reyes series meant and still means a lot to me, as it's what a lot of readers of mine experienced first. I'd love to do more with this setting and cast, but unless these reissues absolutely blow up with massive sales, I can't justify writing more of these vs. other books with better sales prospects.

This book also got a very light touch-up, just a couple of clarifications, a couple changed references, and updating language I've since learned not to use.

Thanks to the team at Deranged Doctor Design for the great new covers for the series! It was an amazing experience working with them and reminded me how fun art direction is.

Thanks to Creative Jay for excellent production design and formatting for these new editions.

Thanks to Meg for everything all the time.

And thanks to you all reading the books, whether you're returning to the series or finding them for the first time.

Newsletter

Find out more about Mike's books, appearances, get bonus stories and more by subscribing to his newsletter at michaelrunderwood.com/newsletter